The Bastard Son

by
Myrle Clarkson

PAGE PUBLISHING, INC.
New York, NY

First originally published by Page Publishing, Inc. 2016

ISBN 978-1-68348-168-3 (pbk)
ISBN 978-1-68348-169-0 (digital)
ISBN 978-1-68348-170-6 (hardcover)

Printed in the United States of America

This story is dedicated to my four wonderful children: Debbie, Roxy, Jonie, and Joe.

And I apologize to these wonderful four for not being a better father figure in their lives.

Sorry, guys,

Dad

ACKNOWLEDGMENTS

A big thank you to my personal editor, Rig "Roxy".

CHAPTER 1

The Birth

This is a true story, and I'll let you know later how I know that it is true. It starts way back in the time of flappers, speakeasies, Prohibition, and even the Italian mafia, and it all takes place in that big windy city of Chicago. Yep, Chi Town. Most of this takes place in the suburbs around that town and starts the first of June 1933 to be exact.

Now, you know I cannot use the real names of the people for obvious reasons and that the dates and times will be a little off. It starts with a fifteen-year-old girl, Irene. Irene is a bit of a tramp; she runs the streets and does as she damn well pleases. She stays out all night, only goes home when she needs something, and does not get along at all with her mother. But she does get along with her stepdad, mainly because he never says anything to her about her ways. She hasn't always been like this. Her behavior changed when she lost her brother, whom she loved very deeply and looked up to. He was killed in an auto accident a few months earlier, and she just sort of snapped. But even though she has this bad lifestyle, she is still in school, which is where she meets Antonio, Tony. Now he is a very handsome young man, a full-blooded Italian. He is not an athlete of any kind, but he has lots of money in his pockets and is the only kid in the school with a new car, which he drives everywhere even though he isn't even old enough to have a driver's license. Of course, all the boys are very envious, and all the girls adore him. But he is going with Irene.

The reason Tony has all this is that he has a very wealthy and powerful father, Salvatore, who is a big man in the booze operation for the mafia. He has a big office downtown and claims that he is the head of the Garbage Department. In fact, Irene's mother, Bess, is a booze hauler for the mafia. Bess and some others have new autos and small trucks with the engine blocks so clean that the alcohol is simply put in the cooling systems. This drives the feds nuts, because when they stop one of the transporters, they never find anything illegal.

Bess is married to her second husband, Rick, who is a very nice man who would give you the shirt off his back. He looks kind of mean because earlier in his life, he was kicked by a horse. He has a very ugly scar on the right side of his face and a glass eye. The man worships the ground that Bess walks on, and there is nothing that he won't do for her. His dream is to retire someday and move to the foot-hills of California, where he would buy a little ranch and run some horses. Rick is a tool and die maker and has a very good job with a large implement company. He and Bess are making very good money together. They have a really nice place on the river with a guest cabin; they even have a cabin cruiser. Rick is an almost-full-blooded Indian, and his father was a council chief of the Cherokee nation.

The hot days of summer have gone by. It is now the first of November, and it is Irene's sixteenth birthday. Tony has taken her out and they are now parked somewhere. She tells Tony that she is about six months pregnant with his kid. Then she says, "So, Daddy, what are you going to do about it?" This announcement sort of knocks the wind out of Tony's sails. He stutters around, and he doesn't know what to say. Irene continues. "You know, we are going to have to figure something out about this."

Tony gets his second wind now and says, "Irene, you don't have to worry about it. I will take good care of you and help all that I can."

"What about the kid?" asks Irene.

"Yeah, the kid too. I hope it's a boy," says Tony, "and maybe we will even have to get married."

It's past Thanksgiving now, and Irene is home getting a few of her things. She has just showered and is standing in front of the mir-ror, looking at her big belly and getting ready to strap herself down with an old girdle. She has been wearing it under loose-fitting clothes to keep from showing. Just then, Bess comes in. She spots Irene and exclaims, "Well, you got yourself pregnant, didn't ya, girl? What the hell did I tell ya about that, huh?"

Irene whirls around, "Don't you worry about it, Maw. I'll take care of it."

Bess retorts, "How, little Miss Know-It-All? What are you going to do? And who in the hell is the father?"

"Don't you worry about it, Grandma! Hell, Tony and I might even get married!" Irene snaps back.

"Tony?" Bess yells, "Are you talking about Sal's son, Antonio, that you go to school with? Well, I'll be damned. That's who it is, isn't it? Married? How goddamn dumb are you, girl? Sal will never let him anywhere near you. The only thing Italian about you is the dressing you put on your salad. You better wise up, daughter dear. You have some difficult times ahead and some important decisions to make. You better get that dumb-ass thought out of your head that you and Antonio are going to be together, because it ain't going to happen. You do know that the state will not let you keep the baby because you are too young, and I am not going to raise another kid. I have already done that."

Irene snaps back, "And you did a piss-poor job of it too, didn't you, Maw?" She dresses quickly and heads for the door. Bess tells her to sit down, that they will talk things through, and that she will try to help her. "No, Maw, I am not going to let you have a damn thing to do with my kid. It's my problem and I will take care of it," Irene says defiantly. She slams the door shut as Bess hollers, "Well, you better talk to someone, a counselor or somebody to get help from!"

Winter has come, it's very cold out, and the ground is covered in snow. School is out for the holidays. Irene and Tony have been arguing a lot because Tony has not told his parents anything yet and Irene thinks he should. To make matters worse, she has found out he has been messing around with other girls. The holidays come and go, and the kids are back in school. Irene and Tony are still bickering back and forth, and no major decisions of any kind have been made.

With one exception: Irene tells Tony that if the kid is a boy, his middle name will be Michael, after the brother she loved so much.

It's now early March 1934. It's late, 10:00 or 11:00 p.m., and the two are parked somewhere, arguing somewhat. Irene hasn't been feeling well for the past couple of days and has been cranky. Then, out of nowhere, she lets out a scream. Tony asks worriedly, "What's the matter? Is it time? Has the time come?"

She moans, "I don't know. I feel some pain! Maybe the kid is just moving around some. Hell, I don't know!" But after a few more sharp pains, Irene tells Tony to take her to the hospital right away.

At the hospital, the admittance staff needs information. Irene tells them everything. Tony just gives his name and admits to being the father, nothing else. As Irene is taken into a room, the doctor looks her over then turns and says, "Well, kids, be prepared to be parents in a couple hours."

The couple of hours seems like forever. Medical people scurry in and out every few minutes. Finally, a nurse says to Tony, "We will see you in a little bit." They wheel Irene into the delivery room.

As Tony walks into the waiting room, Bess comes around the corner. She says, "The nurse told me that my daughter is in the delivery room and the father is in the waiting room."

"Yes," says Tony, "they just took her a few minutes ago. Are you Irene's mother?" Irene nods her head. He continues. "Irene tells me that you and her do not get along very well, but don't worry. I will take good care of her."

"Yeah, right," Bess responds. She raises an eyebrow. "And what about the baby?"

"Oh yes, and the kid too!" says Tony. The time passes while the two sit there and wait and eyeball each other.

Soon, the doctor steps in and says, "Well, you must be the mother and now a new grandmother! And you, young man, are the father of a brand-new baby boy!" He tells them that the new mother is doing fine, and the baby too. Except that the baby's forehead is flat, not at all rounded like it should be, because of the girdle worn to conceal the pregnancy. He tells them not to worry though, because with daily massaging, the forehead will smooth out nicely because the baby's bones are still very soft. He also tells them the new mother will be back in her room shortly and they will bring in the new baby too.

Irene is back in her room with Bess and Tony; a nurse brings the newborn in for them to see, and she asks if they have a name for him yet. Irene proudly states his name will be Wilton Michael and he will be called Willy.

Bess is pleased. "That's very nice to name him after your beloved brother."

Another nurse steps in and says to Tony, "Come with me, Dad. You have a birth certificate to sign." He follows the nurse out the door.

He returns a few minutes later and remarks, "I can't believe I am a daddy."

Irene responds, "Well, you are, and you better get home and tell your folks. I am tired and need some rest now anyway." Tony agrees, tells her good-bye, and leaves. Bess starts to say something, but Irene cuts her off. "Same for you, Maw, now that you have seen little Willy."

Bess nods. "Okay, dear, I will be back later." She kisses her daughter on the cheek, and the door closes softly behind her. Everyone is gone now, and the room is quiet. Irene lies there, cradling her son in her arms, her son born out of wedlock. The bastard son has arrived.

CHAPTER 2

Surprise, Surprise

It's almost breakfast time when Tony walks in. His Dad, Sal, is sitting in the kitchen, drinking coffee. He hollers, "Junior!" That's what he calls Antonio when he is pissed. "Junior, where the hell have you been? You have been out all damn night. Explain yourself right now, and it better be good!"

Tony replies, "Well, just settle down a little, Grandpa."

Sal yells, "Grandpa your ass. You show me some respect, Junior!"

Tony answers, "I am, Dad. I am just trying to tell you that I am a father. That makes you a grandfather!"

Sal looks at Tony in disbelief. "Father? Grandfather? What in the damn hell are you talking about? Have you lost your goddamn mind?" So Tony begins to fill his father in on everything. Sal just explodes. "Now you listen to me, Junior. I am no grandfather, and you are no father. You got that? So you helped some little tramp out that you go to school with, and no one knows who the father is."

"But, Dad," Tony insists, "I signed the birth certificate as the father."

Furious, Sal screams, "What? You did *what*? I can't believe that you are my kid. For Christ's sake, Junior, what the hell have you got yourself into now? It was only a year ago that I got you out of that jam when you rammed your car into some people, now this! When are you going to get some smarts? You will not see that tramp or her kid again. You got that? And furthermore, you are not to leave this house again until I say so. Tell your friend to get your stuff from school. I am getting you enrolled in that new school on the other side of town on Monday. Remember what I said. You are *not* the father, and you don't know who is, and you keep your ass away from that girl and her kid. You got it? Now get upstairs to your room and stay out of my sight for a while!"

Sal leaves to find his right-hand man, Big Mike, who is never very far from him. He tells Big Mike that he wants to know everything about this little tramp and her family, and he wants to know by noon. Big Mike is very good at his job; he has no trouble finding out all the information that Sal wants.

It's early afternoon now, and Sal pays a visit to the Catholic church. He talks with the good Father Francis. He tells Father Francis that his son, Antonio, has been trying to help one of his classmates. He relays the story of a young girl who is somewhat rebellious and has been running the streets, who has gotten herself pregnant, and God knows who the father is! His son, Antonio, drove her to the hospital last night, and she delivered a baby boy. Sal continues. "I think it would be a good thing for you to do, Father, to talk to this girl and convince her that the best thing, and only thing, for her to do is put the child in the new orphanage. You know, the orphanage that we built, where the sisters would take good care of him. She won't let her own mother have the child, and the state surely won't let her, and heaven knows what the state would do with the child." Sal continues. "Then someday, when the time is right and she has her own place and is older, she can get the child back."

"Well," Father Francis responds, "my question to you, Sal, is this: what is all your concern in this matter?"

"You see, Father," Sal explains, "Antonio isn't the sharpest kid in the world, and in his trying to help the girl, he signed some papers at the hospital, including the birth certificate claiming he is the father when, in fact, he has never even been out with the girl." Sal continues. "So, Father, my concern is that if some or any of my so-called 'enemies' get wind of this and think that I am somehow connected with this boy, that might very much put him in harm's way." With that, Sal hands Father Francis a very fat envelope. He says, "So I can rest assured that his name will be changed or misspelled a little and he will be neatly and quietly tucked away for a little while?"

"Oh yes, Sal, by all means, consider it done! And by the way, thank your lovely wife for the fund-raising charity work she has done," answers Father Francis.

"I assure you I will, Father. Oh, and will you let the girl know that her doctor and hospital bills are taken care of?"

Days pass, and Sal is satisfied that his son is out of the mess. Bess doesn't know for sure where her grandson is, and Irene, thinking she has done the right thing, has put little Willy in the Catholic orphanage. Irene has gone back to school and hasn't seen Tony around anywhere. She wants to know why he didn't come back to the hospital to see her. She is friends with Joan now. Joan is the daughter of Jane, her mother's neighbor. Joan and Irene are in no way best friends, but they do speak to each other in a friendly way. One day, Irene asks Joan if she has seen Tony lately. Joan responds that she has not and that the word is out that he has transferred to another school on the other side of the city. "Well, I guess my mother was right," mumbles Irene. And that was the end of that.

The next few days, Irene does a lot of soul searching and thinking about what will be the best thing for her to do now. She decides that she should quit school, get a job, and make some money. After all, that's what it is going to take to get a place of her own and her son back someday. She starts looking around town and in the newspapers, and one day, down by the main part of town, she sees a sign. It's in the window of a little greasy spoon–type café that reads "waitress wanted." She marches inside and tells the guy, "I am your new waitress." He looks her over and responds that he thinks she looks pretty young. Irene counters quickly that yes, she is young, but she is also a quick learner. He tells her that he likes her attitude and eagerness. Irene grins and says, "How about I start tomorrow?" And so begins Irene's new job.

CHAPTER 3

Her New Man

The café where Irene works is around some industrial areas and a few bars, so the clientele is mostly male. Of course, sometimes the guys might have a little too much alcohol in them. This makes them try to get a little too friendly with the waitress. Irene takes it in stride. And like she has assured the owner, she is a quick learner. All the guys seem to like her, and she is quick with a comeback. When they tease her, she can put them in their place and make everyone laugh. Four or five months go by, and late one afternoon, a good-looking guy named Jake comes into the café. His real name is Gerald, but everyone knows him as Jake. He spies Irene right away and asks her what time she gets off work. She retorts, "Too late for you, old man."

Jake raises an eyebrow. "Well, babe, you're pretty quick with your lip. I kinda like that. Now bring me a cup of coffee and a burger, and then we will make some plans."

"Well, you can count me out," she snaps. "You would just be in my way and slow me down." This makes a couple of fellows in the next booth howl with laughter.

Now it turns out that this café is Jake's favorite place to eat, and he comes in quite often. Sometimes he has had a little too much to drink, but most of the time he is happy-go-lucky and just wants to shoot the bull with someone. Eventually, Jake wins out, and he and Irene begin to date.

Around the first week of November, Jake comes into the café with a big guy, not fat, just a really big man. He introduces Irene to his brother, Dale, who goes by the name Butch. Jake tells him that Irene is his new girlfriend. After some small talk, the brothers decide to go to their favorite watering hole for a beer or two. Jake asks his big brother what he thinks of his new girlfriend. His brother says, "She's a schoolgirl, Jake, and too damn young for you."

Jake laughs and says, "Aww, you're just jealous. She's very pretty and just my type."

"No, Jake." Butch shakes his head. "I am telling you, she is too damn young and she is going to be nothing but trouble. Mark my words on that. You better stay away!" But Jake doesn't mark his brother's words, and in fact, he invites Irene to Thanksgiving dinner with Butch and his girlfriend, Anna. The four of them have a great time. The two girls develop a bond; they get along great, like two peas in a pod. Irene learns more about Jake, like the fact that he drinks too much and it's best to keep him away from hard liquor. Hard liquor just makes him mean, but beer, beer just sort of keeps him mellow. The four continue to go out together and become fast friends. It's Christmastime and the girls do their Christmas shopping together. Everything is just fine. They get together again on New Year's Eve, and they ring in the new year, 1935.

In the meantime, Bess has found out where little Willy is. She goes to see him once in a while. She has been massaging his forehead, along with the sisters, and little Willy's forehead now has a nice round shape. Bess has been talking with her husband Rick, wondering if maybe they should take little Willy to raise.

Butch and Anna have set a date, the first of April, to get married. It's only a few months away, and Irene and Anna are busy getting things organized for the big event. Irene will be the bridesmaid, and Jake will be the best man. Spending so much time with Anna, Irene learns a few more things about Jake. Like the fact that he has lost quite a few jobs around town even though he is a pretty good mechanic. When he got drunk on the hard stuff, he wouldn't show up for work the next day. After a couple of times, he would be fired. But big brother Butch is doing a pretty good job of keeping him away from the hard stuff. If Jake only drinks beer, he does all right.

Jake likes his beer, and he has a couple of watering holes that he likes to go to after work. And Irene know all this.

Now the big man, Butch, is just the opposite of his brother. He is a social drinker. He only stops after work for a beer or two, mainly for occasions, like a friend's birthday. He works at the boxing gym, where he trains young fighters and teaches them to box. For a short time, he was a professional boxer himself, but he had to give it up because his legs wouldn't hold up over four or five rounds in the ring. This was because in college, he was a fullback and his knees had been busted a couple times. But the big brute is gentle as a lamb, and he and Jake both love life, especially family life. The brothers' mother lives with her second husband in central Minnesota. It looks like she isn't going to be able to attend the wedding. When the big day finally arrives, it is a fine day for a wedding. It is not too cold and the sun is shining. It is a small wedding with family and friends, and it goes off without a hitch.

CHAPTER 4

The Plan

The honeymoon is over, and Anna and Butch move from their separate apartments into a much bigger apartment. The cold weather has left and the flowers have bloomed. The foursome, Anna, Butch, Jake and Irene, celebrate the Fourth of July 1935 with drinks, a cookout, and fireworks. Soon after, Anna announces that she is pregnant, and the big man is so happy, he throws another party, but no drinks for Anna this time! A few weeks later, Irene is pretty sure that she is pregnant again herself. She is hesitant to tell anyone, but she has to confide in her good friend Anna. Anna is happy for her and says that Irene should tell Jake, and they should marry and get a place of their own. Besides, Anna hopes, this will keep Jake from staying with her and Butch so often. Irene agrees to think it over.

Meanwhile, Bess has been thinking a lot about little Willy and spending more time with him. He is now almost a year and a half old; he has been walking for some time and is jabbering away and beginning to put words together. Late one night, Bess asks Rick what he would think about getting Willy for them to raise. Rick tells her that he would agree to that. Bess says they should think on this for a while and see how much it would change their lifestyle. After a few months go by and Bess and Rick have given it a lot of thought, they decide to do it.

It is now late September, and Bess strolls into Salvatore's office. There are a few wiseguys in the office and also Big Mike. Sal is behind his desk, his feet are up on it, a cigar is dangling from his mouth, and a drink is in front of him. Sal looks up and says, "Well hello, Bess, what brings you here to my office? I sure hope that you are not in any kind of trouble." He blows out a big ring of smoke, and the guys all chuckle. She tells him no; she is not in any trouble. She asks how he knows her name. Does he know her? "I sure do, honey," Sal points out. "I make it a point to know everyone that I can, especially those that I might be in contact with one way or another."

Bess straightens a little and begins. "Well, I will get right to the point, but first, I am not saying that you are involved in any way in what I am going to ask you. I do know, however, that you are a very powerful and influential man and can get things done. First, I am going to quit the work that I am doing, and I want to get my grandson out of the institution, the Catholic orphanage, and take him home to raise."

Sal leans back in his chair and blows out another puff of smoke. "Well, Bess," he says, "I don't know about you quitting your job. You probably know a lot about the business you are involved in, and there would be some people who would like to know about some of the work that you've done. There might be a problem there."

"No, sir, no problem at all," Bess replies. "I would have to be pretty stupid to say anything about something that I know nothing about, and I have a little boy that I want to see grow up." Sal sits there, staring into space, twirling his cigar. "You have a point there, Bess, a very good point." Finally, Sal speaks again and says, "You probably know more than you care to say. So if I was to help you and it was to benefit me in some way, that would mean you would have to take the boy and get clear out of the state of Illinois. You would have to sell your very nice place and move." Bess sits there a moment or two, staring back.

She stands up and says defiantly, "I'll do you one better than that. I'll take the boy and move to the west coast, California. That ought to be far enough. What do you think of that?"

Sal looks squarely at her and says, "I think we have a deal, Bess. When do you think you might be ready to leave?" She answers, "In about three months, the first of next year, or better yet, right before

Christmas. That would make a nice Christmas present for Rick and me. I will keep you informed, Sal."

"No need, Bess," he responds. "I'll know when you are ready to go."

That night, Bess tells Rick that they have three months to get things sold and find a ranch in California. She tells him he needs to check into a job transfer to the San Fernando Valley area, if that's where he wants to be. He is delighted, thinking about the horse he has always wanted. Bess starts right in. That first week, she talks to people and gets her plan in motion. The real estate people arrive and put a sign in the yard. Jane, the neighbor, comes over to see what is going on. Bess tells her that she and Rick are leaving and taking the grandson, moving to California.

It is now around the first of November. Irene and Anna and the brothers have just celebrated Irene's eighteenth birthday. Anna is still trying to get Irene to tell Jake that she is pregnant. Late one afternoon, with only a few customers in the café, Joan walks in. She and Irene were friends in school and see each other from time to time. Joan and her friends like to come in for a coke and a bite to eat under the pretense of seeing Irene but really to check out the men who frequent the café. Joan casually asks Irene if she is moving to California with her mom. Irene is shocked and asks her what she is talking about. Joan tells her that her mother has a "for sale" sign in the yard and is moving to California with Rick and her grandson. Irene fumes and stomps off to the kitchen. Now Irene begins to wonder how is she going to stop this. She starts to formulate a plan of her own.

The first thing Irene does is seek legal help. The legal aid people hear her story and learn that she is now eighteen and the legal mother with the birth certificate. They tell her that if she were to be married and have a decent place to live, they see no reason why she could not have her son. That very night, Irene asks Jake if he loves her. He says they get along very well and have fun together, so he supposes he does. "Jake, then why haven't you asked me to marry you?" Irene wants to know.

"Well, I guess the money and the timing haven't been right," Jake replies.

"Well, would the timing be right if I told you I was pregnant with your child?" she asks. A shocked Jake tells her that yes, the timing is right. Irene and Jake make plans to marry. They decide to get married around Thanksgiving. Irene tells Jake she wants a small wedding with friends and family and Butch and Anna to stand up with them. Jake confides to her that he has been saving money for a car for them instead of his motorbike, but he knows the wedding must come first.

Irene finds an apartment close to Butch and Anna's. Jake asks about furniture, and they are in luck because after Butch and Anna combined their two apartments, they have leftover furniture they can use. Butch has a friend with a truck, and Irene asks about using it to get her bedroom suite from her mother's house. The next weekend, they head to Bess and Rick's. Irene tells the brothers to wait in the truck for a few minutes while she goes in first. Bess is sitting at the table, papers strewn in front of her. She looks up at Irene, and Irene tells her she saw the "for sale" sign. She asks where they are moving to. Bess responds, "Rick and I would like someplace warmer, get out of the snow and cold. We are going to California. Would you like to go with us?" Irene tells her no, she is just there to get her bedroom furniture. Bess says, "Sure, you can have it, dear, but first there is something we need to talk about."

"Not now, Maw," Irene snaps. "I am too busy. I am going to get the boys to come in and get the furniture now."

Thanksgiving weekend arrives, and Irene and Jake are married by the justice of the peace. They celebrate with a few friends, and Jake gets drunk. The first of December, Irene meets with the legal people. She shows them her place, the birth certificate, and the marriage license and tells them about her and Jake's jobs. They say they see no reason why she shouldn't be able to get her son within a week or two, and they will keep her posted.

The next few days are worrisome for Irene. She wants to tell Jake about Willy but can't seem to find the right time. He comes home from work and a few beers, wants to fool around, then passes out or just goes to sleep. The legal team stops by and tells her that she will be able to get little Willy on Friday, the eighteenth, a week before Christmas. What a Christmas present! They assure her they will accompany her to the orphanage and make sure everything goes smoothly.

The day before, Anna stops over to see if Irene has any more Christmas shopping to do. She remarks on how Irene has been jittery, uneasy, and not at all herself. She asks if everything is all right. Irene bursts into tears, crying and trembling. She tells Anna the whole story about Willy and how guilty she feels because she hasn't been able to get him before. Anna wants to know what Jake thinks about all this. Irene replies that she hasn't told him yet.

"Oh no," Anna shrieks. "My god, you have made some mistakes, but this is a big one. You should have told him! I don't think that this is going to set very well with him. What about the father, is he around?" she asks.

Irene explains, "No, he's not. He's a kid I went to school with. I did try to tell Jake several times, but he was drunk or would fall right to sleep. I thought I would have more time, but my Mother stuck her nose in, and I had to step things up a bit, and here we are. Will you go with me tomorrow to get my son?" she asks tearfully. Anna tells her that yes, of course she will go with her. Irene dabs at the tears in her eyes and tells Anna she is sorry to get her in the middle of all this.

"Don't worry about it, Irene," Anna sighs. "You have a long road ahead of you and I will help you all I can."

CHAPTER 5

No, No, Hell No

The day is finally here, and Irene gets little Willy without any problems. The girls are back at Irene's place, talking to the little guy as he walks around. He looks at the new surroundings, points and jabbers, and runs here and there. The day goes by very fast, and Anna has to leave and get supper started. As she leaves, she tells Irene that if things get really bad, to come on over. Irene thanks her but tells her she hopes that Jake will hear her out.

Jake comes in the door. He looks at Irene and little Willy and asks her who she is babysitting for. She tells Jake to grab a beer and come in and sit down. Irene takes a deep breath and says, "His name is Willy, Jake, and he is ours."

Jake raises his voice. "Stop the bullshit, ours my ass!" Irene explains that he is her son, and she is going to raise him, and he will be theirs. "Your son? What in the goddamn hell are you talking about?" Jake explodes. Irene tells him that when she was in school, she had gotten pregnant. "Who is the damn father?" Jake wants to know.

"Just a boy I went to school with," Irene answers.

"So," Jake demands, "where has the little bastard been the last couple of years?" Irene tells him that he has been in an orphanage. "Well," Jake bellows, "I'll tell you what. You can just take the little bastard right back to the damn orphanage! And how come you didn't tell me all this in the first goddamn place?" Irene tries to explain that she wanted to, but the timing was never right. "Well then, why is the timing right now?" Jake yells.

"Because," Irene answers, "my mother is trying to take him, and he is *my* son."

"So let your mother have the little bastard!" Jake hollers. Irene starts to cry and asks him to please not call the boy that. "Why?" Jakes sneers, "That is what he is. Look it up if you don't think so. He is a little bastard, and you can let your mother raise the little bastard. We don't want him or need him. Everything was just fine without him. Is that why you wanted to get married? So your little bastard could get out of the institution?"

Irene fires back, "No, Jake, I am pregnant with your child too, remember? Everything would have been just fine if we had more time. It just didn't work out that way. And it's not like I cheated on you or anything; I had Willy before we ever met!"

"Well, babe, I don't give a damn. I am not raising some asshole's little bastard. I am not going to do it. I don't want him in my place, so you get him the hell out of here. Take him back where he came from, give him to your mother, throw him into the goddamn Chicago River! I don't care what you do with the little bastard, but you better have him gone before I get back, or I will get rid of him for you, do you understand?" And with that, Jake slams the door and leaves. Irene sobs. Little Willy, scared and crying, clings to her leg. *No Christmas spirit here*, she thinks, *and there won't be for a long time.* She sighs, gathers up little Willy's things, and heads for Anna's place.

Irene tells Anna and Butch what happened with Jake. Butch shakes his head and says, "I know what Anna has told me. After all this time the four of us have been together? You should have told Jake a long, long time ago, back when you started seeing each other. I know you mean well and have a good heart, but it will take some time to get Jake over this, if ever! I know where he is. I'll go and try to talk to him."

Butch finds Jake at his favorite watering hole. He is drinking boilermaker's and beer, together. Butch knows it is best to let him drink like this until he is drunk enough to haul him home. He sits beside him and says, "Well, little brother, I heard about the boy. That was certainly no way for you to find out, dumped on you all at once like that."

Jake looks up at him. "That bitch! Do you suppose she planned this just to get that bastard son out of that place?"

"No, Jake, I don't, and remember, she is carrying your child." Butch reminds him. "I think that her mother tried to get the boy, and it was just a quick decision that she felt she had to make."

"Well, I am not raising the son of a bitch bastard; no way I am having another man's bastard son in my house!" Jake fumes.

Butch replies, "Jake, do you remember what I said to you when I first met Irene? Do you? I said she was too young for you and that she was going to be trouble, and you said that I was just jealous. Do you remember that? And another thing, you know what our Daddy would say to you right now? He would say you made your bed, now lie in it."

"Well, Daddy just might have done that, Butch, but not me!" Jake snarls.

"Look, tomorrow, after you sober up, you and Irene are going to have to get together and work this out one way or the other," Butch points out.

Jake slams down his drink, "There is nothing to work out. The little bastard goes, and that's all there is to it." A few hours later, Jake is reeling, slurring his words, and as Butch knows, will soon pass out. He loads him in the car and takes him home. Irene helps Butch put him to bed. Butch asks her where Willy is, and she tells him that he is at his house with Anna. Butch agrees this is a good idea and tells her that she shouldn't have any trouble with Jake the rest of the night. He tells her to talk to Jake the next day and, if Jake gets mad, not to let him hit her. If he does, she should get to his place right away. Irene hugs him and says, "Thank you, big brother, I sure wish Jake was more like you."

But Jake isn't like Butch at all, that's for sure. On payday, Butch never has to pay for a bar tab from the week before. He likes the finer things in life and isn't afraid to work hard for them. He even takes on extra work once in a while. He likes to go to the big city and get tailor-made suits, Italian at that, made just for him. And when he gets all dressed up, he looks like a big shot mafia guy, but of course, he isn't. He isn't shy about spending money when he has it, and he is a good tipper; that gets him a lot of respect. It isn't unusual for a maître d' to take him and his party, bypassing others, to the best table in a fine-dining room or speakeasy. He drives the biggest and blackest car he can find. He loves to go fishing. No, he is nothing like his brother. They are two very different individuals, but he loves his brother, and there is nothing, nothing, he won't do for him.

Saturday morning, Irene wakes up before Jake. She is working the early shift so she can spend the afternoon with her son. She is having a wonderful time with little Willy, trying to get him to say "mommy" as Anna looks on and laughs. Little Willy is running around, laughing, pointing, and even trying to say "mommy." It gets late, and Irene decides to go home and try to talk to Jake. His morning hangover should be gone by now, and he should be sober and easier to talk to.

Jake strolls in the room and comments that she must have gotten rid of the little bastard. "Damn you, Jake. I told you not to call him that, and no, I didn't, and I am not going to, as you say, get rid of him," Irene declares. "He will stay with me, and that is something that we are going to have to work out."

"No, Irene, I am not," Jake huffs. "Why should I raise some son of a bitch's bastard kid? I can't do it. When I see him, I see you in bed with some asshole."

"Oh, Jake, grow up! I told you, I was younger, in high school, and the father was a kid himself. Who the father is makes no difference. He's not the problem; you are!" exclaims Irene. "Well, I don't give a damn. He is not welcome in my home," Jake insists.

"Come on, Jake, he's just a little boy. He's done nothing wrong. I did all the wrong things, and now you say he has to pay for it? He has already spent almost two years of his life put away!" Irene pleads.

"Well, take him back. You don't need him; we were doing fine till he showed up. We have our own, *my* little boy coming soon, and that's all we need. We were getting along and happy, huh? Just leave him where he's at."

"He's at your brother's place, and thank God your brother is not like you!" Irene retorts.

"If Butch and Anna like him and want him, leave him there, and you can go and see him now and then. If my dumbass brother wants him, let him have the little bastard, problem solved," Jake declares. Irene shakes her head and the tears flow. Nothing is resolved, it's getting late, and Jake goes to bed. Irene sinks into a chair, tears streaming down her face. No harmony or Christmas feeling in this household tonight. She thinks about what her friend Anna had said about the long road ahead of her. A long road ahead of her indeed.

Irene wakes up on Sunday morning, realizing she must have spent the night in the big chair. Jake is up and gone already. After a cup of coffee and a quick smoke—she had quit but is smoking again—she heads over to spend the day with her son. It's peaceful at Butch and Anna's place. She watches as Butch chases little Willy around, and Willy peeks around Anna's legs, giggling. *Boy, if only it could be like this at home*, she thinks. *Willy is very happy here, but is this right?* she wonders. Irene plays with Willy, and then, when he is napping, she tells Butch and Anna how the talks with Jake are going nowhere. They invite her to stay for supper, and later, as she is getting ready to leave, she turns and asks them if they would mind if she spent the night. After all, she has never spent a night with her son. They say of course she can, and what a night it is. Irene lies in bed with her son, all snuggled in. He is as close to her as he can get. She has noticed that he seems to crave attention and love. He longs to be close to someone. She knows she has to do something and soon; she just needs to think it through.

The next few days are about the same. Irene spends as much time with her son as she can. She tries to talk Jake into letting her bring her son home to live with them. But nothing has changed. Jake isn't going to give an inch. It's December 24, Christmas Eve. Irene is off work early and home changing clothes. They are heading to Butch and Anna's to spend Christmas together. There's a knock at the door, and Irene opens it to find Bess. She lets her in, and Bess remarks, "Well, daughter dear, I just want to congratulate you on getting the jump on me and getting my grandson out of that awful place." She looks at Irene's stomach. "By the looks of it, I see that there will be two grandkids. Anyway, that is what I had wanted to talk to you about, was getting him out of there. I planned to tell you about the deal I had made to get him out of there. Then I had hoped that the two of us could come up with something."

"What deal?" Irene asks.

"Oh, never mind, it doesn't matter. I see you are married now and have little Willy. By the way, where is he?" she asks as she glances around. Irene says quietly that he is at her sister and brother-in-law's and then starts to cry. Bess asks her what the matter is, and Irene tells her mother how Jake does not want anything to do with Willy and won't even allow him in the home. Her mother asks her what she plans to do, and Irene says she is not sure. She knows that she will stand her ground, though, and she might even give Jake an ultimatum.

"Well, dear," Bess says, "you are a young woman now, with soon-to-be two children to raise. I believe it is time we stop the bickering between us and try to get along, do you agree?" Irene nods her head yes. Bess continues. "I love you, daughter, and I'll do anything I can to help you. The door is always open if you need to get away or need a place for Willy to stay. I'll be more than happy to spend some time with my first grandson, and I promise I won't try to take him away from you."

"But what about you moving away?" Irene asks.

"Well, the deal wasn't through yet when I found out that you had taken Willy from the orphanage, so we decided to stick around awhile. Like I said, the door is always open. There will always be a place for you." Bess hands her a sack with Christmas gifts for her and Willy, wishes her a merry Christmas, and leaves. Jake arrives home shortly, and they head over to Butch and Anna's.

When they walk in, Butch is chasing Willy around. The little guy is laughing and giggling with delight. Butch claps his brother on the back and says, "Merry Christmas, little brother, just like old times, eh?"

"It would be, except for that little bastard over there," Jake mutters.

It is quiet for a moment or two, then Butch says, "Jake, I love you to death and I know you have been dealt a bad hand, and no man wants a ready-made family, but you have one. It is not this little boy's fault that he is here; he damn well wouldn't have asked for all of this if he had a choice. You will show a little kindness while you are in my home. You know what? You might even like him if you would give him a chance; he's a pretty nice little guy. Now damn it, let's have a beer."

"Well, big brother, if you think he is so damn nice, then you keep him," Jake snarls. Butch puts his hand up and tells Jake not another word.

They relax with a couple of beers and get a kick out of watching a very excited Willy open his gifts. Except Jake, that is. The foursome enjoys a meal, opens gifts, plays cards, and has a pretty good time. Anna declares that she hates to be a party pooper, but they have a big day ahead of them. Her sister and her husband are coming to visit. Anna tells them she loves her sister very much and can't wait for them to meet her. She asks Irene to come over early in the morning to help her, and Irene assures her she will.

It's about noon, and Anna and Irene have the dinner almost ready. Butch has stayed out of the kitchen and is playing with Willy. Jake has just come in, and not far behind are Anna's sister and brother-in-law, Dorothy, or Dot as she is also called, and Joe. They live in a fairly large city in the state of Indiana. Joe has a very good job with a large machine plant that makes parts for different companies around the state. They have no children because they don't want kids. The dinner goes very well and the food is great. The men, with their bellies full, are in the front room, snoring. Even little Willy is fast asleep. The women are in the kitchen, cleaning up and chatting. Plans are made to do the same on New Year's Eve and New Year's Day. It is decided that Joe and Dot will spend the night there.

The girls are starting to show now. Both are about six months along. Butch is working a lot as there are a couple of big fights coming up. Jake hasn't been himself for the past couple of weeks. Irene works when she can. She likes the early-morning shift so she can spend the afternoon with her son. He can say "mommy" very clearly now and is putting lots of words together. It's the end of December, and Irene is waiting for Jake to come home. She has tried to talk with him for days, but to no avail, and without much effort from him. She has made a decision, and he will hear her out, come hell or high water!

Jake comes through the door, and Irene tells him to grab a beer and sit down. He asks what is going on, and she says, "I want you to just hear me out. This is not going to be easy, what I am about to say, nor do I like doing it, but I am at the end of my rope. Number one, you do not want my boy around. Number two, I have my son now, and I am not going to abandon him again and I am going to raise him. Therefore, it looks like I am going to have to leave and get a place of my own and move out. So do you want a divorce or what?"

"Wait a minute," a shocked Jake says. "What are you saying? Where would you go?"

Irene answers him calmly, "I have a job, and Anna will babysit, and with tips and wages, I hope to keep a cheaper place. Hell, I don't know, I might even have to go live with my mother for a while."

"What about the baby, my son?" Jake fires back.

"Your son? If it is a boy? Well, then you will know how it feels to be away from him. And I will have two sons to raise. I'll try to have my son out of your hair shortly after the first of the year." With that, Irene slams the door shut and walks out.

She spends the night with Anna and Butch and her son. Anna agrees with her, that although she might not be doing the right thing, she had to do something. She leaves the next morning, telling Anna that she will be back in the afternoon to help with the New Year's Eve festivities. She walks through the door and Jake is there. He tells her it is her turn to grab a beer and sit down. This surprises her very much, but she does as he asks. He starts by saying that he does not want a divorce. He does not want her to leave, even if the little bastard, boy, is to come and live with them. He asks, "Would you do your best to keep him away from me? During the workweek, feed him early and put him to bed before I come home from work and not let him run through the home in the evenings. And let him stay with Butch and Anna on weekends and holidays when I am home." She looks at him skeptically. He continues. "Well, it will be a start, and give me some time to get used to him being around, don't you think?"

Irene thinks for a moment then says, "Jake, tell me something. Would you agree to stay away from the hard liquor and just drink beer? You are a much more mellow guy then." He nods his head yes. "Hell," she continues, "who knows? You might even like, not love, but like, little Willy."

Jake smirks, "Not a chance on that. You can get that idea out of your head. And when he gets older, he can spend summers with his grandparents."

Irene smiles. "As you said, it's a start. We can try it and see how it goes, but no promises."

CHAPTER 6

More Trouble for Jake

It's New Year's Eve at Butch and Anna's. Dot and Joe are there, and Irene is busy helping Anna. Jake arrives and Butch notices that he is in a festive mood, much better than the one he has been in lately. Butch and Anna are aware of the deal that's been made between Jake and Irene and hope for the best. They enjoy a nice meal, and after little Willy is in bed, the little group enjoys wine and beer and welcomes in the new year. Hello, 1936.

The new year starts out cold, with more snow. They all go back to their daily routine. Butch is busy with some new fighters and also some veterans. There are some big events coming up in about six weeks. Anna is getting bigger, Jake is only drinking beer, and Irene is keeping little Willy away from Jake. Willy has the run of the house during the day, but before Jake comes home, Irene puts Willy and his toys over in one corner. She tells the little boy, "Daddy will be home soon and he will be tired and cranky from his long day of work. You have to stay away from him and not bother him, so you stay right here and play with your truck." Willy is confused. He really loves it at Butch and Anna's place. It's a lot different than here with Mommy. Mommy is the only one who chases and plays with him. But this is the daily routine, and it seems to be working for everyone, for everyone except Sal, that is.

Big Mike and the guys are sitting around talking in Sal's office. Sal is standing at the window, watching the snow fall. Sal turns to his right-hand man, Big Mike, and comments, "It's been a month now, and that damn kid is still here. He should be a long way from here by now." Big Mike nods in agreement. Sal tells Big Mike he's decided it's time they do something about it. Big Mike asks if it is Bess's fault. Sal answers, "No, Mike, it's not her fault. Her daughter outsmarted her, that's all. You have to give her credit, the little tramp. She knows how to take care of herself." Sal continues with the plan. "So, Mike, you are going to have to take one of the boys and pay a little visit to that drunken mechanic husband of hers. But not at his house. Catch him at one of his favorite watering holes." "And, Big Mike," Sal chortles, "don't break any of his arms or legs. He's going to need them to be able to move away." The guys roar with laughter at this. Sal continues. "Work him over pretty good. Make sure he gets the message that I want him out of here. I want him and his ready-made family out of town. If he doesn't leave, let him know he can expect another visit in a week or so."

Big Mike nods. "Sure thing, boss, consider it taken care of."

The very next week, Jake is at the local pub, having a drink with friends. He is having a good time, laughing, and telling stories. Jake leaves his barstool and heads to the restroom. He's standing at the urinal when two guys come up behind him. Big Mike turns Jake around and hits him, right in the mouth. He says, "My boss wants you to leave town. You are to move far away from here." With that, the other guy nails him in the face. The two hit Jake a few more times and Jake falls to the floor. "The boss wants you to take your ready-made family and leave town, and if you don't get the message, we'll come back and remind ya." With a few kicks to the ribs, they head for the door. The bartender hears the commotion. He hollers at Jake, wanting to know what he is doing in there. The bartender comes in as the goons push past him and out the door. He looks at Jake on the floor. His nose looks busted, his mouth is bleeding and one eye is starting to swell shut. Jake's friends and the bartender get him into a booth. They ask if he wants an ambulance. Jake shakes his head no. One man leaves to get Butch. Butch walks in a few minutes later. He takes one look at his brother and says, "Jake, are you fighting again and drinking hard liquor?"

Jake says, "No, Butch, no. I just went into the pisser and two guys came in and jumped my ass."

"But why?" Butch wants to know. "Who are they?" Jake moans that he doesn't know. "Well, think, damn it, think. You must have pissed somebody off. Do you owe anybody money?" Butch demands. Jake says no, he doesn't owe anybody any money. "Goddamn it, something is wrong! Did they say anything to you?" Butch asks.

"They said the boss wants you to move, get the hell out of town, that's what I got out of it. And if I don't, they'll see me again." Jake answers.

Butch is exasperated, "*Think*, damn it! You must have done something to somebody to get this kind of attention. Can you walk? Let's get you home and have Irene help clean up these wounds."

Irene glances out the window and sees Butch helping Jake up the stairs. She asks if he has been in an accident. Butch explains that a couple goons worked him over, but they don't know why. Jake tells her he will be fine if they will just help him clean up his wounds and get into bed. Later, Butch leaves and tells Jake to stay put for the night. They meet the next day and decide that it will be best for Jake to stay away from the bars for a while. Butch is going to ask around town and in the gym to see if anybody knows anything.

A week goes by and nothing happens. But the brothers come up with a plan. Jake will go back to the bar, but this time Butch will be sitting back in the corner booth. Jake is to keep an eye out for the guys who worked him over and give Butch a signal if he sees them. It's the third attempt of this plan, and on this occasion, Sal's two thugs walk in. They sit down and order a beer, thinking that Jake hasn't seen them. Jake gives Butch a nod and heads to the men's room. He's standing at the urinal, but this time, he isn't doing anything. His hands are free and his feet are planted firmly; he is ready. The two come in, and just as before, one guy reaches and grabs Jake by the shoulder and swings him around to hit him. But Jake is ready, and this time he lets his right hand fly and punches the fellow right in the mouth. The second guy rushes up to help his partner but Butch is there, and Butch's big fist really does some damage! The two brothers throw punch after punch until the bartender hears the commotion. The thugs scramble for the back door again. But this time, they are doing the bleeding, with swelling eyes and a hanging jaw that looks like it's busted. Jake comes out with his fists raised in triumph. Butch grins and slaps his brother on the back. They celebrate for a few minutes, then Butch says grimly, "What in the hell is going on, little brother?"

Jake is puzzled. "What do you mean? We just kicked their asses!"

Sternly, Butch says, "Now you listen to me. I recognize those two. They are Sal's men. Just what in the hell have you got yourself into?"

"Nothing," Jake responds. "And it doesn't matter. We kicked their asses, and they won't be back."

"The hell they won't," Butch bellows. "Sal won't stop until he gets what he wants. He will send four guys next time. We have to figure out what this is all about. *Think.* What did they say to you again when they worked you over?"

Jake answers, "I told you, they want me to leave town. They said to take my ready-made family and get the hell out of here."

"Christ, Jake," Butch explodes. "They are talking about little Willy! But why the hell does he want the kid gone?"

They head back to Jake's place. Irene looks at them and asks what happened. Jake tells her how they set the goons up and had gotten the better of them this time. Butch paces the floor. He turns to Irene and says, "Now, Irene, tell me the truth. Did you go to school with Sal's son?" Irene nods her head yes. With his eyes fixed firmly on her, Butch demands, "Is he the father of Willy?" Irene stammers and looks at her hands. Butch continues. "It's Sal's men that are after Jake, and they want Jake and his 'ready-made' family out of town. There has to be some sort of connection. That's it, isn't it?"

"Yes," Irene admits quietly. Butch throws his hands into the air. Irene continue. "But my mother was trying to get Willy first."

"Wait a minute." Butch whirls around. "But doesn't she have her place up for sale?"

"Well, she did, and she did say something about a deal." Irene remembers.

"That must be it. She made a deal with Sal to take Willy out of the state! But you found out about it and got Willy first. Sal is the boy's grandfather!" Butch exclaims.

"Well, good, Irene," Jake pipes up. "Just let Sal have the little bastard. He has money. He can raise him, and I won't end up in the Chicago River."

"No, don't you see, Jake? Sal don't want him! He's an embarrassment to him and his family! That's why he wants him gone, and before anybody can find out about him," Butch shouts. "You, little brother," he warns, "you need to keep your mouth shut, like at the bar, talking about the 'bastard son' as you call him. Keep your mouth shut so nobody else figures this out, or you may end up in the damn river."

"All right," Jake says, "but I don't want to leave town." Butch tells them that he has an idea that might work; he just needs a little time.

Monday morning, Butch walks into Sal's office. There's Sal, his feet up on the desk, a cigar in his mouth, and a drink in front of him. Big Mike is there and a few of Sal's other men as well. Big Mike spots Butch and points and heads toward him. Sal puts his hand up and stops him. Now Sal is a big man himself but not as big as Butch. Sal eyeballs him, saying, "You *are* a big guy, Butch. I hope you are here for a job, after seeing what you did to my men. I could use a man with your talents."

Butch replies, "No, I don't need a job. I have one."

Sal responds, "I know what you do. I am sort of in the same game myself. I've sponsored a fighter now and then, and I do a little betting on the side." Butch asks how he knows his name. Sal responds, "You used to be a pretty good fighter, you were going places, until your legs gave out. I know you like big cars and very fine suits. You get a lot of respect around town. Some even think you're connected with my people." Sal blows a big puff of smoke. He sits up in his chair and says, "So why are you here?"

Butch clears his throat and says, "I'll get right to the point. I know that you want my brother and his family a long way from here.

I want to make a deal with you." The guys in the office roar with laughter.

"A deal?" Sal says. "A deal? My last deal didn't go so well, but all right, what do you propose?" So Butch begins, "Well, you already know where I work, and well, I know a lot of different things about fighters. Like who isn't feeling up to par, whose left jab isn't working very well, who's having muscle cramps, things of that nature. I think maybe this information could be valuable to someone in your profession. In exchange, you could call the dogs off my little brother, at least long enough for him to get on his feet. He has bills to catch up on, and his wife is due to have a baby soon. But I will see to it that he does leave town."

The room gets very quiet. Sal twirls his cigar round and round. "You make a very good point, a very good point," he says. The room is still so quiet you could hear a pin drop. Butch nervously waits, then Sal says, "I have a better idea." He points his finger at Butch, "Now, you know anything we discuss or decide on here is just between you and me. Your brother is not to know anything; he has loose lips when he drinks." Butch nods in agreement. "Now then," Sal continues. "You remember when you first quit boxing? You weren't doing any training then; you were just sparring with the heavyweights to keep them in shape?" Again, Butch nods yes. "You remember Tony G.? He was the fat heavyweight who wasn't much of a fighter because he moved too slowly. He was big. He had a punch that if he hit you, man, it was lights out, baby! Well, I know you had a beef with this guy, and I know it's you that knocked him on his fat ass in the ring one day."

"Sure," Butch says, "I know him. And he slipped that day."

"Slipped my ass!" Sal retorts. "The only slip he made was getting you pissed at him. People say he quit boxing because of it." He taps his cigar ash. "But now let's get down to business. You know about the fight coming up in March between our own Chicago Kid and the Golden Boy from California."

"I do," says Butch, "and I will be the one giving the Kid his workouts."

"No." Sal shakes his head. "That's going to change. The Golden Boy is coming here in about a week, and he wants to work out with you. The boy is talented, that's true. But he is a little too cocky for his own good, and some of us are getting a little, shall we say, concerned. Now he loves to be around the press. He loves to show off his jab with that smirk on his face. So now here's the deal. The main event is Friday night. Wednesday afternoon, he will be in the ring with you. The press will be there, talking with him and taking photos. When those cameras flash, I want you to belt him hard enough that he is on his ass in that ring; put him down good. Then you get the hell out of there, don't talk to nobody, you got it?" Butch is quiet. Sal asks, "Well, big man, do you take the deal or not?"

Butch looks hard at Sal, "You mean all I have to do is drop the boy wonder? And everything will be taken care of? Then we have a deal." Butch holds out his hand. Butch turns to leave, and before he does, Sal opens his desk drawer. He takes out an envelope and hands it to Butch.

"Here, ringside seats to the fight. Take your brother and have a good time. Oh, and here's a tip for you. Take all the money you can get your hands on, and bet it all on the Golden Boy."

CHAPTER 7

A Boy and What? A Girl!

A few months later, Butch is in the ring, working with the Golden Boy. Anna's sister, Dot, has been coming to help her out from time to time. Jake is back at his favorite bar but just drinking beer. Irene is doing a good job of keeping Willy away from Jake during the week, but one day, Jake steps on a toy truck. He gives it a good kick, sending it across the room and putting a hole in the wall. He swears and hollers. "That little bastard's toy is in the way!"

"Damn it," Irene says. "Stop it! That could have hit him." Jake mutters under his breath and sinks in his chair. Willy is learning to stay away from Daddy, that Daddy scares him. When he runs to Irene, crying, Jake says that he is a sissy, scared of his own shadow. "Damn it, Jake," Irene points out angrily, "you are the one making him that way. He is going to grow up resentful toward you."

"Good," Jake scowls, "the feelings will be mutual."

It's Wednesday before the big fight, and Butch is in the gym, doing what he's supposed to. He finishes up and heads to the bar to see Jake. He asks his brother if he has been able to save any money. Jake says sure and asks why he wants to know. Butch responds by pulling the two fight tickets out of his pocket. Jake's mouth drops open and Butch grins. "I got them through a little promotion at work; nothing too good for us, right?" He continues. "Now Friday, payday, don't cash your paycheck. I'll meet up with you. I want to place a bet for us."

"Okay," Jake says, "but Irene won't like it."

"She doesn't need to know about it," Butch answers.

Friday night, the brothers are in their seats at ringside. The bell rings, and the first round of ten starts. The first couple of rounds are uneventful, with lots of dancing and jabbing by both boxers. Jake keeps hollering out for the Chicago Kid to make his move and get to work on this California clown! It's the fifth round and the Kid goes down; he gets back up and the crowd is going crazy. Jake remarks to Butch that he is getting a little worried; they have a lot of money riding on their boy, the Kid. The rounds continue with more of the same. Then in the middle of the eighth round, it's over. The Chicago Kid is in the center of the ring, knocked out cold. Jake stands up and shouts obscenities at the Kid. Then he notices that Butch isn't nearly as upset as he is.

Jake asks, "How bad is it? Did we bet it all?" Butch tells him that they did. Jake sits back down. "Damn, Irene is going to be pissed."

"Well, don't say a word to her, Jake. You two come over tomorrow night, and tell her to wear her best dress. I'm taking us to dinner and a show, and I'll explain it all to her then."

"Christ," Jake explodes, "why the hell are we going out to celebrate after such a big loss? Are you nuts? You've had too many blows to your big head!"

The next night at dinner, the girls are having a wonderful time, relaxing and laughing. Butch is thoroughly enjoying himself too. It's only Jake that's a little edgy. He's downing his beers, waiting nervously for Butch to tell the girls the bad news. Finally, Butch reaches into his pocket and says, "This has been fun, but I can't stand it any longer." He hands a very fat envelope to Irene. Her eyes widen; she looks inside and gasps.

She looks at Jake, "You bet on the fight?"

He stammers, "Yeah, but we lost!"

"No, we didn't, little brother." Butch beams. "We won big, very big!" Jake looks at him in disbelief. He grabs the envelope, looks inside, and grins. "You bet our money on that California clown, and you let me think we bet on the favorite?"

Butch nods and smiles. "But listen to me." He turns serious. "There is enough money here to pay all your bills and for the baby on the way. Stop running up bar tabs. Pay as you go. And slow down some. You have a family, and that should come first. Also, a friend of mine has a car for sale. It's at a very good price, and you should look at it tomorrow. You would be crazy not to buy it." Jake grins and thanks his big brother repeatedly. They enjoy the rest of the evening, and it's a very good night for the foursome.

The money brings a big change in the lives of Jake and Irene, and Jake does buy the car. It's the latter part of March now, and little Willy is two years old. Anna has been in and out of the hospital a few times, false alarms each time. Irene has allowed Bess to watch little Willy some, and Bess loves every minute of it. It's the first week of April, and the next false alarm turns out to be the real deal for Butch and Anna. She delivers a healthy baby boy. They name him Johnny, after Anna's father, John. Butch is thrilled and can't wait to get to the bar to tell everyone about his new baby boy. He buys drinks for the house but only beers for his brother. Jake comments, "All right, you got your little boy, and in a few weeks, I'll have mine." But it doesn't quite turn out that way. No, not that way at all. In the middle of April, Irene gives birth to a beautiful baby girl. They name her Rosie. Jake can't hide his disappointment that he didn't get a son, but in time, he grows very fond of little Rosie.

CHAPTER 8

A Tragedy Strikes

After Rosie's birth, the weather warms up nicely. As they head into summer, Butch and Anna are very happy with their new son, Johnny. They still keep Willy on the weekends, and Willy is very fond of Johnny and loves being with the three of them. Jake holds and plays with his daughter. He warns Irene that Willy is to stay away from his little girl. When Daddy is gone, though, Willy gets to see Rosie and touch her and even try to talk to her. He is learning to stay away from Daddy; he is very scared of him and just watches him from the other side of the room. Jake still yells obscenities at him, and a frightened Willy still clings to Mommy. At Butch and Anna's, he tries to call Butch "Daddy," but Butch insists that Willy is to call him "Uncle." He is learning that life is very different over at his uncle's place. Anna and Irene get together with the kids quite often, and the bond grows even stronger between the two. Butch is still working with fighters, and nothing is ever said about the incident earlier in the year. The foursome, with their children, spend the entire summer together.

Rosie and Johnny are growing fast, and Willy is too. In November, Irene discovers she is pregnant again. They have a nice Thanksgiving, and it's December already. The weather is cold, and the snow keeps Irene and Anna indoors with the kids. Anna's sister, Dot, comes to visit and takes the girls out to do their Christmas shopping. The three families spend the holidays together again at Butch and Anna's. The kids are excited by the pretty twinkling lights and the gifts; Willy is especially excited for Christmas. He knows he has to stay away from Jake and Rosie. Butch tells Jake he thinks it's time he starts paying some attention to Willy; after all, he is going to be around for a long time, and it would be better for everyone. Jake says the boy is in his home; that's enough. Irene is raising her own bastard son. Besides, he will have his own son soon; just wait and see. Butch says, "Jake, I don't know why you are so stubborn. You know, if we get to take a trip up to see Mom again, she will like the boy, no matter where he came from."

It's March 1937 and time for Willy's third birthday. It's cold and snowy still, but you can tell spring is just around the corner. Johnny's first birthday is in early April, and Rosie's is right behind. The weather turns warm and summer comes to Chicago. The little ones are excited about the big Fourth of July celebration. They love the fireworks and pretty lights but are afraid of the loud noises. Irene starts to get pretty uncomfortable as she is due any day now. Rosie and Willy are already at Willy's second home, the one he likes best, in preparation for the birth. A few days later, Irene goes into labor. Jake can't control himself; he finally has his boy! He is so proud. The boy will be named Dale, after his brother, but they will call him Little Butch. He can't wait to see his brother and buy a round of drinks and hand out cigars. Jake tells Butch how happy he is that they each have a boy and there are two boys in the family now. Butch reminds him that actually, with Willy, there are three. Jake says, "No, Irene's bastard son is not family. He is not one of us and never will be." It's a good thing that Irene is in the hospital that night, because Jake hits the hard liquor.

A couple of days later, Anna takes Willy and Rosie to see their mom and new baby brother in the hospital. Dot is at home with little Johnny, and Butch plans to stop by later. Anna and the kids come in the room. Jake is already there with Irene. The adults talk excitedly while waiting for the nurse to bring little Butch in. The room is set up with the head of the bed on the inside wall, and Irene is looking at the big, long window on the outside wall. The bottom half of the window is open as high as it can go because it is mid-July and there is no air-conditioning. Under the window is a long, but not tall, radiator, used for steam heat in the wintertime. The window has a screen on it, but the S hook to hold it in place is not fastened. Willy climbs up on the radiator. He sits on the windowsill with his feet dangling. Anna and Jake are at Irene's bedside, chatting with her. Rosie, seeing Willy, wants to be in the window with him. Willy helps her climb up. The nurse brings the newborn baby in and hands him to Irene, then she steps back out of the way.

And then it happens. Either Rosie or Willy or both lean back on the screen. The screen pops out, and both children are falling! The nurse sees what is happening and screams. She lunges forward and manages to grab a foot. She grabs Willy, but she can't get to Rosie. Rosie falls the full four floors to the concrete below. The scene is chaotic. Irene and Anna are hysterical. Jake, seeing that Rosie is gone, heads for the stairwell and races down all four floors. He is on the ground, holding Rosie and hysterical himself. Medical personnel come running and rush Rosie into the hospital. Butch arrives on the scene. Irene and Anna are given sedatives and they wait, wait to hear something about Rosie. The doctor finally comes into the room and looks at the anguished parents. He says solemnly that she is gone. The little girl did not make it.

"He did it!" Jake screams. "That little bastard killed my girl, my Rosie!"

"No, Jake, no." Butch shakes his head. "It was a horrible, terrible accident. You said yourself they were both in the window. Hell, it could've been him or both. He was just closest to the nurse."

"But it wasn't him, was it?" Jake snarls. "It should have been him, then Irene and me would have had our own family. I should have never let him back in my home. I should have gotten rid of the little bastard myself. I should have done something, Butch. I should have done some goddamn thing to that little bastard son of a bitch."

Father Francis happens to be in the hospital this afternoon, visiting some sick parishioners. He hears of the tragedy and goes to help. He walks from the room where he has just given Rosie the last rites. Jake is sitting in the room with her. Butch takes this opportunity to head back upstairs to check on the girls. The nurse tells him that Irene is heavily sedated and will be for the rest of the day and night. Anna is crying. Butch comforts her and tells her to take Willy and go home. Irene is out for the night, and "There is nothing else you can do for her," he reasons. He tells her that he will stay with Jake. She asks how Jake is holding up, and Butch replies, "He is in bad shape. I think that he will kill Willy if he gets his hands on him now. Keep Willy at our place, and don't let anybody take him unless I say it's okay." Anna agrees and turns to leave. He tells her he will see her the next day; he intends to spend the night with Jake.

Butch sees Father Francis returning to the room where Rosie is lying. Jake is still sitting there, looking at his daughter. Father Francis gently asks Jake if this lovely girl is his daughter. Jake nods yes. "Well," Father Francis continues, "she must be a very special little girl, so young and beautiful and with a heart so pure that God wants her by his side."

Jake says bitterly, "He should have taken someone else and not her."

Father Francis continues quietly. "I understand that she was sitting with her brother, you know. They both could have fallen."

"That's not her brother!" Jake screams. "He is a bastard son, and that's who should have fallen, not Rosie!" The father thinks for a moment. "So your wife, Irene, is the mother of Rosie, and she is also the mother of the boy you call the bastard son?" Jake nods. "So the boy is Willy. My, how he has grown!" Father Francis remarks.

Jake snaps his head around. "So you know Willy? Are you the priest who put him in the orphanage? Why'd you have to cause me all this goddamn trouble by not keeping the little bastard where he belongs? Now, because of you, my little girl is gone."

Father Francis clasps his hands. "I am very sorry for your loss," he begins.

"Oh, kiss my ass! You Catholics are all alike!" Jake explodes.

Butch, standing to the side, grabs his brother's arm. "Come on," he says. "Let's go and get you a drink."

At the bar, Jake starts drinking boilermakers. He tells Butch, "I know that little bastard had something to do with Rosie's death. He was very jealous, you know; he would always sit in the corner staring at us when I would play with her. I don't want him in my home ever again!"

Butch counters, "Well, I'm sure he was watching your every move with Rosie, my god! He was told he has to stay away from you, and then you play with her? He probably wondered what the hell he would have to do to have Daddy play like that with him."

"I am not his daddy," Jake screams, "and I don't want to be!"

"But he doesn't know that, for chrissakes, Jake, and he's just a little boy. And he was falling too, remember?" Butch reasons.

"Well, he sure lucked out, didn't he? It would have been good if it would have been him. Rosie would still be here if Irene would have left him where he was at. Or better yet let her mother have him. He would be on the West Coast by now and completely out of my sight." Finally, Jake has had enough to drink and is ready to pass out. Butch takes him home and puts him into bed. The next day, Butch and Anna go to see Irene. She is still sedated but visiting with Father Francis. She tells him how bad she feels that she hadn't gotten Rosie baptized. The good father tells her not to worry, that he baptized the child before he gave her the last rites. Jake enters the room just as Father Francis is leaving. The priest tells the parents that if there is anything he can do to help with funeral arrangements, to let him know. A grief-stricken Anna bursts into tears. She sobs, "I should have watched the children more closely."

Irene assures her that it wasn't her fault. "If anything," she says sadly, "we all should have watched them better. But then, the nurse had just brought in this little guy." And with that, she holds up the newborn baby. "How could we not have looked at this darling little guy?"

"Yeah," Jake says glumly, "I got my boy, but what a price to pay!" What a price to pay indeed.

CHAPTER 9

Pregnant Again

A funeral is held for the little girl and she is buried. An overwhelming sadness hangs over everyone. July goes by slowly for the foursome as they try to get back to some kind of normalcy. The weather turns hot as the days slip into August. The men continue to work, and Jake sticks to drinking beer only, no hard stuff. He bonds with his precious new son, Little Butch. Irene and Anna get together with the kids as often as they can. Willy asks a lot of questions and is more confused than ever. When Daddy stops over to Butch's place with the new baby, he watches Daddy give the baby attention. It has been over a month since Rosie's death, and Willy is still at Butch and Anna's. Irene knows that she is going to have to make a stand to get Willy back home. Irene and Anna have just had a tearful day, packing up Rosie's things. That night, Irene tells Jake that she is bringing Willy back home. Jake says no, he has caused enough trouble and pain, and he doesn't want him around Little Butch. Irene doesn't back down. "Jake," she says, "they are brothers, and I am going to raise them that way whether you like it or not. Besides, it's not like he's going to come running to you saying 'Play with me, Daddy.' He is scared to death of you! He will stay as far away from you as he can! He spent almost two years of his life in that damn institution and now most of the time with Butch and Anna. And the hell of it is, he likes it better over there. He's treated like family there, and he and Johnny are bonding like brothers. He *has* a brother here, at home. How would you like it if somebody took your brother away from you?" She continues. "Do you remember our deal, when I said I wouldn't promise anything? Well, the time is here, and if you plan to do something about it, then do it now." With that, she slams the door and leaves.

Irene does what she says; she brings Willy home. Not much changes, except Willy spends a few more weekends at home now. Jake plays with his son, Butch. Summer flies by, Thanksgiving comes and goes, it's already December. It's a cold and snowy evening, and Irene and Anna have just told their husbands that they are both pregnant again. Butch jokes, "What have we started here, little brother!" The harsh winter fades into spring, and with it brings the children's birthdays. At their annual Fourth of July celebration, Butch makes an announcement to his brother. He tells him that his time is up. A confused Jake asks, "What in the hell are you talking about?"

Butch explains, "Well, I had a visit from Sal the other day. He says you have had enough extra time, and he wants you out of town before the snow flies."

"Oh, he said that, did he?" growls Jake.

"He did," Butch says patiently. "And I will be gone by then too. Anna and me and the family, we are going south, to Indiana, around where Anna's sister and Joe live. Why don't you come that way too?"

"I don't know." Jake shakes his head. "I'll have to think about it. But I know it won't be hard to get Irene to move if Anna is going. But what the hell will you do down there?"

Butch explains, "Joe has a job lined up for me at the machine plant where he works. He said that the plant just got a new contract to make airplane parts for the government. He claims this airplane stuff is gonna be a big family business. Hell, with your mechanical knowledge, I'll bet you could get a really good job there."

Jake scratches his chin. "I don't know, Butch. Like I said, I'll have to think on it."

It's mid-August, and Irene is back in the hospital. She delivers another baby boy. He is named Melvin, after Jake's dad, but they plan to call him Mel. A few weeks later, Anna gives birth to a baby boy also. He is named Douglas and will be called Doug. Jake and Butch are very pleased with their new sons, but Butch tells Jake that he is done; two kids are enough for him.

CHAPTER 10

The Big Move

The days pass quickly. Butch tells Jake that he will be leaving on the fifteenth of November for Indiana. He asks Jake what he has decided to do. Jake tells his brother that he and Irene have talked it over, and they have decided to move to central Minnesota. He explains that this way, they will be closer to their mother. Besides, she can spend time with her grandkids. "That's great!" Butch says, "and we can come and see you in the summertime."

"Yep," Jake agrees. "And"—he chuckles—"I know I'll find work somewhere, because everybody needs a good mechanic, don't they?" He tells Butch that they plan to leave a few days before Thanksgiving so that they can spend the holiday with their mother. The brothers continue discussing their moving plans. Butch has a truck rented for the fourteenth, and Jake assures him he will be there to help him load it. Irene has most of their furniture sold already, and the car will be loaded down with bedding, clothes, and kitchen stuff. "Leave room for the kids!" Butch jokes.

"Yeah," Jake grunts, "you want one?"

It's a busy time for everyone. Moving day has come and gone for Butch and Anna, and moving day is finally here for Jake and Irene. But Jake plans to move in the middle of the night. Jake hasn't told his brother, but he has gotten a little behind in his bills, with Irene not working much and more mouths to feed. He plans to skip town and leave the bills behind. He will have his last paycheck, plus the furniture money, but it isn't much. Irene hasn't told him, and isn't going to, about the money Bess gave her when she took the kids to say good-bye.

Jake is in the driver's seat; Little Butch is propped up on some pillows. Irene is holding Mel in the passenger seat, and Willy is fast asleep on a mound of blankets in the backseat. The family drives through the night. When the sun comes up, they stop for coffee and breakfast. The main highways, few and far between, are paved, but most of the roads are not. They don't travel very fast. Around noon, a rear tire goes flat and there is no spare. Jake unloads stuff from the trunk to get to the jack and the tire-repair kit. He jacks the car up, removes the tire and wheel, patches the tube, and gets them back on the road. This takes a lot of time, and it soon grows dark. The kids are hungry and cranky. They decide to stop at the next small town and get a cheap room for the night. They pay in advance and leave the next morning at daylight. They drive on and are about half way to their destination when the engine begins to make a loud knocking sound. Jake knows that this isn't good and pulls over immediately. He opens the hood and takes a look; he hollers obscenities. He climbs back in the car and tells Irene that they can't go any farther. He grimaces. "There is oil all over the motor, an oil line has blown, or there is a hole in the pan, or some goddamn thing, or a piston rod has gone out!"

"Can't you just put more oil in the motor?" she asks.

"No, damn it, the damage has already been done," he sighs. He knows there is a small town ahead. He figures if he can get the car restarted, he can limp into town for some help.

The car starts, noise and all, and they manage to make it to the next town. They pull into a lot in front of a big old building. The sign reads, "Fred's Welding Shop, Farm Equipment and Auto Repair." The place has one gravity-filled gas pump, with the handle on the side. You pump the gas into the glass on top where it's marked half gallon or full gallon. You fill this with as much gas as you want to buy, then you take the hose and let the gas run down into your tank. Jake stands by the car, hood up, looking at the motor. A voice behind him says hello and asks if he needs help. Jake points to the engine, "I sure do, but I got a big problem here."

"Yes, you do," the man says. "That looks like one big oil leak."

"Well, it's worse than that; the motor ran out of oil, and there is at least one piston rod going out too." Jake replies as he wipes his forehead with the back of his hand. "You wouldn't know it by the looks of my car, but I am a good mechanic," he tells the man. The man extends his hand and introduces himself as Fred.

Jake shakes his hand and says, "Jake, Bad Luck Jake."

Fred smiles, "Mr. Bad Luck Jake, you say you are a mechanic and a good one? Maybe your luck has changed." Jake assures him that he is a good mechanic and has his own tools. "You see that sign up there?" The man points to the building. "That's me. I own this place. What you probably can't see is the sign in the window over there that says "Mechanic Wanted." Jake tells him that if he is offering him a job. That would sure take care of some of his problems, but he has a family here. "Now just a minute, just a minute, follow me," Fred says. Jake follows Fred to the end of the building. Fred points and says, "See that house back there? That's mine and it's empty. That's part of the deal. What little rent I charge can come right off your wages. Now before you say anything, let's walk back to your auto and tell your missus."

In the car, Jake and Irene talk it over. Irene says that they don't have many options right now, and Fred is making them a very generous offer. She asks Fred if they would be able to get in the house today? And would they be able to have some heat to get warm? Fred explains that there is plenty of wood and coal. He tells them it's a small two-bedroom house with electricity, but no plumbing or water. He tells them the toilet is an outhouse out back. He adds that there is a well and a pump close to the front for drinking water and cooking. There's a cookstove that burns cobs or wood and a heat stove that burns coal or wood. There's plenty of furniture and two beds. He asks if they would like to walk over and take a look at it. Jake and Irene look at each other and then nod yes. They decide that the house will do just fine. Fred gets the key and lets them in. Irene sweeps the place out and starts a fire. The men get the car to the front door and start unloading it. Fred asks if they need anything for supper and tells them that there is a little grocery store about a block and a half away. It closes in an hour though, he warns. Irene puts Mel down on a pile of blankets; she tells Jake to watch him and Dale, and she and Willy head to the store. When she returns, the men have the car unloaded. Fred leaves, telling them he will be back in the morning to discuss the rest of the details. He tells them that if they will put a pot of coffee on, he will bring the sweet rolls. Jake and Irene feed the kids and get them to bed. Over a bowl of hot soup, Jake sighs, "This sure isn't where I wanted to be right now, but I guess we are lucky to have this!"

The next morning, not only does Fred bring over sweet rolls, he also brings a small hen turkey for dinner the next day. Irene thanks him repeatedly. Fred blushes and explains that up until about ten days ago, a young fellow worked for him. He had lived in the house with his wife and small daughter. Fred continues. "He was my mechanic. He just up and left, and I don't know why. That turkey was for him. He's gone now, so it's yours. You see, on Thanksgiving and Christmas, I give all my employees turkeys, all two of them," he says with a laugh. "My other employee is Al. He's a welder. He does nothing but weld farm machinery. Now, Jake, your job will be mostly to work on cars, take care of customers that come in for oil and belts. I sell a lot of radiator alcohol in the winter. These old guys around here have cars that get stuck in the snow, and you know for yourself it doesn't take much to boil the alcohol away. That and help keep the snow out of the driveway. And if you run out of things to do, you can take machinery apart for Al and me to weld."

Jake asks, "Fred, is there much business here in this little burg of a town?" Fred smiles and asks where they are from. Jake answers that they are from the big city of Chicago. Jake tells him they were heading to central Minnesota to be near his mother so she could see the grandkids.

"Well," Fred says, "you are only nine miles from the Minnesota border. And in answer to your question, yes, this is a small town. We have a church, a store, a one-room schoolhouse, and a post office. We also have a telephone office, a beer joint, and a hardware store where you will get coal, cobs, and wood from, and of course, my shop." They sip their coffee and Fred continues. "You already know you have no inside plumbing. The whole town is like that. All twenty-two homes and the businesses too. So here you are in the north central part of Iowa, only nine miles from the Minnesota border. This town is surrounded by small farms, mostly ten to fifty acres. There are very few tractors. Most farmers have an auto or pickup truck, and there are lots of horses. Hell, if it wasn't for the horses, these farmers wouldn't get to town in the wintertime! Those county snowplows don't come through here very often. It's not unusual for us to be snowed in here for seven to ten days. Anyway, most of my work comes from the farmers. So here's what I can do." Fred writes a number down on a piece of paper and passes it to Jake and says, "I'll give you that much money plus the house with the electric."

Jake eyes the paper and answers, "Okay, but you know, we aren't going to stay here forever. When I get my car fixed, we will be leaving."

Fred nods. "I understand that. Just tell me a week for so beforehand. Now that pay is for a week's worth of work, without missing any days, and that's six days a week. Once in a while, though, we do quit early on Saturdays."

Jake responds with a smile, "When do I start?"

"You start Friday," Fred says as the two men shake hands. "Oh, and, Irene, my wife, Mary, says that if you ever need someone to watch the children, she would be tickled pink to watch over them for you. She loves children, and we never had any of our own."

Irene smiles. "Please tell her thank you, and I will probably take her up on that. And thank her for the delicious homemade sweet rolls."

Fred pats his stomach and chuckles. "Well, she loves to bake, and since she just has me, well, you can bet she will be bringing cookies for those kids!" He tells Irene that the shed out back has a little wagon in it that she can use to bring home groceries, and the kids can play with it. Irene thanks him again. Fred stands to leave and says, "Come on, Jake, let's go find Al and see if we can get that car of yours in the back corner of the building. That way, it will be inside when you want work on it." He adds with a grin, "That is, in your spare time." He tells them that if they want, he can get them a line of credit at the lumberyard and the grocery store. "But each week," he warns, "I gotta pay them off out of your paycheck. That fella that was here before you? He left in the middle of the night, owing them both, and I promised them that would never happen again." The men leave to go find Al and get the car moved. When Jake returns, he says to Irene, "Fred's right. It sure is different around here. I have to go outside and use the outhouse in the cold!" Irene reminds him that it could be a lot worse for them.

Jake tells Irene to give him some money as he wants check out the local beer joint. Irene busies herself with the children and makes supper. Later that night, Jake plays with little Butch as Willy looks on. Willy has been asking his mom a lot of questions and is curious about the new place.

Thanksgiving comes and goes, and they settle into a routine. Jake works hard at his new job. It's cold out but without too much snow on the ground. Irene checks out the town. She finds the post office and mails a letter to Bess. The next few weeks go by pretty smoothly. Then one morning a few days before Christmas, after Jake has already left for work, Irene notices a car stopping out front. She watches as the door swings open, and to her surprise, out steps her father, Jim! She races to the car, and after lots of hugs and kisses, she brings him back to the house to meet the children. There is much excitement and the questions are flying! She finds out that he still works on the dairy farm in central Iowa. He tells her he had gone to the big city to find her after he heard that he had grandchildren. When he couldn't find her, he looked up Bess. Bess told him about the letter she'd gotten from Irene and where to find her. So Grandpa Jim gets to meet his grandkids! After things settle down a bit, Jim and Irene have a very long, and much-needed, talk. Jim is very pleased when he sees Willy's birth certificate and that he has been named after his only son. Jake comes home for lunch and meets his father-in-law, although not much is said between them. Irene tries to convince her dad to stay for supper, but he says he can't because he doesn't like to drive after dark. He says his good-byes, but before he leaves, he unloads sacks of groceries and Christmas gifts and gives Irene some cash. Over supper that night, Jake asks Irene about her father. She only tells him what she wants him to know. Without thinking, Jake says, "I suppose he liked your kid the best."

Irene answers with a laugh, "Jake, he liked *all* my kids the best!"

The snow starts to fall as the family celebrates Christmas and the new year, 1939. Willy plays with the used sled he gets for Christmas, but he just pulls it all around the yard by the rope until some older boys come over and show him how to use it. They show him how to slide down the hill behind the outhouse. It isn't a big hill, but it's big enough for the boys. They also show him another trick. Out in the street, the snow gets packed down by the horses and the sleigh runners. They show him how to hold his sled up, run a little, then slam it down and lay on it and slide! What fun Willy has! Willy can't wait to show this trick to his mom. Jake is standing in the front room with a beer in his hand. Willy comes busting through the kitchen door and slams the sled on the floor. But the sled stays put, and Willy goes sliding on his nose into the front room. Jake doubles over with laughter. "Look at your little bastard now!" Willy hangs his head, just now realizing that it only works on snow. Jake continues to laugh and sneers, "You can sure tell he ain't one of mine!"

It's been a rough winter on both Jake and Willy, being cooped inside the small house. Willy asks his mom why his daddy doesn't like him, why he treats him like that, and why he can't see Uncle Butch anymore. Irene always responds that he is too young to understand and that someday she will explain it to him. Jake still calls Willy a bastard, and Irene does her best but doesn't seem to be able to keep them far enough apart.

The winter passes, and Jake hasn't done much work on the family car yet. Fred's wife, Mary, brings homemade cookies for the kids and visits Irene. She watches the kids while Irene goes to the store and Willy goes with her. The days and weeks pass, and it is Willy's fifth birthday. Mary brings a big cake with candles and all. They celebrate in the afternoon, before Daddy gets home. Irene tells Willy that now he can start school, but Willy isn't so excited about this.

The winter gives way to spring, and the flowers start to bloom. Irene plants a garden. She buys a fan as the cookstove in the little house makes it very hot in the summertime. Little Butch turns two, and there's a big birthday party in the backyard on that hot July day.

CHAPTER 11

What? Another Boy!

The day is finally here. Mary is babysitting with the boys, Dale and Mel, and Irene is enrolling Willy in school. But Willy isn't going to be in first grade; he can't start first grade until he is six years old. This class is the "getting acquainted" class. He will learn things like how to get along with others and how to follow instructions. He will hear stories and finger paint and play. While it's called a one-room schoolhouse, it actually has more rooms. There's a cloakroom for coats and overshoes, a small library room, and the room where all the desks are. The teacher will teach Willy's class plus three others, with fifteen students altogether. That first day, Irene leaves Willy with the teacher and walks home. It's such a beautiful day that Irene takes the long way. When she gets home, there's Willy! No way is he staying in that place without his mommy, he informs her. But in the next few days, he gives in and stays at the school and quickly realizes that he likes it. He is so proud to come home and tell his mother what he has learned. He thinks maybe his daddy will like to know too but finds out that Daddy doesn't care, and it won't make Daddy like him any better. Willy walks to and from school with his sledding buddies. After a few weeks of school, he tells his mom that the kids in school and his buddies call him Will. He likes this a lot better and wants to be called Will at home too.

The weeks pass, and Mary has been a godsend to Irene. Jake continues to work on the car in his spare time. Soon, it's Thanksgiving again, and like last year, Fred gives them another turkey. And Irene knows she is pregnant again. Winter arrives, and Jake plays with his boys when he isn't working on the car. Mary helps Irene with the children. Will learns a lot in school and spends the winter sledding down the hill with his buddies. It's Will's sixth birthday, and spring is around the corner. Then the weather turns hot and school is out for the summer. One day shortly after school is out, Grandpa Jim surprises everyone with a visit. He brings toys for the kids and groceries for the family. He enjoys the day with them then asks Irene if Will can spend the summer with him. Irene says yes; she knows it will be good for Will to be around a father figure. She also knows it will be good to get him away from Jake for a while.

Will is thrilled to go home with Grandpa Jim and spend the summer with him and Grandma. He follows Grandpa everywhere. He even gets up at two in the morning with him to get the cows from the pasture. Gramps lets Will hold the flashlight while Grandpa hollers "Come, boss, come, boss" and all forty-eight cows follow them back into the big red barn. The cows go into the stanchions, where they get milked. Grandpa measures out the mixture of corn and oats and feeds them. The cows get milked then get turned back into the pasture. The milk is put into big cans with tight lids and put into a cooler until the truck hauls it away. The milk house and machinery all get cleaned. In the barn, the gutter where the manure goes has to be cleaned. This is Will's least favorite part. Each day, Will helps Grandpa. Every morning Grandma makes a big breakfast of bacon, eggs, oatmeal, orange juice, pancakes, and toast. After breakfast is Grandpa's nap time, so Will goes with Grandma to pick blueberries. Or he watches the other workers put hay and straw away for the wintertime.

One cow is much shorter than the rest. Grandpa says she is a shorthorn and the only one in the bunch; the rest are all Holsteins. Will pets this one and scratches her ears. When Grandpa isn't looking, he gives her a handful or two of the ground grain. It isn't long until she wants more. When Will is outside, she comes right up to the fence where he is. He pulls out some of the green grass and clover growing in the fence line and gives them to her. This becomes a daily event, and the workers soon laugh about the little boy and the little cow.

One day, Grandpa Jim talks to Will about his mother, Irene, explaining to the young boy that she is his daughter. He tells the boy that he had been married to Grandma Bess at one time and that Irene is their little girl. He says that he loves his daughter very much and is sorry that he hadn't been around much while she was growing up. Will seems to understand and nods. "I love my mom very much too, Grandpa."

"How about your dad?" Grandpa Jim asks the boy. Will doesn't answer for a moment.

Then he quietly says, "No. Does that make me bad? Am I a bad boy, Grandpa?"

Grandpa Jim quickly replies, "No, of course not! But why do you ask that?"

"Because he don't like me," Will responds, "He calls me bad names, and Mom gets mad when he does that."

Grandpa Jim pats the little boy on the shoulder. "Well, I know it's hard for you to understand, but someday you will."

"Mom says that too." Will nods. "But he plays with Dale and Mel and tells me to get out of the way. Don't tell him or Mom, but, Grandpa, sometimes I hate him. I wish he was gone."

"I wish I could help you," sighs Grandpa Jim. "Someday this will all be behind you," he assures the boy.

The next day is Grandpa Jim's day off. He tells Will that after breakfast, the three of them are going to the city. They stop in to see friends, and while the men are visiting, the ladies take Will shopping. He gets new school clothes, and boy, is he excited!

Back at home, Jake is still working on the car. He tells Irene that he needs money for the new car parts. He tells her he wants the money that her father gave her. Fred can get the parts for him at cost, but he still needs the money in advance. Irene suggests he use some of his beer money. Jake explains that the motor is all apart and cleaned. Once he has the new parts, the target date for them to leave is the first of November. Hopefully, they will be at his mother's by this Thanksgiving. Jake informs Fred of the plan and writes to his mother and informs her too. It's the first part of July, and Irene isn't feeling well, although her due date is about a month away. She is grateful she has Mary's help each day. Then one hot day in mid August, Irene goes into labor. Mary runs and get the two ladies next door then runs to the telephone office and calls the doctor. She assures Irene that the two ladies will take good care of her. After calling the doctor, Mary runs to get Jake. The women are in the house with Irene, and Jake stands outside with Little Butch and Mel. They hear grunts and groans then a scream. All is quiet, and then they hear a baby cry. The doctor pulls up; he races past Jake and inside the house. He comes back out a few minutes later and declares that the women have done a very good job, and everyone is just fine. "And you, young man," he says as he points to Jake, "you are the father of another boy!"

CHAPTER 12

Made It This Time

Mary exclaims, "Jake, you must be a hell of a man, four boys!"

"No," says Jake with a smile, "I have three." The new baby boy is named Kenny, after Jake. The next few days are very hot, and Irene gets some much-needed help from Mary. August rolls into September, and Grandpa brings Will back home. Will knows of the new baby and is excited to see his new brother. As before, Jim brings big bags of groceries and supplies for the family. Will excitedly shows his mother his new school clothes. She reminds him that they are for school only; he must change into play clothes when he gets home from school. After Grandpa Jim leaves, Jake remarks to Irene, "I see he got your kid new stuff."

Irene snaps, "My dad is not like that. He knows all the kids are his grandkids. But they weren't with him. He doesn't know their sizes. He left money for me to buy them clothes with. Now damn it, does that make you happy?"

Will starts school even if it's only for a couple months. Irene gets back into a routine with the kids and the new baby. Jake has the car nearly finished, and it's close to the first of November. The letter Jake gets from his mother informs them that she has a house for them, right across the street from her. It's furnished and ready to move into. She explains that the lady who had lived there has passed away. She has worked out a good deal for them. Her friend has agreed to rent them the house, and the furniture too, for only a little extra each month. Once again, Jake has lucked out.

Moving day is here. And like before, the car is loaded with bedding and kids; stuff is even tied on the back. The only difference this time is that the bills are paid up, and they are not leaving in the middle of the night. They say good-bye to Fred and Mary. Fred tells them that if they ever get back that way, to be sure and stop in, and with hands waving and the horn honking, the family drives off.

A few days later, they arrive at another grandma's place. This is Grandma Elsie, and her husband is Dewey. Dewey is Elsie's second husband. Her first husband, Jake's father, was killed in the war. Dewey is a very quiet guy who keeps to himself. He stands beside Elsie, and they greet the family as they arrive. Elsie spots her son; she hugs and kisses him then Irene. She grabs the little ones, kissing and hugging them, all the while cuddling the baby. Jake proudly points out and names each one. The newborn, Kenny, then Mel, then Little Butch, named after his brother, and finally, Irene's little bastard, Will. Will stands there, head down. But what happens next delights him. Grandma Elsie stands up tall. She points to her son and says, "Now let's get one thing straight here and now. Butch and Anna have told me how you treat this little fellow and the names you call him. I will not tolerate this kind of nonsense around me or in my home, do you understand me?" Will knows he is going to like this Grandma! Before Jake can answer his mother, Will moves closer to her and grabs her leg. Jake mutters something to the boy, but Will just smiles.

Grandma Elsie takes them across the street and shows them the house they will live in. Irene shouts with joy, "Indoor plumbing!" The next few days are spent getting settled in. Will is enrolled in the nearby school. There's a small grocery store on the street, and Grandma Elsie gives Will some pennies to buy candy with. Dewey tells Jake he knows of several places in town that are in need of a mechanic. Jake gets hired on at one of them and starts work immediately. Irene is busy with kids and housework. Thanksgiving arrives and they have a wonderful day. The family is into a new routine. Grandma is enjoying being with her grandchildren. Things are going great for everyone. Except for Will, who has a new problem. Two brothers live next door to them; one is Will's age and the other is a year older. These boys are the neighborhood bullies, and for some reason, they want to fight Will. But Will doesn't want to fight them, so every day, they chase him home from school. This continues for quite some time until one day, Irene asks Will why he always comes home so winded. He tells her about the two boys. Irene confides in Grandma Elsie, and when she finds out, she wants to talk to the boy's mother. These two are terrors, always in trouble, throwing rocks and causing trouble for everyone. But Jake steps in and says, "No, let it be. Let the little wussy learn how to handle himself." So Will figures out that when they are split up, they don't want to fight; it's only when the brothers are together. He watches them closely and manages to avoid them, especially when they are together. He is careful not to start anything and avoids any trouble. Winter arrives, and with it the snow and cold. The family has a wonderful Christmas thanks to Grandma Elsie. And things go better for Will, also thanks to Grandma Elsie, because Jake isn't as mean to the boy with his mother around.

A few weeks into the new year, Will gets very sick and is sent home from school. A doctor is called to the house, and after examining Will, a big sign is put on the front door. "No one in, no one out, until further notice. under quarantine." Will has scarlet fever. The doctor tells Irene to put a note in the mailbox for the things she needs. Dewey or Elsie are to leave the items on the front porch. Irene can then take the supplies inside. The doctor tells them it will be two weeks, maybe longer, depending on who else gets sick and when. Jake comes home from work, sees the big yellow sign on the front door, and wants to know what is going on. His mother explains it to him and he explodes. "Now that damn little bastard has me locked out of my own place! He's been a pain in my ass from day one, damn him anyway!"

"Now, Jake," Elsie reasons with him, "he's just a little boy. He gets sick like all kids. I remember when you had chicken pox and had your dad locked out! Now check the mailbox for a note from Irene and get on over here. I will fix you supper. You will stay with me until the quarantine is over."

CHAPTER 13

The Big Surprise

Will's sickness lasts about three weeks. The sign comes down and the quarantine is over. It takes a few days, but everything gets back to normal. Jake still drinks just beer, and with Grandma Elsie around, things are pretty good for Will. Elsie helps Irene with the kids and is delighted to be with her grandchildren. Jake has a good job. As long as he controls his drinking, hopefully, he can keep it. That's how he lost every other job, except for the last one. Grandma Elsie throws a nice birthday party for Will's seventh birthday. She treats all the kids the same, much to Jake's dismay.

The weather begins to turn warmer. Summer is around the corner and school is almost out. Elsie announces that on the first week of June, there is going to be a family reunion with her three brothers and their families. Jake is pleased; he hasn't seen his uncles in a very long time. Elsie also hints that there will be a surprise. Everyone is excited, and it's finally the week of the family reunion. The three families are all together at Elsie and Dewey's. The kids are in the backyard, playing. The men are outside with the kids, drinking beer and telling stories. The women are in the kitchen, preparing the food and talking and laughing. A few minutes later, they hear a car horn. The car horn just keeps blaring, honking and honking. The men look at each other, puzzled; the women stop talking and listen. Finally, Jake can't stand it any longer. He stomps around to the front of the house, and there stands his big brother, Butch. "Surprise!" Butch yells. Little brother can't believe it! Everyone is excited, and there is much hugging and kissing. Irene is delighted to see Anna; they have so much catching up to do. Will, too, is excited to see Anna and "Uncle Daddy" Butch, as he had sometimes called him. And even though Johnny was only two the last time he had seen Will, he recognizes him immediately, which makes Will really happy. The two boys, Will and Johnny, take up right where they left off, as if they had never been separated. It might have been that day or one of the following days, but they make a pact. They declare that they are blood brothers. They will get together to see each other as often as they can. They promise to even write letters to each other. This is their pact, and they intend to keep it.

The next few days are fun and hectic. The uncles, Elsie's brothers, are here for just the weekend. But Butch and his family stay for a whole week. One day, Grandma Elsie says it sure would be nice if Dewey, Butch, and Jake take the older boys fishing. The old millpond is a great place to catch bullheads, and they can have a fish fry. She is famous for her fish fries. Her only rule is the fish have to be fried on the back porch, not in the house. The men get the fishing gear ready, cane poles, bobbers, night crawlers, and beer. Grandma Elsie supplies the sandwiches. Butch tells Johnny to get in the car, but the boy says no, he won't. Butch is surprised by this and asks him why. Johnny explains that Uncle Jake says Will can't go, there isn't enough room, so without Will, he isn't going either. Butch booms as he glances at Jake, "The hell there isn't enough room. Now you boys both get into the car!" The boys have a great time fishing. Butch shows them how to bait the hook, watch the bobber, and hold the poles. Everyone enjoys Elsie's fish fry. The whole week goes by quickly. And as it comes to a close, the night before Butch and Anna are to leave, the grown-ups are playing cards. Playing cards is something Elsie loves to do. They are sitting around the table, and Butch glances up over his cards. He looks at Irene and says, "I know Jake don't give a damn, so I'll ask you. Would it be all right if I take Will back to spend the rest of the summer with us? I'll get him back to you before school starts. One way or another, train, bus, hell, I'll drive him back myself." Irene smiles and says yes, of course that will be all right. The boys jump up and down with glee.

Jake grunts, "Hell, you know what I would say. You can just have him!"

Jake is happy to be with just his kids for the summer. And Will has a great time with his second family. He and Johnny make a lot of promises to each other. Then the summer is over, and Will takes the bus back home. Grandma Elsie is there to pick him up. Everyone is glad to see him, and he is glad to see everyone, except for Jake, and the feeling is mutual. A few days before school starts, a man approaches Will and asks him if he thinks he is big enough to handle a small paper route. Will says he needs to ask his mother and takes the man home to meet Irene. The man explains to her that it's just a few newspapers around the neighborhood. He tells her that after school, Will is to stand at the corner. Someone will drop off the papers, and Will can then deliver them, and he adds that a bike or wagon would be nice. "Will doesn't have a bike, but he does have a wagon," Irene says. The man continues to explain that the first few days, he will show Will how to fold the papers and where to deliver them, and on Saturdays he will get paid for a week's work. Irene looks at Will, who is pleading with her and jumping up and down, and she can't say no. Will has a paper route! Now, as luck will have it, one of the houses he delivers to is where the two mean brothers live. Will trains with the man a few days, then he is on his own. That first day alone, he comes to the brothers' house, and there, outside, stand both of them. But what they don't know is that Will has already talked to Uncle Butch about his problem with them. Will takes a deep breath and walks right up to them. He looks the oldest square in the eye and says, "My uncle said to tell you to put up or shut up, and one way or another, after this, you will leave me the hell alone!" Will is glad his mother isn't there to hear him say "hell." He feels his heart pounding and he is scared, but he doesn't waver. The startled boys look at each other and then take off back to the house. Will stands there and grins from ear to ear.

CHAPTER 14

What? Another One?

Summer turns to fall, and the family enjoys a nice Thanksgiving. Then the weather turns cold and the snow arrives. Will bundles up each day and delivers the newspapers. He keeps up with his chores at home; he doesn't want to give Jake any reason to holler at him. He also doesn't want his dad to know about the bike fund he has started from his paper route money. His mom knows, and Grandma Elsie knows and donates some pennies now and then.

Christmas has come and gone, and the grown-ups are ringing in the new year, 1942. It isn't much of a celebration, though, because the country is three weeks into World War II, which began with the bombing of Pearl Harbor on December 7, 1941. Throughout the country, the women are filling the jobs that are being vacated by the men as they get called into the service. Materials like steel and rubber to make cars soon become in short supply. Even items like sugar, coffee, and tea are scarce. All the family can do is learn to get along with less. They listen to the radio and get on their knees and pray for the war to end, or at the very least stay off American soil.

In January, the things of great interest to Elsie, Jake, and Irene are the war and the fact that Irene is pregnant again. In the next few months as the war continues, the government issues tokens and stamps to families according to size for the purchase of staples. For items such as flour, sugar, salt, and cotton, you must have a stamp or token and be in that line to purchase that item. This takes its toll on the family.

In March Will turns eight years old. In the spring, they plant a victory garden, and by summer they enjoy the produce from it. In mid September, Irene goes to the hospital in labor. She delivers Jakes' fourth son. He is named Donny and called Don for short. Dale is now five years old, and Mel is four. The boys have spats now and then. They scream and throw things. Dale likes to drag Will into the fights even though Will isn't a part of it. Jake spanks either Dale or Mel, whichever he thinks deserves it. He always spanks Will, saying he's the oldest and should have known better.

The winter drags on and Jake gets restless. He resents his mother complaining about his drinking. She says he shouldn't drink so much because he has all those little mouths to feed, plus she always sides with Will. All this gets to Jake. He tells his mother that the railroad is needing section men really badly. He tells her that they are paying better wages than he makes, and the job is not too far away. Jake is ready to move again.

CHAPTER 15

What? Not Again!

Early in the summer, Jake moves the family to a little town in southern Minnesota. He gets a job with a section gang on a small railroad. He works with four other guys, and their job is to keep the track in good shape. They replace railroad ties that rot out, fix broken rails, keep the snow off the switches, and anything else that might delay the train. They are on call all the time. If a storm blows up, they have to make sure any debris is cleared off. It's a heavy job, but it is a good-paying one. The town is small, much like the other little town they lived in. This one has twenty houses. In addition, there's a locker plant where they process beef and pork and a creamery that processes milk from all the nearby farms. When Irene sees the three-bedroom house they will be living in, she isn't very happy. It's another house with no indoor plumbing. And this time, the well and pump for water is not even in the front yard; it's a block away.

Jake hits it off immediately with the men he works with. He really likes a guy named Bubba. Bubba is a lot like Butch in some ways. He is a big man, well built and very strong, and very smart and soft-spoken. He doesn't dress fancy or drive a big car, but like Jake, he likes a cold beer. He especially likes a cold beer on a hot day after work. Drinking doesn't change his demeanor; it just makes him hungry for a home-cooked meal. Bubba, and the other men, are single.

Irene is faced with a lot more work. Besides Jake, she has five mouths to feed. All the clothes have to be washed in a big old tub with a washboard. There is no water, much less hot water. It's the job of Little Butch to bring in the cobs, or kindling, for the cookstove. It's Will's job to get all the water plus the split wood and coal for the heat stove. But it's summer now, and Will only has to worry about the water. He starts looking for ways to make some money. He helps older people carry their groceries. He asks to mow their yards and never charges anything; he only takes what money they give him. He gets a paper route; eighteen of the twenty homes get the evening paper. As far as he can figure out, he is the oldest boy in the town. He meets three boys that he gets along with very well. He also meets a big fat kid who is a year younger than him. This kid is a bully. Will figures out that if there are two or more kids together, the bully doesn't bother them. He stays away from him and avoids any trouble.

By late summer, Will has put away more change in his bike jar. He already had a pretty good amount when he left Grandma Elsie's. One day, walking past the hardware store, he looks in the window and there it is. The prettiest red and white Schwinn bicycle he has ever seen. It has a headlight, horn, rearview mirror, and a mud flap with a big red reflector on it. Will can't believe his eyes; it's a beauty! He goes in the store and over to the bicycle to get a better look. A voice behind him says, "Hey, son, you wanna buy that bike?" Will turns around and sees an older gentleman struggling to get up from his chair.

"Sure I would, mister," Will tells him, "but I am not sure I have enough money saved up yet. I am saving money. I suppose by the time I get enough, though, this beauty will be sold." The man asks him how much he has saved. Will tells him he doesn't know, but he knows his jar is getting pretty heavy. The man tells the boy to get his money and come back, and maybe they can make a deal. Will races out the door and isn't gone long; he only lives a block and a half away. The man smiles when he returns, and they count out the coins together. The old man tells the boy he has a good amount saved. He thinks he can make him a deal. He asks him how he earned his money. Will tells him that he has a paper route, he mows grass, and in the winter he shovels snow. The man asks, "Do you think you could come in here once or twice a week and sweep and clean up? And in the winter, shovel the snow off the front sidewalk?"

"Yes, I can!" Will assures him. The man takes the money that Will has saved and says that it will be the down payment. He tells him that he will put his name on the bike and hold it for him so no one else can buy it. Then in the spring, they will see how much he has earned toward it.

"That's the deal," the man continues, "but only if it is okay with your mother." The man hands Will a receipt and tells him that if it's not all right with his mother, to come back and he'll refund his money. Will is very excited and thanks the man over and over again. He runs to the window and touches the beautiful bike that he is one step closer to owning.

He says, "My name is Will. Put it right there on the handlebar, okay?"

At home, Will can barely contain his excitement. He hands the receipt to his mother and talks a hundred miles an hour. She smiles and tells him to slow down and tell the story. He tells her about the man and the bike and the job. He looks up at her and asks, "It's okay, Momma, ain't it?"

She nods. "I think so, Will. I wish you would have said something first, but it's all right. Under one condition, though: you have to keep your part of the deal. Can you?"

"Yes, Mom. He nods enthusiastically. "I can!"

CHAPTER 16

Hot Water

It's a rough summer for Will. Jake has two guys that he works with, Bubba and another fellow, over on the weekends. Bubba and the other guy are pretty nice. They are great with the kids; they love to play with them. They are single, with no family of their own. Irene always has them stay for dinner because they really love home cooking. Irene is a really good cook; she can make anything taste great. After a few times, Bubba never again comes over empty-handed. He always brings a roast, a chicken, a ham, or something. Jake finds out that the guys like the hard stuff, liquor, especially whisky. But the county is dry, meaning they only sell beer. The guys tell him that there had been a bootlegger in town. The bootlegger would drive twelve miles away to a town in the next county, a wet county. He would buy whisky and bring it back and resell it. This sounds good to Jake, and he becomes a bootlegger. He sells the flour and sugar stamps and tokens to the guys, who give them to their wives for baking. Jake uses the money and buys a case of whisky, which he stashes under the bed. Irene does not want the hard stuff around, but Jake tells her that they can use the extra money. He reasons that he can keep enough money from the sales to replace the case each time, and the rest of the money can pay for his beer, leaving her with more household money. Jake resells the whisky to the guys, but the problem is, they stay at Jake and Irene's to drink it. They offer Jake a drink or two, and he gets drunk with them. He calls Will bad names, and things get bad for Will. Jake tells Bubba about the little bastard that he is raising. He hollers to Irene, "Hey, he's getting older. When the hell are you gonna tell him who he is?" When Jake starts drinking, Will escapes to the outside and finds something to do. One day, Bubba follows him outside and talks to him.

Will responds, "It's all right, Bubba. He hates me, and I don't like him much either." And that's how Will spent the rest of the summer, trying to stay as far away as he can from his daddy. Will and Dale get enrolled in school. Will is in fourth grade; Dale is in first. It's a one-room schoolhouse, like before, but actually has a couple of rooms and a basement. There is no water or plumbing. Two out-houses sit in the back, one for the boys, one for the girls. There is a cloakroom inside and a stand with a bucket of water with a dipper on it, which everyone drinks from. Will continues to get good grades in school and is on the A honor roll, which he has been on since first grade. He thinks being on the honor roll will make his dad like him more, but it never does. It makes his mom proud though.

One day close to Thanksgiving, Bubba brings over a great big turkey for the family. Too bad his daddy isn't more like Bubba, Will thinks. At the end of November, Irene tells Jake that she is pregnant again. Soon the weather turns cold, and along with it comes the snow. Jake tells Will that when his other chores are done, he has another job for him. He is to take the big tub on his sled and go to the rail-road yard. Big chunks of coal fall to the ground from the railcars, and he can bring them back to the house and put them in the coal shed. Will does this, plus he always does his other chores. He keeps plenty of coal and wood on the porch and two buckets of water inside for drinking and cooking. On wash day, he hauls two big tubs of water. He doesn't like wash day. His mom has to work very hard that day. First she has to dip the water into smaller pans to heat on the stove. Then she has to bend over the washboard in that big tub and scrub all the clothes. Having all these babies and all the hard work is hard on Irene. It wasn't that many years ago since that day she had walked Will to first grade that the teacher had thought she was Will's sister. Now she looks old, and she is only twenty-five years of age.

One day after Will is caught up on his chores, he is at the cream-ery with his friends. There is a lot of snow on the roads, and the boys are excited. They know the farmers are coming to town with their horses and sleighs to sell their milk. This is where the boys have fun! When a sleighs leaves, they hitch a ride on the back with their sleds and ride out of town. The farmer always knows they are back there. Sometimes he will even shout when they meet another sleigh going to town, "Hey, there's your ride back to town!" Back at the creamery, the boys stand by the pipes on the side of the building to stay warm. The little door on the side opens up, and a young man steps out.

He jokes, "Are you warming up for your next ride?" Will tells him yes, and the man says he can remember doing the very same thing when he was a boy. Now he works inside where all the heat is.

"Why is it so hot in there?" Will asks the man.

"Well," the young man explains, "it's on account of all the hot boilers in there, making all this steam you see and feel coming out of these pipes."

"Boy, I sure wish this was close to my house over there," Will tells him. The man asks him if it is to keep warm. "No," Will shakes his head, "to make the water hot for my mom on wash day."

The man smiles. "You must be the kid I see over there at the well pump so much." The young man thinks for a moment then says, "Say, I'll tell you what, kid. The next time you haul water, you come over here and rap on the door. I'll give you all the boiling water you can haul."

An excited Will grins, "Really? You will do that?" A couple days later, Will returns and knocks on the door.

The man eyes Will's sled. "If I was to fill that tub, it would probably slop so much over the sides, you wouldn't have much left when you got home." He tells Will to take the tub home and get a wide board to lay on the sled to help distribute the weight. He lets Will use a cream can with a lid on it to haul the water home. "You have to bring the can right back though," he tells Will.

"Yes, sir!" Will says as he heads home with his sled and the cream can full of boiling water. Will shows up at the front door with the hot water, and Irene is thrilled and amazed. She gives the boy a big hug and kiss and tells him how proud she is of him. She asks how he came to get this huge can of hot water. He tells her it's the same kind of can that Grandpa Jim has on his dairy farm and that he can't explain now; he has to get the can back.

It is a very slim Christmas without the help of Grandpa Jim or Grandma Elsie. On New Year's Day, Irene has the turkey in the oven. The men are sitting around, nursing hangovers from the night before. Irene tells them about the hot water and how smart her oldest son is. Jake rolls his eyes and mutters something under his breath. But Bubba thinks this is great and jumps up to go outside and find Will. He finds the boy and tells him how nice it is of him to think about his mother and do that for her. Then his eyes light up! "What you did, Will, just made me think of something! Why didn't I think of this sooner? Come with me!" he exclaims. They hop in Bubba's old pickup, and Bubba drives to the shed behind his house. He opens the door and points, "See that? We are going to give that to your mother!" Will peers inside. He sees a machine. It has big fat rubber wringers on the top, just like the one Grandma has. It's an old Maytag; the sign on it reads "washing machine." Bubba tells Will, "It doesn't look the greatest, the paint is peeling and all, but it runs fine and will do the job."

Will shouts, "Wow! An electric clothes washing machine for my Mom!" He is so happy; he knows what this will mean for his mom. He starts to cry and gives Bubba a big hug.

Bubba pats him on the head, "Hey now, none of that. Let's get this loaded and over to your house." Well, if Will thinks his Mom was excited about the hot water, she is over the moon about the new machine! Irene watches while Bubba and Will bring it to the front porch. Bubba checks it over, oils the gears, plugs it in, and it works fine. He tells Irene it used to be his mother's, but it belongs to her now. Tears brim in her eyes as she thanks him. She tells him to drop off his dirty clothes once a week and she will be more than glad to wash them.

Jake and Bubba do a lot of hunting. They always like to hunt after a fresh snowfall; they say that's when the game hunkers down. They mostly ditch hunt; they drive along a deserted road and shoot out of the open car window. Irene is really good at cooking pheasant and rabbit, and this is the main menu in the winter months. One day, the pair decide to go hunting, but this time, they are going to hunt "dog-style," and they want Will to come along. Irene says no, but Bubba assures her he will look after the boy. He tells her it's something that all boys do in their young life. As Will tugs on his boots, he wonders about the dog part. Did Bubba have a dog somewhere? They drive out along the railroad tracks and park the car. Bubba and Jake take out long guns and begin to walk the tracks as Will follows. Then Will finds out the dog part. It's his job to walk down in the ditch, in the thick undergrowth and through the stickers, to flush out the game. He is the dog! The men walk for some distance down the tracks, with Will in the ditch, then turn and head back, with Will on the other side. They hunt most of the day and end up with several birds and rabbits. They get back to the car, and Will is glad that this part is over. Then Bubba shows Will how to dress out the game and clean it so it's ready to cook. If they don't cook it right away, they wrap it in wax paper and leave it on the front porch in the cold. Will learns something new that day and is very tired that night.

CHAPTER 17

Another Mouth to Feed

That's the way the rest of the winter goes. Will tries to find more ways to earn bike money. Of course, about every day he stops by and looks at it. The old man assures him it isn't going anywhere. It's nearing Will's tenth birthday. The snow is melting, and each passing day makes him more nervous and anxious to get the bike. Then the day finally arrives. The snow is gone, the sun is shining, and Will is riding his brand-new bike home! He even has the papers to show that it is his and how to take care of it. His mom and the boys, even some neighbor kids, all come over to take a look at it. Will wipes it off with a clean, soft cloth, being careful not to scratch it. He rides it back and forth across town, honking the horn now and then. He knows this will be really nice for his paper route; he'll get done a lot sooner. He is in the yard, wiping his new bike off with the cloth again, when Jake gets home. Jake takes one look and bellows, "Where the hell did that come from?"

"I bought it today with my savings and paper route money," Will responds.

"How the hell come you didn't ask me about this?" Jake shouts.

Just then, Irene steps out on the porch. "Why should he have, Jake? You don't want anything to do with him in the first damn place."

"Well," Jake retorts, "It's not all his. The rest of the boys get to ride it too whenever they want." And with that, he walks inside and slams the door. Irene follows Jake inside, and Will takes off on his bike. He knows there is going to be an argument between them. He hates to hear it, and he knows it's about him, but why? *Why doesn't he like me? Why doesn't he want me around?*

Later that night at the supper table, Jake tells Dale that the bike is his also. He can ride it just as much as Will does. Dale looks at Will with a smirk on his face. Dale knows he is his Dad's favorite and can get away with just about anything. He also knows their dad doesn't like Will. He begins to torment Will too; he wants to be just like his daddy. The next few days don't go so well for Will. Dale rides the new bike all he wants then jumps off it and lets it crash to the ground. He never bothers to use the kickstand or lean it against the house because he knows this will really bother Will. Will hollers at him and runs over and picks up the bike. He wipes it down carefully with a cloth. This makes Dale grin a big silly grin. He knows that Will would love to retaliate but doesn't dare because Dale will just tell Jake.

June and July pass quickly, and it is mid August. Irene gives birth to another baby, but this time, Jake gets a baby girl. The sweet baby girl is named after Jake; her name is Linda Geraldine. Now the house is really full with five boys and one newborn baby girl. Irene really has her hands full. It's a good thing she has her washing machine.

Chapter 18

And That's Why

The young girls in town like Irene very much. They come to her for advice and girl talk. They come over to see the new baby girl and hold her. There are three or four that come over quite often. One of the girls babysits on the rare occasion that Jake takes Irene out.

The minister of the Lutheran church, which is the only church in town, asks Will to join Sunday school. He talks with Will about it one day while Will is delivering his newspaper. The minister tells Will that the Lord has the answer to everything. Will thinks this might help him figure out what is going on between him and his daddy. Besides, it makes his mother very proud that he is doing this all on his own. He is also enrolled in a catechism class that begins right after Sunday School. So far, all Will has learned is that he is supposed to be the good guy and turn the other cheek, and he isn't sure about this. He already wishes for something bad to happen to his daddy and this gives him mixed emotions. When the class is completed, the minister plans a ceremony for Will and the other three kids who are in the class. Irene says she will be very happy to attend with Will. The day arrives and Irene has a surprise. She hands him a pair of gray pants, a white shirt and tie, and a maroon sports coat. He grins from ear to ear. He stands dressed in the new clothes, feeling very proud. Irene tells him he is very handsome and will be the best-looking guy there. She is wearing a very pretty dress and looks great. Will smiles; he hasn't seen her look like this in a long, long time. Jake looks up from his chair and hollers, "Where the hell are you going?"

"I told you," she responds, "I am going to that thing for Will today. Did you forget?"

He snaps back, "And where the hell did those clothes come from? That's money we could've used for other stuff."

She stiffens. "Like what, whisky? You don't worry about it. It's from his granddad." She knows this is a lie but doesn't care. She continues. "There is bread in the oven. Take it out when it gets brown on top. I'll put the meatloaf in when we get back. Can you do that?" Bubba, who had been sitting quietly with Jake, tells her he will gladly see to it.

When they return, Jake is feeling the effects of the whisky. He starts ranting and raving. He yells, "Today is the day we tell the little bastard who he really is. He's older now and supposed to be so smart."

"Stop it, Jake," Irene pleads. Bubba stands up and tries to intervene, but Jake won't be stopped. Will knows a fight is coming. He changes quickly out of his clothes. He wants to get on his bike and get out of there fast.

He races down the stairs to make his getaway, but Jake hollers, "Hey, bastard boy, come here! You're going to learn something today!" Will is scared; he looks at his mom.

"Go outside Will," she says. "I will be out in a minute."

Jake continues to holler, "You better tell him, Irene, or I promise you, I will! It's time you stop babying that little wussy!" Irene runs outside; she is crying and so is Will.

She sobs, "If I don't tell you this, he will, and I want you to hear it from me. That man, Jake, he is not your father. He's not your daddy. I had you before I ever met him, and he can't accept that. That's why he doesn't like you and treats you like he does. That's why he calls you horrible names and from day one has never wanted anything to do with you." She wipes her eyes and continues. "I am very sorry for all those things you have had to go through because I wanted to raise you. Lord knows you would have been a lot better off if only I would have let Grandma Bess have you. She wanted to take you far away and raise you and I said no. But I didn't know it was going to be like this." She touches his shoulder. "I am so sorry, Will.

Please don't hate me." With that, she walks back inside. Will stands there a moment, tears streaming down his face.

He hears Irene yell at Jake, "Are you happy now? Are you happy now, Jake? I told him! And I don't think he is ever going to like you any more than you like him!" He gets on his bike and slowly rides away. So many things had been left unsaid. Not a word had been said about who he really is. He rides to the old abandoned farmhouse about a mile out of town. He thinks about what he's been told and wonders what he should do. So many things race through his mind. He reasons that all the fights and arguments are his fault. If it weren't for him, she wouldn't have to stick up for him, and they would all get along better. But wait a minute, he remembers. Butch and Bubba like him. And even though Jake isn't his dad, why does he and his mom have to suffer? *I am not the bastard*, he thinks. *He is the bastard! I hate you, Mr. Bastard!* The tears flow as Will sits and thinks. He knows he loves his mom, so he can't run away. He decides that he will just have to stay away from Mr. Bastard. And someday, when he is older and bigger, he'll get a job and pay him back for every cent he's ever had to spend on him!

It grows dark and Jake is passed out on the couch. Irene knows he will wake later and want to eat. She puts supper on the table for the kids but is worried about Will. Bubba tells her he will go and look for him. He doesn't have to drive far before he sees the little headlight on Will's bike. Bubba pulls the truck over. He puts the bike in the back and tells Will to get in. He turns in his seat toward the boy. He says sadly, "I really don't know what to say. I know this is pretty hard on you, at your age and all. The hell of it is, it didn't have to be like this! You're a good kid, Will. I would have been proud to have you for a son." He sighs, "Well, the only good thing is that maybe now your dad—"

"He's not my dad!" Will interrupts.

"Right," Bubba continues. "Maybe now Jake, knows that you know he's not your dad, will shut the hell up and quit hollering so much about it. Maybe things will ease up now. You two will just have to try to get along some way. I hope so, Will, for your sake. I really do." Back at home, Irene hugs Will as they both fight back tears. She tells him how sorry she is. Will takes a seat at the table, and she urges him to eat his supper.

He says softly, "I sure would like to go and spend the rest of the summer with Butch."

"I know, dear," she says sadly, "but it's too late. School will be starting soon." Will tosses and turns that night. He doesn't sleep at all, but now he knows.

CHAPTER 19

Will and Johnny Together Again

The school year starts, and Will is in the fifth grade and Dale is in second grade. Will's good grades keep him on the A honor roll; he does odd jobs to make money, and he stays away from Jake as much as he can. He makes sure he does his chores so as not to cause any problems. Whenever Jake is home, Will stays outside. He rides his bike when it is warm, and when it's cold, he dresses warmly and rides his sled in the snow. Maybe Bubba is right about Jake just wanting Will to know he has no father and that it is certainly not him, because the name-calling isn't as much as before. Jake still calls Will a wussy once in a while, but they seem to be tolerating each other.

The cold winter arrives, and once again, it's a very slim Christmas. The cold days give way to spring and approach Will's birthday. The year is 1945 and Will turns eleven. The school year winds to a close, and Irene has a great surprise for Will. He is going to spend the summer with his Uncle Butch! He will be with his "blood brother" Johnny, and even though they have been writing letters back and forth, neither of them knew of this surprise. What a summer they have! Cookouts, fireworks, swimming, fishing, bike rides, camping, ice cream, all the things boys love. One day, Uncle Butch has a long talk with Will. He tells him how sorry he is that his little brother, Jake, never took a liking to the boy. He tells Will that if things ever get too bad at home, to be sure and tell him, because Will is always welcome there.

Summer comes to an end, and Will is back home with his mother and the other kids. Bubba is glad to see him. Jake doesn't say a word to him but doesn't call him a name either. The new school year starts. Will is in sixth grade, Dale is in third, and Mel is in second. This year, Will is the oldest kid in the school. There are two other boys in Will's class, but both are younger than he is. The two older boys who were in the eighth grade the year before are now in high school, so that leaves no students in seventh or eighth grade.

One day early in the school year, a man and a woman come into the classroom and speak to the teacher. The teacher stands and asks Will to follow the three of them into the library room. They introduce themselves to Will and tell him they are on the school board. They ask him if he will be willing to go to the basement of the school at the end of each day and fill the coal stoker with coal to keep the school warm through the night in the winter months. Will says yes, he will. Then the lady smiles and says, "One more thing. We would like you to be the patrol captain." She hands Will a brown leather harness and belt. It goes around the waist with a strap in the back, up over the shoulder, and down to the waist again. It has a big shiny brass badge in the middle with the words "Patrol Captain" on it. Will likes the shiny badge and thinks the leather smells good.

Then the man says, "Now, Will, before you say yes, we want you to know that this is a very serious job. You will be leading the children to and from school. From school, you will get them in the right formation. You will take them across the highway, then across the railroad tracks, then two blocks to the telephone office, where they will disband. In the mornings, this is where you will meet." He continues. "We will tell the children how serious this is, and if they don't do as instructed by you, you will report them, because it's for their own safety." He smiles at Will. "We think you can do this. You are on the A honor roll, and your teacher says you follow instructions very well." Will is so excited, he can't wait to get that belt and badge on! In the cloakroom, he finds a long pole with a big red flag on it. He holds the pole and points the flag in the air with a couple practice flourishes. He adjusts his belt a little and pats the shiny badge and grins from ear to ear.

CHAPTER 20

The Christmas Tree Stand

Will races home from school; he can't wait to tell his mom. Irene takes a look at him and says, "Well, Mr. Patrol Captain, look at you! What is all this?"

Dale scowls, "He thinks he's special now. He gets to lead us to and from school and report on us if we do anything bad." Will tells her all about it. He tells her how the man had walked with him and showed him what to do. He relays what the man had said, "Now, you just can't stick the flag, or stop signal, out in front of cars on the highway. You look and wait until there are no cars around. Then you hold it out with the red flag that says 'stop' hanging down. Then, when everyone is across, you get back in front and hold it up high and straight. At the tracks, make sure no train is close before you cross, then go up to the telephone office and you're done." Irene smiles and tells him how proud she is of him, and that he will make an excellent patrol captain. Will wishes he had a dad that he can tell, but he doesn't, and he sure isn't going to tell Jake.

Soon, the kids in school find out that they are going to be putting on a carnival for the parents. It will be around Halloween. Jake also hears about this from the school board member he drinks with at the local tavern. Jake tells Bubba and the school-board guy that he thinks it would be a great idea to have a little boxing match between a couple of the boys. Nothing serious, he tells them, just dancing around, sparring, poking jabs at each other. The boys can wear big, soft gloves. They can make a homemade arena and have the contest during the carnival. The school board member agrees and says they can use the storeroom in the basement of the school. Jake smiles smugly; he has a plan of his own. A couple nights later, he comes home with two sets of boxing gloves. He is tired of hearing about Will being so good at things. He is going to see to it that Little Butch, Dale, is a boxing star. Jake has Will put on one pair of gloves and Dale the other. He instructs Will that he is to cover up his face with the gloves and dance around while Jake shows Dale how to jab and punch him. Will cannot hit back. At first, Dale goes crazy. He swings hard and fast, hitting Will over and over, so much so that he runs out of steam. Dale wears himself out and has to sit and rest. So Jake steps in; he tells Dale to slow down and continues the lesson. With the big gloves covering him, Will is not getting hurt. But he feels used, embarrassed, and ashamed of the way Jake lets Dale pound on him. Later, when Will is in his room with Dale and Mel, he finds out that Dale really wanted to hurt his big brother. Confused, Will asks him why. Dale sneers, "Well, goody-two-shoes, because you have to be so good and do everything right. Daddy says to us, 'Why can't you be more like Will? Why can't you get good grades in school? Why can't you help your mother more?'" So Will finds out that by trying so hard to be good and do things right so as not to make Jake mad at him, he makes his brothers mad at him. He sighs and rolls over in his bed and stares at the ceiling. His brothers don't know that Jake is not his father, and he decides not to tell them.

The day of the school carnival arrives. Dale is about to show the world how to be a boxing champion. The upstairs of the school is lined with tables of homemade treats and the children's drawings. The downstairs has the makeshift boxing ring. A surprise awaits Jake and Dale. They find out that Dale's opponent is none other than the big bully, who is older and much bigger than Dale! Little Butch finds out and tells Jake no, he won't do it. He won't get in the ring with the bully. Jake looks around nervously. He finds the school board member and asks if there isn't some other kid, more the same size as Dale, that will do it. The man shakes his head. "No, sorry, there isn't anyone. I guess it's off then."

Jake's eyes light up. "Will! Will has to do it!"

Will looks up at him in shock. "But I'm older than he is!" The men talk and decide that since the bully is bigger, that makes it even. Will is really unhappy about this. It's just another one of those things that Jake is always doing to him. He knows if he doesn't do it, Jake will make things rough for him at home. Will sighs and decides he will just get it over with. Jake takes the gloves off Dale and puts them on Will. Will steps in the ring; the bully is looking bigger all the time. The man instructs them, "Now, boys, we are going to make this look as real as we can. It's going to be three rounds of one minute each. I even have a little bell here. At the first sound of it, you start jabbing and hitting each other. Not like a real fight, you hit lightly with the big soft gloves, more like a pillow fight. At the end of the minute, you will hear the bell, and you will stop for a breather, okay?" He says further, "And the bell will ring for the second round, and so on, you got it?" But it doesn't go anything like that. The man has the two boys step in the center of the ring and touch gloves. Then *bam*, the bully hits Will right in the nose! There is no bell yet. Will staggers back a few steps and the bully follows, pounding on Will. The man tries to get things under control, but not Jake. He hollers, "Hey, wuss, fight that kid!" Another board member hears the commotion and comes down the stairs. He takes one look at the situation and immediately stops the contest. Will is crying a little, and blood is coming from his nose. His pride and his feelings are hurt more than anything. He hears Jake calling him a big wussy. He knows that he will not live this down for a very long time.

And he is right. The very next school morning, as Will is getting the kids lined up, Harold, the bully, taunts him. "Hey, wussy, you want me to help you get to school?"

Will retorts back, "Hey, cheater, I am not scared of you one damn bit!"

Harold snorts, "What? Trying to scare me, wussy, I am tougher than you!"

Will yells back, "You may be, but you're also dumber!" This comment makes the other kids laugh as they line up and follow Will.

The rest of the school year passes without much incident. The summer is incident free too, and then it's winter again. It's another slim Christmas for the family. It's the first of the year, and Irene isn't feeling well. Will tries to help her as much as he can. One day after school and the patrol group, he is on his way home. He notices a few girls; they go screaming by him and run into a store. They are running away from Harold, the bully. Harold is doing what he likes to do best. He pushes them down in the snow then rubs snow all over their faces. Will walks into the house and sees Irene, lying on the couch. He stokes the fire in the front room and puts some cobs in the kitchen stove. He hears screaming again and looks out to see these same girls running up onto the porch to get away from Harold. Harold stands in the front yard, snow in hand, laughing. The girls ask if they might come in and visit with Irene until Harold leaves. But Irene says no, not today, she just isn't feeling well enough. Harold keeps taunting them, and the girls keep screaming, like young girls do. Irene can't stand it any longer. She begs Will to please do something about the noise. He has to get them to stop the screaming; that's all there is to it. So Will steps outside and walks up to Harold. He says, "You have to leave so the screaming girls can go home. My mom is sick and can't stand all the noise."

Harold jeers back, "Who's gonna make me, wussy boy? Not you, that's for sure. Even your dad says you're a wussy." Harold gives Will a big shove. Will falls backward against the front porch and lands in the snow. His hand grazes the Christmas tree stand that his brother Dale was supposed to have put away. The stand is wooden, made of two small two-by-fours. Will stands up, Christmas tree in hand. He raises it up high and brings it down right toward Harold's head. It's a good thing Harold raises his arm over his head, because that's right where it smacks him, on his arm. Harold runs off crying. The girls come off the porch, laughing. They thank Will and head for home. Will goes inside and Irene thanks him, but he doesn't say a word about what he has done. He helps his mom by setting the table, and he heats the soup for supper.

Later that night, the family sits down at the supper table. A few minutes later, there's a knock at the door. Dale goes to the door. He comes back followed by a big woman and Harold, with a big white cast on his arm. She asks Harold as she points to Will, "Now, Harold, is that the boy?" He nods yes, it is. The woman glares at Jake, "Your son broke my little Harold's arm, in two places, and you're going to pay for it."

Jake looks over at Will. "Did you do that?" Will nods his head yes. Jake raises his voice, "I can't hear you!"

Will manages to say, "I guess so." Irene jumps up from her chair.

She looks at the woman calmly and says, "I am so sorry for your boy's broken arm." She then relays to the woman the story of what had happened that afternoon. Upon hearing this, Jake pushes his chair back from the table.

He looks at the woman angrily, "Now you get your fat ass out of here, and take your fat-ass little Harold with you! And if he doesn't want his other arm broke, stay the hell off my property!" The woman grabs Harold and storms out the door. The house is very quiet. Dale and Mel smirk at each other, but Irene gives Will a little wink. Will sits in his chair, stiff as a board. He waits, wondering what is going to happen next. But Jake never says a word. Later that night, the kids are all upstairs in bed. Will overhears Jake downstairs with Irene. He grunts, "Well, maybe he ain't a wuss after all."

Early in the morning, Will and the kids are awakened by the sound of voices downstairs. There is quite a commotion, and Will tries to go downstairs to find out what is going on. He is met on the stairs by Jake, who tells him to stay upstairs and to keep all the kids upstairs until he says otherwise. He tells him, "Your mother is very sick. Some ladies from next door are here, and the doctor is on his way. So stay upstairs and keep the others quiet. She will be all right, I promise." After what seems like a very long time, Will and the kids are told they can come downstairs. Irene is lying on the bed. She smiles weakly at them and tells them she is fine, and in a day or two she will be up and around. She assures them she will be okay. The neighbor ladies make breakfast for the children. They help them get ready for school and pack their lunches. As he heads out the door, Will overhears one of the ladies says something about a "miscarriage," whatever that is.

CHAPTER 21

Another Death

Early one school morning, Will is at the telephone office, getting the patrol ready. He walks over to Harold. "Hey, you want to call me a wuss again?" Harold shakes his head no. "That's good," Will replies confidently. And this is where he tells a little lie, "Because my Dad says it's okay for me to break your other arm! Stay away from me, and leave the girls alone too."

Springtime nears, and with it Will's twelfth birthday. School is out for the summer. Will gets another job. This one is working at the store once in a while. He stocks shelves, sweeps the floor, and even candles eggs. The eggs are in a box, with a lightbulb through a hole in the box. He holds the egg up to the light to tell if it's a good egg or not. He is still saving money, but this time, it's for a car. He gives his mother money, and she is supposed to let Jake know that he is paying his share. Jake has eased up on Will some, and the name-calling is less, too. Will still does his daily chores plus the paper route and any other odd jobs. He would like to see Johnny again; he misses him. But he knows he needs to work and keep paying his fair share to Jake.

School starts again in the fall. Then the winter arrives, and Will is older and stronger and can shovel more snow. He saves enough money to give his mother extra to use for Christmas.

They celebrate the new year, 1947. Will turns thirteen in the spring. One day in March, Will has the patrol lined up and they are on making their way home from school. They are just a few feet away from the telephone office when they hear a loud train whistle. It just keeps blaring and blaring. Then they hear a tremendous crash, and Will and the children turn around to see a truck get hit by the train. A huge ball of fire shoots into the air! The children gasp and point. Will instructs them not to look back any more and to go straight home and tell their parents. Will races home and tells Irene what he has just seen and heard. He heads out of the house to do his paper route. Irene warns him to stay away from the wreck. He tells her he will try, but his paper route goes right by it. He goes about his route but stops for a while. He sits on his bike, a safe distance back, and watches the wreckage site.

Jake comes home just before supper. He tells Irene he is only there to catch a quick bite to eat because there has been a truck and train wreck down by the gas station. He tells her the crew has to repair and clean up the site, and he will probably be there all night. The next day is Saturday, no school. Jake comes home briefly to get a bite to eat and a quick nap then heads back to the accident site. Over a sandwich, he tells Irene how it could have been much worse. He explains that if the truck had been close to the gas station, the whole corner would have blown up. He tells her the scene is really grim; the driver died in the crash and burned to death, and the whole scene smells horribly.

The school year comes to a close. One day early in the summer, a man from the school board and an attorney come to Will's house. They spot Will out in the yard and ask him if his mother is home. Will tells them yes, and the man explains that they would like to talk to him and his mother. They follow Will into the house. They introduce themselves to Irene and say, "We are here to give you and Will a heads-up. We would like you not go anywhere for the next two weeks. There is to be an inquest about the truck and train accident that happened in late March. We will give you the date soon. But we want Will present. And his parents, or at least one parent, should be there also." Irene is taken aback and asks what this is all about? The attorney continues calmly, "Now don't get too alarmed. Two insurance companies are battling over the accident to see who is to pay. They want all the facts and want to talk to anyone and everyone who was anywhere near when it happened. I will be in touch. Now can I count on a parent and Will to be there?"

"Yes, of course," Irene nods. "We will be there."

It's a very warm day, and Will is in the backyard, working on his bike. Jake comes home from work and is inside talking to Irene. The windows are open, and Will can hear everything being said between the two. Irene tells Jake about the inquest coming up. Jake explodes, "You mean that bastard was involved in that death too? What did he do this time?"

Irene hushes him, "No, no, it's nothing like that. They want to talk to each and every person that was anywhere near the accident."

Jake huffs, "Well, you can bet your ass something must be up. You go and protect him. I'll be at work."

The next day, Will asks his mother, "What did Jake mean, 'involved in another death'? He thinks I was involved in Rosie's death, don't he?"

"Will," Irene quickly points out, "'involved' only means you were there."

Will's lip quivers. "No, he thinks that it was *my* fault, that I was fooling around or maybe even gave her a shove."

Irene hugs the boy, "No, Will, no, all we know is that you helped her get up there on the window ledge. It was a horrible accident." She starts to cry and fumbles for a tissue. "The screen wasn't latched. It could've been you or both of you."

His eyes fill with tears as he looks up at her. "I am sorry, Mother. I am sorry."

A couple days later, Will spots Bubba coming from the out-house. He gives him a serious look and says, "Bubba, I want you to tell me the truth. I know my dad, um, Jake, has told you everything about me being a bastard and all that." Bubba nods yes. The boy blinks hard. "He thinks that I am to blame for little Rosie's death too, don't he?" Tears begin to roll down his face. "Mom just says that he thinks I am 'involved,' and she gets upset when I try to talk to her. I know there's something she isn't telling me. I suppose I could have been more involved in some way." He continues softly. "And that would make him think that way, right? Why wouldn't he think that? She was his only daughter and me the bastard and not his son, right?"

Bubba gives the boy a big hug. "Will, some way or another, you are going to have to put this behind you. But okay, let's just say that your Mom is right and Jake just thinks that yes, you were just involved." Bubba lowers his head and doesn't say any more. He pats the boy on the shoulder and walks toward the house. Will stands there, eyes filled with tears. He knows in his heart that Jake wishes it could have been him and not Rosie who fell out of that window that day.

At the inquest, tables and chairs are set up around a head table. People are there from the railroad, the trucking company, and the insurance companies. Will sees a lady who he now remembers was driving a car, across from the patrol, at the corner by the telephone office. She had turned around to go the other way after the wreck. There are some other men in nice suits, the school board guy, his representative, and Will and Irene. One by one, people go up and sit at the main table. Two men question them. Will watches and waits nervously. Soon, it is his turn. When asked about that day, Will tells them that he and the children left the school like always. They crossed the highway and came up to the railroad crossing. The man asked Will if he knew where the truck was at this time. Will says he isn't sure, but he thinks it was the same truck that was on the drive at the gas station. Then the man asks Will if he could see or hear the train? Will says that yes, he could hear the train whistle as it was about to come around the curve on the other side of the depot, but that he couldn't see it yet. The man looks up from his notes. "Will, why did you take the patrol across the tracks if you knew the train was coming?"

Will responds, "Because I knew there was plenty of time to make it because it wasn't in sight yet." Will walks back and takes his seat beside his mother. The attorney tells him he did a good job. Irene smiles at him, and he breathes a sigh of relief.

Finally, a man at the head table stands up. He announces, "It's very evident that from where the truck was stopped, the driver saw the patrol over on the right side of the road. He saw them cross the tracks. If the patrol had stayed there and waited for the train to go by, the driver would have done the same." Now the man in the nice suit at Will's table stands.

He clears his throat and begins, "You may be right about that, yes. It could have been like that. But let's talk about what we know for sure. First, we know that the truck did not have chains on his tires. We know that the incline going up and over the tracks was hard packed with snow. It was indeed slippery, and the truck could have lost traction. We know that the patrol did have plenty of time. As Will says, they were at the telephone office, which the lady in the car verifies. Now then, we also know that if Will would have kept the patrol there, and the truck driver would have tried to go anyway, we would have had children in that fiery mess!" The man sits back down and leans back in his chair, pleased. There are hushed tones from the head table. Then a few minutes later, briefcases snap shut and people begin shaking hands. The man at Will's table tells Will and Irene, "This is done and over with. I promise you that you will never hear another word about it." He hands Irene some money, saying, "Thank you, this is for your time. Take Will to lunch."

CHAPTER 22

Another Boy

Will is enjoying the summer. He thinks Bubba must've said something to Jake because Jake isn't calling him names as much. Jake does get his little digs in to Will, though, when he is drinking, but not as bad as before. Will is keeping busy doing anything he can to earn extra money. He does odd jobs and also does yard work for some older people around town. He wants to buy all his own clothes and give his mom some money too. And besides these expenses, he wants to save money for a car someday.

It's the end of August, and Irene is pregnant again. School starts in the fall, and Will knows it will be his last year at this school. The teacher tells him that if he stays on the A honor roll through the rest of the year, his name will be put in a book. She tells him it will be a record for a boy to do it; so far only the girls have. He will be the first boy to go all the way from first grade to eighth grade on the A honor roll, and he will get a paper with a state seal on it.

The year is pretty normal for Will and his family. Winter comes and with it a lot of snow that has to be shoveled. But shoveling snow means extra money for Will. Spring arrives, and in May 1948, Irene delivers the baby. Jake is once again the father of another boy. This baby boy is named Roger.

Will is now fourteen years old. He graduates from the eighth grade on the A honor roll. He is excited because in the fall, he will go into the ninth grade and be a freshman in high school.

CHAPTER 23

A Blood Disorder

Early in the summer, Will starts to have some difficulties with his joints. His joints swell up and are very painful at times. Irene puts a variety of different ointments and salves on his joints, but it doesn't help much. Will's elbows and knees swell at various times, causing him tremendous pain, so much so that he cries. Jake's response is that Will is just suffering from growing pains that everybody gets, and the wuss needs to be a man. He says Will needs to quit riding the damn bike all over town and he will be all right. Will does stop some of his activities, and it does seem to help a little.

Fall rolls around and it is time for school to start. Will finds out where the bus stop is and what time he needs to be there. He must be there early because the bus stop is the farthest the bus can travel away from the school, about twelve miles. There are three or four kids at the stop, and Will is the only new one. The others are older; two are juniors and one is a senior. They are the first ones on the bus, then the bus will stop and pick up more on the way. Will is not prepared for the difference between the one-room schoolhouse, with the toilet out back, and this new great big place. Now he has to go from room to room for different classes. This school has a lunch room, where they make the lunch, lockers to keep your things in, a track and a football field. But it doesn't take Will long to figure out the routine. He is embarrassed, though; the other kids in his class all have nice clothes. He is the only one in the overall pants. They all know each other and do things together. In study hall, they all like to sit together and talk and laugh. Will sits at a table at the other end of the study hall with a fat boy and a girl who is feeling just as much out of place as Will is. These three sit together every day. Will has been in the new school for about a month when one morning he can barely get out of bed. His knees are very swollen, and all his joints are very painful. Irene tells Jake that they are going to take him to the doctor in the bigger town about nine miles away. Jake only agrees to take them because he is out of whisky.

The doctor gives Will a thorough examination and takes some blood samples. He gives Irene a written prescription for some pain pills. He tells them that Will has a murmur in his heart. When Will gets home, he is to stay flat in bed and stay still until they hear from him. He tells them he will come to the house after he has the results of the blood tests. Irene is very upset at this news. The doctor calms her. He tells her not to get too worried; he just doesn't want Will up and running around even if the swelling goes down. Later, when the doctor gets the results, he explains it to them. He tells them that the corpuscles in Will's blood, the red ones and the white ones, are battling. The red ones are destroying the white ones. The treatment is bed rest and shots of quinine, which he will administer, and quinine pills, to be taken daily. Will asks the doctor, "How long will this take?"

The doctor shakes his head and says, "Here's the hard part. The best I can tell you is that it will take at least two months, up to ten months." Will grimaces. The doctor looks at Irene and continues, "Let's hope for the best. But let me tell you, after a few days, he is going to be feeling fine, just like nothing is wrong. But if you don't keep him down, he will damage his heart very badly."

The next problem is that there is only one bed downstairs, and that is Jake and Irene's. Irene wants to put Will in their room and she and Jake move upstairs with the kids. Jake says no. Will tells his mother that he will sleep upstairs; he doesn't want to cause any trouble between her and Jake. So it is decided that Will stays on the couch during the daytime then walks very slowly up the stairs at night. Each morning he comes back downstairs. The doctor is right. Within a few days, Will is feeling better and the swelling is down.

Some of the evenings, the kids play games with Will. But the days are very long and boring. One day, Will talks with one of the older girls in town who goes to the same high school as him. She talks to the principal, who talks to Will's teachers, and they send the schoolwork home with her to give to Will. When he finishes it, she takes it back to school for him, and this keeps him busy. He manages to get caught up on all his schoolwork. This arrangement is working out pretty well. While the weather is nice, Jake and the guys drink their booze outside. But when the weather turns bad, they come inside to drink. Jake complains that Will is sprawled out all over the couch and the guys don't have any place to sit. On these nights, Will goes upstairs early.

The winter comes and goes, and in the spring, Will turns fifteen years old. One day, near the end of the school year, Will's teacher from the old one-room school visits him. He tells her that he is all caught up on his schoolwork and that he would really like to take the year-end test to see how he has done. She thinks this is a great idea. She contacts the principal of his school and gets the test. She returns a few days later and administers the test to him, and Will passes! He is going to be in the tenth grade, a sophomore. Irene hugs him and tells him how proud she is of him.

A week later, the doctor comes by and does another blood test. He tells them he has good news; the last blood tests were very good. He smiles at Will. "If this blood test is the same, I think that you, young man, have won the battle! You will be able to go on with your life as it was before." Will and Irene and the kids all shout for joy. The teacher from the one-room school is there. She asks Will if he got the news that he passed the year-end test. He tells her that he knows he passed and thanks her for all she has done for him.

She winks at him and says with a laugh, "But just a minute. I do have some bad news. You are no longer on the A honor roll. You passed with Cs and Ds." With this news, Will chuckles and rolls his eyes, and everyone laughs.

The doctor returns in a few days and gives Will a clean bill of health. He tells him to take it easy for the next week or so, to finish the last of the pills, and to come in to the office soon for a final checkup. Everyone is very happy, but no one is happier than Will. It has been a long eight months. The kids all laugh at him because none of his clothes fit anymore. Poor Will has gained twenty pounds! It is June 1949. Will is back to normal, and Irene is pregnant again.

CHAPTER 24

The Big Date

It doesn't take Will very long to start looking for jobs. Dale has taken over the bike, and Jake says that the paper route is Dale's too. Will is convinced, more than ever, that he really owes Jake, and he wants to pay his own way. He goes to the store to see if he can get some of his old cleanup jobs back. But the main boss isn't there. Disappointed, he turns to leave. As he does, he hears a man say, "Hey, Will, how are you?" The voice belongs to Oscar, a man from his paper route. Oscar tells him that Dale has filled him in on Will's illness. Will tells Oscar that he is well again and doing fine, but he is looking for some odd jobs. Oscar smiles. "Good for you, Will glad to hear you are better. Hey, my brother Tom and I bought the locker on the edge of town. We sure could use some help. Why don't you come by tomorrow and we'll talk?" Will tells him he will be there the first thing in the morning.

At the plant the next morning, Oscar shows Will around. There are holding pens off to the side where hogs and cattle are put, and these pens have to be cleaned every so often. There's a kill room, it's all cement, and hoses and hot water. It needs to be cleaned once a day, sometimes twice, and needs to be disinfected as well. There's a big cooler and a chill room, where the butchered meat goes. Off to the side, there's a smokehouse, where the bacon and ham is cured. In the front, the meat is cut up. It is cut into chops, steaks, and roasts, and the hamburger meat is ground. The meat is packaged and put into a big, sharp freezer. Oscar explains to Will that in addition, three neighboring towns have freezers with numbered lockers, where processed meat is kept until needed. Farmers bring hogs and cattle in to be butchered and packaged. Then, depending on where his farm is, the processed and packaged meat is delivered to the locker that the farmer rents. Oscar also tells him that besides this operation, the brothers also buy hogs and beef that they process and sell to restaurants and grocery stores. He explains that it is quite a bit of work for the two of them, and even though the war has been over for a couple years, a lot of the servicemen are still overseas. He says that good help is hard to find, especially in the smaller towns. Oscar looks intently at Will then states, "If you want to work for us, Will, you will start out by keeping everything clean. Then I'll show you how to bone out meat and grind up hamburger, and who knows after that! I'm sure we will need you three full days a week and maybe a few part-time hours. So what do you think?"

Will nods enthusiastically. "I am ready to start! But you know I have school in the fall, and the bus doesn't get back very early in the afternoons. That would just leave Saturdays, and even though you're closed on Sunday, I could clean for you that day."

Oscar thinks for a moment then gives a little laugh. "So when do you want to start?"

Will smiles. "Right now."

Oscar chuckles. "But, Will, we haven't even talked about your pay yet!"

Will responds, "I know I am just a boy, but I am sure you will give me a fair wage." Oscar says yes, they will, and the two shake hands and agree for Will to start by the first of July.

By mid July, Will already loves his new job. He learns very fast and is already grinding hamburger. He also wraps steaks, chops, and hamburger into five-, ten- and twenty-pound packages. The brothers are pleased with his work and on different occasions send meat home with him. Will likes the soup bones and roasts, and even though they are free, Irene tells Jake that Will pays for it out of his salary. True to their word, the brothers pay Will a fair wage. And each week, Will gives Irene money. Several mornings, the brothers arrive at the plant and find Will already there, cleaning out the pens and hard at work.

One day, Oscar hands Will a key and says, "Here. If you're going to be here so damn early, you just as well open up the place." This makes Will feel really special. He knows that Oscar and Tom place a lot of trust in him; he vows to himself to never violate that trust.

The pills are all gone, and it's time for Will's final checkup with the doctor. The doctor concludes that this will be Will's last visit. He tells him that he does have a faint heart murmur still, but it shouldn't cause him any problems. No problems for now, at least not at this point. The doctor explains that someday, when Will is really old, way down the road, if he is under stress, then it may cause him problems. This is good news to Will and he grins. The doctor claps him on the back and wishes him well as he jumps off the table. Irene and Will turn to leave, and the doctor remarks that he is glad Will has lost all the weight he had gained. The three of them laugh, and Will leaves the doctor's office a very happy boy.

It's a week or so before school is to start, and Will is very nervous. Oscar asks him what is wrong. Will tells him that school is about to start and he doesn't want to lose his job. "I suppose you will find someone else right away, huh?"

Oscar pats him on the shoulder. "No, Will, I'll tell you what. There's Saturdays yet, and I don't know about Sundays. You know, we usually work till five then clean up that last hour to be out of here by six. You could certainly be here by then. Clean up and lock up. We will just wait and see, okay?" Will nods and breathes a sigh of relief.

It's the first day of school, and even though Will has better clothes this year, he still feels out of place. He is given a card from his classmates, signed by each of them, congratulating him on passing into the tenth grade. They also have a gift for him. They give him a very nice shirt. He thanks them graciously and smiles. He sees all the old faces and spots a new guy. He notices that this guy is very good-looking, has a muscular frame, and is a big hit with all the girls. Then a funny thing happens at the very first study hall period. The new guy walks right past all the seats that are being saved for him. He walks right over to Will's table and sits down beside Will. Will finds out that he had transferred to the school in the middle of last school year while Will was gone. So although he is new to Will, he isn't new to the others. He tells Will that he has a brother who had a blood disease similar to what Will had, and the brother had to have complete bed rest too. Will finds him to be a very down-to-earth kind of guy, not at all like the rest of them. He, like Will, loves his mother very much. He also has to do chores, and he lives on a farm, so he has even more chores than Will has. He doesn't have to ride the bus to school though; he has his own car.

In Will's class there is a set of twin girls. They are very cute, but they are not identical. You can tell them apart easily, and they don't act the same either. One is very outgoing, and the other is very shy. Will finds out that his new friend is dating one twin, the outgoing one. If she is in study hall, his friend sits with her. But most of the time, she isn't there, so he sits with Will. It's still early in the school year, in the first month, and one day in study hall, the new friend turns to Will and asks him if he dates anyone. Will shakes his head, "No. In the first place, I don't have time. And in the second place, I don't have anybody to date."

His friend continues. "Well, you know I date the one twin, right?"

Will says, "Yes, I know, and she is very smart and nice looking too." Then what the guy says next nearly gets Will kicked out of study hall.

"Her sister wants me to ask you if you would like to go with us to the movies sometime."

"What?" a shocked Will screeches.

The study hall monitor looks over and snaps at him, "Quiet down. There are people trying to study in here!" Will is dumbfounded and at a total loss for words. He finally manages to say that yes, he would like that, but has to check at home. His friend tells him to find out, and if Will can make it, they will set it up for Saturday night. He will pick up Will first and then the girls. Will is a nervous wreck. He gets home and tells Irene all about it. She thinks this is great and says that yes, of course, Will can go. Will is excited and scared at the same time and asks Irene a million questions.

The big night finally arrives. Will is ready to go. He is all slicked up, not too much oil is on his hair; it's just the right amount. His mom tells him he looks very handsome. He stands nervously, looking out the window, waiting for his friend. Jake comes in. He has been at the tavern all day, drinking beer. He spies Will, all dressed up, and asks what the hell is going on. Dale pipes up, "Will's got a date!"

And Mel adds, "With a girl!" Irene tells Jake that Will and a couple of his new friends are going to a movie.

"Well," Jake snarls, "good, Dale can go too. He would like to see a movie and have some popcorn, wouldn't ya, Dale?"

Dale grins. "Sure I would, Dad!" Will's chin drops to the floor.

Irene steps in. "Damn it, Jake, wait a minute. You can't do that to Will!"

"The hell I can't," Jake roars back. "If Will goes, so does Dale!" Will senses a big fight, or worse, coming for his mother, so he tells her it's okay. Irene clenches her teeth and storms out of the room. An excited Dale runs upstairs to get ready. The car pulls up at the end of the yard, and Will walks outside with his head down. He tells his friend that something has come up and he can't go. The friend sees a tear in Will's eye and asks what is wrong. Will glumly explains that he and his stepdad don't get along and that his stepdad tries to make his life as miserable as possible and he's doing a good job of it.

"So you can't go then?" his friend asks gently.

Will kicks the gravel with his toe. "No, if I go, I have to take my twelve-year-old brother with me. Dad says he would like to see a movie too."

The friend looks up. "Is that him? On the porch?" Will nods yes. "Well, go and get him. We will all go!"

"What?" Will cries, "I can't do that. How embarrassing!"

His friend grabs his arm. "Look, I don't want to go alone. I would rather have too many than not enough. Come on, Will, it'll just be some kids going to a movie." So Will relents, and Will and Dale go to the movies. But later, Will wishes he hadn't agreed to it. Dale is trying to be the center of attention and making a fool of himself. Will is embarrassed to tears and can't wait for the night to end. Monday comes and Will dreads going to school. And it's even worse than he imagined. All during the first couple of classes, the girls look back at Will and whisper and giggle. Then in study hall, the girls point and laugh at him. The science teacher, who is the study hall monitor, demands to know what is so funny. The girls all just point at Will. The teacher comes over to Will. She says sternly, "So what are you doing to these girls to make them act so silly?"

Will drops his head. "I am not doing anything." She walks behind him, declares that he must be doing something, and strikes the back of his neck with her ruler. Then Will just snaps. He jumps up and grabs the ruler. He throws it on the floor and storms out the door. All the while, the teacher is hollering at him, telling him to get back there or she will get the principal. Will marches down the stairs. He opens his locker, takes out his belongings, and slams the door shut. The principal comes around the corner. He huffs, "Get in my office right now, young man!" But Will walks right past him and out the front door. He is done with school. He decides to hitch a ride home. As he is walking, along comes the school bus that he should be on. The driver pulls up beside him and asks him if he wants a ride home. Will gets on the bus. He rides in silence, up front by the driver, the rest of the way home.

CHAPTER 25

Where's Irene?

Will gets home from school and tells his mother what happened. Will tells her adamantly that he is done with school; he isn't going back no matter what she says. He tells her he plans to work more, help the family out with money, and someday pay Jake back for every cent he ever spent on him. He also tells his mother that he will do whatever Jake wants as long as he lives there, but someday—*someday*, he stresses—that will change. Irene sighs and shakes her head. She isn't very happy with her son's decision, but she also knows it is all Jake's fault. She knows she will never get Will back in school and that something is going to have to give between Will and Jake.

The brothers at the locker plant, Oscar and Tom, are glad to have Will back, and Will is very glad to be back. One day at work, Oscar asks Will if he can drive. Will replies that he can; Bubba taught him a year ago in his old truck. And, he adds, whenever he had a doctor's appointment, his mother had let him drive. Oscar grins and says that's good, because the two of them are going to take a little trip. Will loads the fifty pounds of meat in the little green-panel delivery truck. Oscar gets in the passenger side and tells Will to slide behind the wheel. They are going to deliver the meat to two stores in the neighboring town, eight miles south. Oscar shows him how to pull up to the rear entrance of both stores, where to put the meat in the coolers, and then how to get the tickets signed. "Now," Oscar continues, "I am going to show you how to get to the Country Club. It's easy, a few turns and just a little bit up the street. Can you do this on your own?" Will assures him that he can. "Good!" Oscar explains, "Because next Saturday, you are going to have to. You know how much Tom and I love to golf, and Saturday, we are in a golf tournament. Here's the plan. Saturday morning, we'll stop by the plant to see if everything is okay. We will go golfing and you will have to deliver the two meat orders. Clean the place up, leave here about three o'clock, deliver the meat, then come and pick me up. Tom and his wife are going to stay longer. Do you need any directions or anything?" Will tells him confidently that he can handle it.

Saturday arrives, and Will delivers the meat on time. He is on his way to the country club to pick up Oscar when he notices flashing red lights and a police car behind him. Will pulls over to the side of the road. A police office walks up to the van and asks for Will's driver's license, and of course, Will doesn't have one. Then the officer leans into the window and questions him, "Where have you been? Where are you going, and what have you been doing?" The officer also wants to know if there are any other kids with Will. Will tells the officer that no one else has been with him. He has been working, doing deliveries, and he is on his way to the country club. The officer eyes him suspiciously and then takes Will to the police station. At the station, a couple more cops get involved. They ask him again about other kids being with him. Again Will says no, no others. They ask him if there is anyone who can verify his story. Will tells them again about his boss, Oscar, at the country club. One officer spots the bloodstained apron that Will has taken off. He goes to the country club and brings Oscar back with him, and is Will ever happy to see his boss. The officers tell Oscar the reason they stopped Will is there had been a report of kids in a similar green van breaking out school windows. Oscar verifies Will's story, and the officers tell Oscar and Will they are free to leave. On their way out, one officer chides Oscar, "Get a licensed driver to deliver your meat."

This comment irritates Oscar. He snaps back, "With all the men still overseas, do you know how hard it is to get good help? You can come and get the damn meat yourself or go without!" The officer holds up a hand. "Now wait a minute. Cool down. Maybe we can work something out." He thinks for a moment then says, "Anytime the kid is going to do deliveries, let us know, and we will escort him to his stops. How's that?" Oscar calms down and nods that will be fine. "But, kid," the officer continues, "get your driver's license as soon as you can."

The following Monday at work, the brothers tease Will about his run-in with the cops. Oscar ruffles Will's hair and asks him if he was scared. Will nods. "I sure was. I didn't know what was going on! And was I ever glad to see you show up. And when you started in on them about getting their own meat or going without, boy, I thought they would put us both in jail!" Oscar laughs. "I showed them, didn't I?" Will nods and chuckles.

"Hey, Will," Tom chimes in, "Oscar says you are saving every dime you get your hands on. What are you saving for?"

Will answers, "A car. I want a car soon."

Tom smiles and nods. "That's what all young boys want. I remember when I got my first car."

Oscar chortles. "Yeah, it was my old one."

Tom responds, laughing, "You got everything first. All I ever got was hand-me-downs." Then Tom snaps his fingers. "Hey, what about that car in the backyard? It was going to be my work car, but then we got this place with the delivery van. It's been just sitting there for a little over a year. It was running fine then, but it wouldn't start when I tried it a couple weeks ago. With a good tune-up, I'll bet it will run again." He continues, "Hell, why don't you sell it to Will? You don't need it! Or better yet, just give the old car to him!"

Will glances at Oscar and asks him what kind it is.

"Hell, Will, you and the car are the same age. It's a 1934 Model B Ford. It needs a little work and maybe a tire or two. It could use a coating of black tar on the soft top because the snow sat on it all last year. What do you think? Are you interested?"

"Yes, I am!" Will answers excitedly. "But how much do you want for it?"

"I'll tell you what, Will. Can you get someone to help you pull it out from behind my house and take it someplace to work on it? Then when you get it running, drive it down here to see me. I will give you one hell of a deal, one you won't be able to pass up." This sounds great to Will, and he thanks Oscar repeatedly. They decide Will will get the car on Sunday. The rest of the week, Will is on cloud nine. He flies around the plant and the brothers can hardly slow him down.

Will tells his mother about his deal for the car. Bubba hears him and tells him that on Sunday he will take his pickup and help pull the car back to the house. And if he wants, he will help Will get it running. Will thanks him and tells him that will be great. He knows Bubba is a good mechanic and he can learn a lot from him. Besides, with Bubba's help, he won't have to ask Jake for a thing. The next few days, the two keep busy working on the old car, and Will learns a lot from Bubba. Bubba has his own tools, and he shows Will how to clean and regap spark plugs, find and replace bad wires, and install ignition points and condensers. Irene looks out the back window from time to time. Watching Will and Bubba work on the old car together makes her sad; she wishes that could be Will and Jake, but she knows that will never be. Finally, Bubba and Will get the old car running. Bubba stands by the car, wiping his hands on a greasy rag, grinning from ear to ear. Jake walks out to the backyard, beer in hand. He chortles, "She sounds good, Bubba. Looks like I'll have another car to drive." Bubba glances over at Will and gives the boy a wink, and Will never says a word. The next few evenings, Will keeps working on the car. He puts some black tar on the top; he takes the seats out and beats the dust off them. He washes the old car and cleans it until it sparkles. The next day, he drives it to work to show Oscar. Oscar steps out of the door and smiles. "You and your dad did good, Will. It really sounds good and even looks pretty good!"

Will blushes. "It was my dad's friend, Bubba, who helped me." Oscar puts his hand on the boy's shoulder.

He says, "I hope it runs another fifteen years, Will, and you don't owe me a dime. It's all yours. Consider it a bonus for all your hard work and the extra work, that you've done around here."

Will's eyes glisten with tears. "I don't know what to say. You guys have treated me so very good. Are you sure, Oscar?"

Oscar smiles. "Oh yeah, Will, I am very sure!" Will is grateful for the car. He never abuses the use of the car, and he never takes it for granted. He never takes it joy riding. He does use it to get another job though. He picks up a Sunday rural paper route. This way, he can drive the car and get paid for it. It isn't a big route, only about an hour or so, to all the farms surrounding the town. But it's extra money for Will, and he gets to drive his very own car.

One night in November, just before Thanksgiving, Will comes home from work to find Jake very upset and talking to the babysitter. Jake tells her he will be right back, and he heads to the telephone office. Will questions the girl and finds out that his mom has hired her to babysit the kids. Irene told the girl that she didn't know when she would be back, and she has taken Jake's car and left. She has just up and left. Will is devastated. He slumps down on the couch, his head in his hands. What he can't understand is why she left him there. After all, he is the one who doesn't fit in. How could she do this to him? How could she leave him there with Jake? Will knows he is being selfish and only thinking about himself, but he is heartbroken. He tries to put himself in her shoes and think about her wants and needs. Who knows what she has been going through trying to keep peace in the family? Then Jake bursts back through the door. He tells the girl he should be back in the morning and not to leave until he gets back. The girl nods and says she can stay. Then Jake turns to Will. "Get your car. I am driving. We're going to where your mother is, at Grandpa Jim's." Will stares back at him. He knows that it's about 175 miles away.

They drive most of the way in silence. They stop once, and Jake gets a beer and Will a soda. The whole drive, all Will can do is wonder why. Why would his mother do this to him? It makes him very sad to think that she could leave him. When they finally arrive at Grandpa Jim's, Irene gives Will a big hug and says that she is glad to see him. Then Grandpa Jim takes Will out to the front porch. He tells Will that the two grown-ups have a lot to talk about and they should let them be. Grandpa Jim asks Will questions about how things are at home, but all the while, Will just tries to hear what is being said between his mom and Jake. He doesn't answer any of his grandpa's questions; he is too busy trying to overhear what is being said inside. He hears his mom say that she is sick and tired of the way things are and she just wanted to get away for a while. She says angrily, "We have a full house and another one on the way. We're short on money and we can't always get the kids what they need. I'm damn tired of you drinking that whiskey, Jake, and picking on Will all the time." She continues hotly, "I don't mind you correcting him or punishing him when he is wrong, but you do it constantly! According to you, he can't do anything right. His whole life, up until the time you wanted him to know he wasn't yours, all he ever did was try to please you, to make you like him and do things like the other kids do with their daddy." Bitterly, she adds, "Well, Jake, I hope you're happy. You got him so he hates you. Oh, he will respect you, but deep down inside, he hates you! Then you put him up against Dale and Mel and even make them mad at him. But when you made him take his younger brother on his first date, that did it. You made him feel embarrassed and humiliated. I think that's why he quit school." Her voice quivers as she continues. "He does more than his fair share of the chores. He gives us half of what he makes for wages, plus he gives most of what he has left for Christmas." Will leans forward in his chair and listens intently.

He hears Jake say, "I'll stop the bootlegging and stay away from the whiskey. But I can't love, or even like, Will as one of my own, especially after Rosie."

Irene's raises her voice. "Now, Jake, stop it! He knows what you think about that, and you don't have to love or even like him. It's a little too late for that anyway. Just give him some room. Cut him some slack. He's fifteen years old, and in a few more years, and he'll probably be clear the hell away from you."

Will doesn't hear any more of the conversation. He sighs and slumps in his chair. He turns to Grandpa and starts answering his questions. He fills him in on everything he wants to know. Then Grandpa Jim stands up; he looks at Will thoughtfully and says, "Will, I hope that I live long enough to see you claim what is rightfully yours." With that, Grandpa walks into the house, leaving Will alone on the porch.

Jake and Irene finish the conversation in the house. Things are better between them, and they decide to head home. The good-byes are said, and before they leave, Grandpa Jim hands Will an envelope of money. He tells the boy to give it to his mother when Jake is not around. They start the long drive back, Jake driving his car, with Irene sitting close beside him. Will follows behind in his car. He drives home deep in thought, his mind racing, thinking about all that he has overheard.

CHAPTER 26

The Big Wind

Back at home, things are better for Will. Jake leaves him alone, and the two of them just sort of tolerate each other. Thanks to Grandpa Jim, the family has a pretty good Christmas. The new year, 1950, comes in quietly for the family. One snowy morning in late January, Dale and Mel go with Will on his Sunday paper route. The roads have deep snow on the edge where the plows have pushed it. Will drives carefully down the country road but somehow manages to get the car stuck in the snow. He goes to the trunk to get the shovel, but no shovel. Dale has used it and didn't put it back. So Will decides they will have to push the car out of the snow. But this doesn't work because Dale and Mel can't do it by themselves. So Will has a plan. He pulls the choke knob out a little bit to make the motor run a little faster. The motor revs up, and he hops out of the car to help the boys push. But the car takes off across the road and into the ditch! This makes Will very unhappy, but it makes Dale and Mel laugh with glee. Will walks over and surveys the situation. Hands on his hips, he looks down at the car. The good thing is, the ditch isn't very steep, and there is no deep snow there either. Even better, just a little farther up, there's a field entrance from the road. The field is frozen hard, so Will has another plan. He just drives the car over the frozen field and up to the fence. He hops out and opens the gate, and they are back on the road again. The three laugh heartily. Will smiles at his good fortune. Then Will looks at his brothers and warns, "Now, don't you tell Dad about this." But blabbermouth Dale can't wait to get home and tell Jake all about it. So Jake declares that Will has put Dale and Mel in danger, and the only time he can use the car now is for his Sunday paper route, and he must go alone. Soon it's March and Will's birthday, and he turns sixteen years old. At the end of March, Jake becomes a father again. Irene delivers another boy, who is named Jerry. Talk about a full house! Besides Will, there are six other boys and one girl. That's a lot of mouths to feed and a lot of clothes to wash. Will feels sorry for his mom and the amount of work keeping up with the demands of a large family places on her.

One day, Will finds out from his mom that after school is out, there is going to be a family reunion. It will be the first of June and held at Jake's uncle's place, about 120 miles away in central Iowa. He hears that Butch and Johnny will be there and is pretty excited about this. He also finds out that during the summer, there are going to be free movies every Saturday night in the parking lot of the grocery store. Will thinks this is going to be a good summer! A couple of days before the reunion trip, Will pleads with his mother to take his car too. He wants to show his car to Johnny. But Jake says no, that it would be a waste of gas to take two cars. He says that his car is big enough. But then, Jake has a thought. He says if Will is to buy the gas, then they can take his car. Jake tells him how much money he will need. Will glances at his mom, unsure what to say. He sees the wink she gives him, and he tells Jake they have a deal.

Will is delighted to see Johnny at the reunion. Even though Will and Johnny write letters to each other, it is great for them to be together again. They still consider themselves as true blood brothers. Will asks his mom if he can take Johnny for a ride in his car. Irene isn't sure, but Jake says yes as long as he takes Dale, Mel, Kenny, and Doug. And no funny stuff, he cautions. The boys take off in Will's car. They drive down the street, honking and waving at all the girls they see in town. Will and Johnny laugh, and the boys all have a great time.

Later that afternoon, Will isn't so sure he likes what he is hearing. He overhears Jake talking with one of the uncles. The man tells Jake about a job at an auto dealership in town. The place would hire him in a minute, he tells Jake. He adds that the town has lots of places with cheap rent. Will knows that the railroad has been unhappy with Jake about all the time he misses from work. Will doesn't like the sounds of this; he knows what Jake is up to. He also knows there is nothing he can do about it. At the end of the reunion, Will and Johnny say their good-byes. They promise to keep writing to each other.

Back at home, the free movies in the parking lot are great. The movies start at dusk. There are short logs set up with planks across them to sit on, facing the homemade movie screen. The kids get there plenty early; there is free popcorn and Kool-Aid for a few cents. The farmers in the area bring their kids into town for the movies too. Will meets a farm girl that he likes. She sits beside him and they munch popcorn. One night they watch *Tarzan of the Jungle*. The younger kids watch them and giggle.

One Saturday, the weather is particularly hot, sticky, and cloudy. Just before dusk, the clouds get really dark, they roll rapidly across the sky, and the wind picks up. The kids are milling around, looking for their friends and finding seats on the planks. Suddenly, a county sheriff's car comes racing up, lights flashing. The deputy yells, telling everyone to take cover; there is a tornado heading that way. The farmers quickly find their kids, load them up, and head for home. People everywhere are scurrying; parents anxiously look for their children. Will jumps up off the plank and finds Donny. He spots Jake and Irene, who have Dale and Mel with them. They quickly head for home as the sky grows darker and darker. Jake opens the trap door to the basement and yells for everyone to get inside. The basement is a dark, musty-smelling old hole, but they all cram inside. Everyone is scared; the youngest are clinging to Irene and crying. They hear creaking and groaning and loud noises overhead. There's a big thud that shakes the entire house. Then, just like that, it's over. It is eerily quiet. Jake opens the trap door and comes out first. He looks around and then tells them it is safe for everyone to come out. Bubba pulls up just then. He jumps out of his truck and asks if everyone is okay. The house is dark; there is no electricity. Irene lights some hurricane lamps. Jake and Bubba tell everyone to stay inside; they are going to drive through town and see if anyone needs help. When they come back, they report that some trees are down and some houses have roof damage, but everything's seems to be okay. As for the thud, the roof has a hole in it from a big limb that fell off the tree in the backyard. Jake remembers there is a piece of plywood in the shed big enough to cover the hole. The two men get a ladder, hammer and nails, and get to work covering the hole. Inside, Irene makes a big pot of chili and homemade bread for everyone.

At daybreak, Will and the older kids can't wait to get out and look around town. The first thing they see, right across the front yard, is a strip about ten to twelve feet wide. It is just plain dirt; the grass is entirely gone! In the gravel parking lot, they see two cars. The windows are broken out on one side, and all the paint is off that side. The cars look like they've been sandblasted. On the edge of town, across from the creamery, the telephone poles look fuzzy. Will thinks they look like they need a shave because of all the hay and straw that is sticking out of them. Two big stacks of hay that had been in the field are gone. The hay is strewn all around town; it's on the houses and in the streets. The boys spot a couple of chickens running around that have hardly any feathers left on them. Donny manages to catch one. He takes it home with him, and Jake remarks that it would go good with some dumplings. But Donny won't hear of it. He says that the chicken is his, and he is going to take good care of it!

CHAPTER 27

From Bad to Good

It takes a couple of weeks for the town to get back to normal. Will continues to enjoy the rest of the summer movies, and he enjoys sitting beside the girl too. One day, he spots some men up on the roof of the local tavern. He watches them put up a long, high pole, with a wing-shaped attachment on it. He wonders what it could be and asks Bubba about it. Bubba tells him that it is for the new television set that is going to be in the bar. Will gives him a funny look and asks what it is for. "Well," Bubba explains, "it's like a radio, but you can see stuff besides just hearing stuff. You'll be able to see a boxing match or any game while it's going on." Will frowns and thinks it must be for rich people. Bubba smiles and adds, "The bar owner says we should be able to see the boxing match next Friday night, so come in then and take a look!" Will nods and tells him he will. The next day at work, Will asks Oscar what he thinks of the television set. Oscar tells him he thinks it is really going to be something but costs a lot of money.

"Just what I thought," Will sighs. "You'll have to be rich to have one."

The next Friday night, Will and a friend go to the tavern. Bubba, Jake, and about six other guys are all looking at a big radio with a round glass in the front with what looks like a snowstorm on it. Will laughs when he sees it. "You can look out your window in the wintertime and see that, and it don't cost ya anything!" Will thinks right there and then that you would have to be pretty dumb to buy one of those things, and he heads back outside.

The younger kids in the family start school, but they aren't there for long. Jake tells the family that his uncle is coming the first of October with a truck to help them move down to where his uncle lives. Will tells his mother that he really doesn't want to go. Irene gives him a long look. "Well, Will, there are younger boys than you out there on their own. Do you think you are ready for that? You have a pretty good job, but you would have to find a place to live, cook for yourself, pay for heat, and pay all your bills."

Will thinks it over for a minute then says quietly, "No, Mom, I'm not ready. Besides, you and the family need my help." Irene smiles and puts her hand on his shoulder.

She nods. "That's true. But the day will come when we will have to get along without your help, and believe me, son, you have made a big difference. There were times when I don't know what I would've done without you." She gives him a quick grin. "Besides, it might not be so bad. It's a whole lot bigger town, and there should be a lot of places for you to work. Jake is going to be a mechanic again, for the Kaiser Dealership. And his uncle got us a place to live with more bedrooms, just what we need".

Will has a hard time telling Oscar and Tom that he is leaving. The brothers really hate to see him go. They are very fond of Will. Oscar tells the boy that if he ever gets back that way again, to be sure and stop in and see them. Will assures them he will and hugs them good-bye.

The family moves to the new location. And what Jake hasn't told them is that the new place is two miles outside of town, a farm-house. And guess what? No plumbing and no running water! Irene is furious when she finds out. "No, Jake, damn it, no! I want water and an inside toilet!" Jake promises her that if she will just make this place do through the winter, they will move into town in the spring. Right after they make the move, Jake's car quits working. He decides to use Will's car, or as he calls it, his "second car."

It takes a few days, but the family gets settled in. Then Jake announces that he has a job for Will. He tells Will that a farmer a few miles farther out from town needs a hired hand. Will really wants to work and will take anything at this point. The job includes room and board and pay, with the bulk of the pay going to Jake. Jake says he heard about this job when he was working on the farmers' pickup. Jake tells Will that he will get the family car fixed or get a different one, so Will can have his car back. With his car back, he will be able to come home once in a while. Irene isn't too happy about this arrangement but decides they can give it a try.

Will starts his new job with the farmer, and right from the start, he fears that he is in a bad situation. The room that is his is up in the attic. There is an old army cot for a bed and a couple of old wool army blankets. There is only one light, and the farmer controls how long it is to be on. Will rises at dawn and does the morning chores with the livestock. By this time, the farmer and his wife are up, and he meets them for breakfast. There are no second helpings except for coffee and no lunch until noon. There is a lot of work that needs to be done before the snow comes. Some of the bales of hay and straw need to be taken down from the hayloft and stacked at the other end of the barn. The oats and corn need to be mixed for feed after the ears of dried corn are run through a hand-cranked corn Sheller. The manure needs to be hauled out and spread over the fields. It's Will's job to shovel the manure into the spreader, then the farmer hauls it out to the field. At noon, on the way in for lunch, he must go through the henhouse and gather eggs for the farmer's wife. There are no days off. The next few days, Will follows the routine. He does what he is told, and as long as he is busy, it keeps his mind off how much he hates this job. But at night, after supper, he goes to his lonely old room in the attic and thinks. He wonders, what in the hell did I ever do to get into this mess? And worse yet, how am I going to get out of it? The light goes out, and Will cries himself to sleep. Then at daybreak, it starts all over again. One day, the old farmer tells him, "The good Lord meant for man to work from daylight to sunset." The only problem with this is, the man expects Will to work after dark too. Things get continually worse for Will. Finally, one Sunday after breakfast, he can take no more. The God-fearing couple, although they don't go to church, get ready to read from the

Good Book. They like to read for one hour, which they maintain is a good thing. They tell Will that he will have to read with them, that it will not only be good for his soul, but it will help take the laziness out of him. This makes Will snap. He tells them no, he won't do it, and he storms out the door. He heads back to work, frustrated and unhappy. He is so deep in thought that he doesn't even go in for lunch at noon. About four in the afternoon, Will walks into the farmhouse. He says firmly, "I am all done working for you, so take me home." The man gives him a hard look, "Well, son, that's not part of the deal." Will gathers his clothes and heads for the door. It is late October, and there is a chill in the air. Will thinks maybe he will walk across the country, through the fields, to get home. But he decides against it. He figures with his luck, he will probably run into a mean bull or get lost or something. No, he reasons, he better stick to the roads. He walks along and there is not a soul in sight. Finally, about an hour into his walk, along comes a black pickup. The truck pulls alongside Will, and a man in his early forties sticks his head out the window and says, "Hey, young fellow, it looks like you could use a ride!" Will smiles and says he sure can. He runs around and hops in the other side of the truck. The man eyes him kindly and says, "Well, I didn't spot any vehicles broken down along the road, so what are you doing out here walking?" Will tells the man that he and his family are new to the area and that he had been working at a job back down the road. He continues, telling the stranger that he feels bad; he's never done anything like this before, but he'd quit his job, just up and quit.

He adds glumly, "And he won't give me a ride home, so here I am."

The man gives a knowing smile, "I'll bet ya was working for old Pete, wasn't ya?" Will nods his head yes. At that, the man with the kindly eyes bursts into laughter. "How long was ya there?"

Will gives him a puzzled look. "Seven and a half days."

"Well," he says grinning, "don't feel bad. You probably set a record. Nobody has ever worked for that old son of a gun for more than two or three days! No one around these parts will work for him." Then he turns to look at the boy. His eyes brighten and he says,

"You hungry? Hell, you probably haven't had a good meal in a week. What do you say, how about coming home with me? My wife, June, is a hell of a cook. She'll have supper ready, and I'll take you home in the morning."

Will says slowly, "Well, I don't want to cause you any problems or anything." The man assures him it will be no problem, and June will be happy to see a new face.

They pull up to the farmhouse, and Will follows the nice man through the front door. The man introduces his wife to Will, and she extends a hand politely. Mike tells her that he picked up Will coming from Pete's place, and the boy had been there a week. She tells the two to get washed up and she will put dinner on the table. Will can't help but notice that besides being a nice lady, she is also very pretty. Soon he discovers that she is also a good cook, just like Mike said. Supper is meatloaf and mashed potatoes and gravy, Will's favorites. Will tells her the food is delicious and that his mom is a good cook, but there's no way she could make a meatloaf as good as June's. June blushes. "You're probably just hungry from being at Pete's. Now then, do you want ice cream on your apple pie?" Mike grins and looks at Will and gives him a wink.

After supper, the three of them chat. Will finds out that Mike and June are high school sweethearts. The farm had belonged to Mike's folks but was given to him when they passed on. They couple never had any children, not that they wouldn't have liked to. Will tells them that his family is new to the area. They just moved here from a very small town in Minnesota. He tells them they rent the first place outside of town. Mike recognizes it as the old Peterson place and asks Will if they intend to farm it. Will says no, his dad is a mechanic, and they move around a lot because his dad is always looking for better pay. He tells them that Jake is working for the Kaiser Dealership. Mike tells Will he knows the place; a friend of his owns it. He adds that he has already seen Jake, the new guy. They sit in silence for a moment, then June asks Will what he intends to do now for a job. Will says he guesses he will have to go into town and look for a job. She thinks for a moment. "Say, we could use him here, couldn't we, Mike? Look at last year, how far behind you got before spring planting. You were working all day and half the night." Mike looks at his wife and nods. "Yeah, you're right. And this long driveway, we sit so far back from the road, it takes a lot of time to keep the snow plowed off it. I'll bet you already know how to slop the hogs, milk the cows, and other farm chores, right?" Will assures him he does. Then Mike asks him if he has plowed snow before. Will tells him he hasn't, but if he will just show him once how it wants it done, he can handle it. Mike smiles. "I like your attitude. And if you do come to work for us, we will give you room and board plus wages. I'm sure all three will be better than what you had at your last job!" Mike stands and stretches and declares it's time for bed. He says they can sleep on it and talk about it in the morning. June shows Will where the bathroom is and the room that he is to sleep in. She tells him if he comes to work for them, that will be his room. Will looks around. It's a very nice room, with a big bed, lights, and even a small radio. Will sleeps like a baby and is awakened in the morning to the smell of fresh coffee brewing and bacon. He thinks to himself, how can I refuse all this?

After breakfast, Will thanks them for supper and the bed and breakfast and tells them they are some of the nicest people that he has ever met. If they want him to work for them, then he will. He would be really dumb if he didn't! He asks if he can go home first though; he wants to let his mother know about his job change. Mike says sure; he has to run into town anyway, and he will drop him off. He says Will can talk it over with his mom, and he will come back and get him in an hour or so.

Will tells Irene what has happened. She is very sorry about the first job but very happy about the second one. She has a surprise for Will; he can have his car back! Jake has gotten a good used car from where he works. Will says that with his car back, he really won't have to stay with Mike and June; he can drive back and forth to work. Irene agrees that's true but reasons that with Will gone, there is one less mouth to feed and less clothes to wash, plus Will is away from Jake. Will sighs and agrees with her. He says he will try the room and board arrangement again. Mike stops by to pick up Will and meets Irene. He tells her he is glad that Will is coming out to live with them. He draws Irene a little map to show her how to get to his farm. And although Irene doesn't have a phone, he gives her a phone number. He tells her it is to a party line, and she can call out there any time to talk to Will. Mike says that since Will has his car back, he can drive home in the evenings or weekends to see his family. They agree on Will's wages and everything is set. Will hugs his mom good-bye. He drives his car and follows Mike out to the farmhouse. Will drives in silence and smiles to himself. He can't help but think how things have changed, how things have gone from very bad to very good.

CHAPTER 28

Will and Dolly

At the farm, Mike tells Will that the best place to park his car is beside the garage. Here it will be out of the wind and won't get so covered with snow. A dog comes running to greet them, tail wagging. Will loves dogs; he stoops to scratch its ears and pet it. The dog enjoys this and takes an instant liking to the boy; the dog is sure they are now best friends. Will continues to pat the dog and remarks to Mike that he didn't remember seeing a dog last night. Mike tells him that the dog lives in the barn. He has a corner with clean hay and stray, and that's where he stays at night. During the day, he stays outside, checking things out around the farm. June comes out of the chicken house just then. She walks over and gives the dog a pat. She tells Will that his name is Roger and he is a very good watchdog. Will chuckles and remarks that Roger is a funny name for a dog. June replies with a grin. "Well, I named him after a guy my sister dated. He was a real dog." They all laugh, and Roger wags his tail and nudges Will to keep scratching. "But now," June continues, "I am sorry I named him that, because he is such a good dog!"

The next few days, Mike shows Will what needs to be done around the farm. He tells him that June takes care of the chickens. She spreads the feed around and gathers the eggs. But on cold windy days or if she isn't feeling well, they are to do it for her. Mike shows him where the feed is and how much to use. The eggs are to be gathered from the nest, put in a basket, and placed on the porch. He tells him it isn't a dairy farm, so they only milk the cows once a day, in the late afternoon. They feed the hogs once a day. The water tanks, there are three of them, are to be kept full, so he will have to keep his eye on them. He adds that when it gets cold and they freeze over, he will have to bust up the ice two or three times a day. They have an electric feed mixer. He will need to fill it, pull the switch, then watch the tubs so they don't flow over. The cows, there are four of them, and two steers, they will come and go. There are also two horses. He must make sure the barn door is open when it's cold. The horses are on the side with the tall opening, the cows on the side with the short door. Will listens intently; his eyes follow as Mike points and continues, "That little tractor over there? I'll show you how to run it in a few days, when we start pulling machinery in the garage to get ready for spring planting. When the snow comes, there's a bucket and plow on the tractor to move the snow. And of course, any and every tool we need is there in the garage." He stops for a moment and wipes his brow with his hand. He tells Will if he doesn't understand something, to just ask him. "Fair enough?" he asks.

Will nods. "Fair enough."

Mike adjusts his cap and says, "I want you to be able to do things that need to be done without having to ask me. So if you do it right, good. If you do it wrong, well, I must have showed you wrong, or you goofed.

Will smiles at him. "No goofs, Mike, no goofs!"

Mike slaps him on the shoulder, "Like I said, Will, I like your attitude! Now let's go slop the hogs and milk those cows."

The two head for the barn, with Roger at Will's heels. While milking, Mike notices that Will is doing pretty well, but the milk is coming out in a thin stream. He tells Will he will show him a little trick. He puts his hand on the cow. "You see up here? Between the belly and her flank, this bare spot?" Will peers under and sees the spot Mike is pointing to. "Well," he continues, "I want you to put your head right here, up against this spot, and every so often, give her a little nudge or two. See how that works for you." Will does as Mike instructs, and sure enough, the milk starts to flow in a strong, steady stream into the pail.

"Boy, Mike," Will exclaims, "that makes all the difference in the world! How come?"

Mike smiles and says, "That's what the calf does when it is sucking. It's a signal to the mom to let her milk come down a little more freely."

The days on the farm fly by. Mike and June are more than pleased with Will, and Will is very content. When Thanksgiving comes, Will goes home and spends it with his family. Soon it's the first of December, and there is already snow on the ground. Mike teaches Will how to use the plow and where to pile the snow to keep the farmyard open. The animals start coming into the barn at night. Dolly, one of the horses, grows very fond of Will, and he grows very fond of her. They seem to have a special bond. She is nearly blind, but that doesn't stop her a bit as long as she is around Betsy, the other horse. Dolly always knows when Will is around. She bobs her head up and down, as if she is saying yes, as she waits for the apple that Will always gives her. And wherever Will goes, so does Roger. Whenever the work is caught up, Will is in the barn, spending all his free time with Dolly and Roger.

One night at supper, June comments, "Will must really like those apples we picked last fall. That barrel on the porch was plumb full. I told Will he could have all he wanted, and he's made quite a dent in them already." Mike starts to laugh and looks over at Will.

He chuckles. "Will's got a stash of them out in the barn that he gives to Dolly and Betsy!'

June glances at Will, "Well, that's good. Last year, before we could use them all, they started to rot. We fed them to the pigs. That's a good thing, Will, being so good to the animals, especially in this cold weather. Keep it up. Take all you want." She gives the boy a little smile.

Mike throws his head back and laughs again. "Good to the animals? Did you see him yesterday? He had Roger riding on the plow with him!"

Will helps June clear the table. Tonight is game night. Some nights after supper, the three play board games or cards. On the other nights, Will is out in the barn with Dolly and Roger. Will looks at

Mike and June and thinks about how nice they are and what a nice place this is to work. But in the back of his mind, he knows that someday, he will want to be around kids his own age, maybe meet a girl, and do things like other kids. But for now, he is very happy.

One Saturday night before Christmas, Will makes plans to go home. Then he finds out about the sleigh ride. June tells him that this time of year, during the holidays, Mike hitches the horses up to the sleigh. He takes the team into town and gives the children a sleigh ride. Will thinks this sounds great and wants to join Mike. He tells Mike he will get Dolly ready, but first he watches how Mike gets Betsy ready. Mike instructs him, "First, the halter with the bit goes into her mouth and the collar around her neck. Then lead her out of the barn and back them up to the sleigh. The sleigh tongue hooks to the collar then the chains to the double tree." Will nods and listens. "But we're not done yet," Mike continues. "We have to hook the bells up to the leather straps. Then there's clean fresh straw for the back, and June will bring out blankets, hot cocoa, and coffee." Just then, June comes out of the house with her arms full. She grins at Will and winks at Mike. "Well, now that we have a new driver, you, mister, are going to cuddle up with me in that nice straw in the back!"

Mike laughs. "Sure, Will can drive the team!"

Will quips, "Sure I will. Just show me where the horn and head-lights are!"

Mike walks over to the horses and picks up the reins. "Well, my boy," he says, "you take these reins in your hands. When you want to go left, pull the left one back toward you. The farther you pull it, the sharper the turn, same way for the right side. You wanna stop, you pull both and yell 'whoa.' You notice we have Dolly on the right? That's to keep her away from the cars. So when you get on the road, stay clear to the right, as long as the snow isn't too deep. We don't want Dolly working any harder than necessary." Will hops up on the driver's seat, and Mike and June get comfortable in the back.

Will holds the reins and says, "Giddyup." Nothing happens. Mike bursts out laughing. Will looks back at him puzzled.

Mike explains, "You gotta hold the reins up a little higher then snap them down on their butts. Not too hard, just enough to signal them when you say 'giddyup.'" Will does like Mike says, and that does it! The horses take off, and the sleigh heads for town. First, they drive by the church on the edge of town and pick up some kids. They go in a big square around the edge of town. More and more children join them. The kids laugh and drink hot cocoa. Some of the young boys take turns sitting up front by Will. The horses whinny from time to time; they seem to prance, and the bells ring out in the December air. Everyone has a good time, and as the day comes to a close, Will drives the team back home.

Back at the farm, Will pulls the sleigh up to the front of the house. June hops out; she tells the boys to hurry up and she will make some more cocoa. Will tells Mike to go inside too; he can handle putting the sleigh and the horses away. Mike jumps off the sleigh and says with a laugh, "Are you sure, Will? Oh, I know, you just want to give Dolly another apple."

Will grins. "No, I am going to give her two!" Mike smiles and tells him to give them another scoop or two of feed while he's at it. Will puts the sleigh away and feeds the horses. He pats Dolly one last time for the night. He hears her whinny softly, and he smiles to himself as he closes the barn door tight.

Christmas arrives, and Will goes home to see his family. June sends with him a couple of pies, a box of cookies, a few dozen eggs, and a big duck that she has wanted out of her freezer. Jake is pleased; he likes roasted duck and hasn't had it for quite some time. Things are better between Jake and Will, but of course, they aren't around each other very much anymore. The family enjoys a nice Christmas, and at the end of the day, Will heads back to the farm. He walks into the house, and June hands him two very nicely wrapped packages. Will takes the gifts from her, but his eyes are on the floor and he feels very sheepish. "Naw, this ain't right," he stammers. "I didn't get you anything."

June smiles kindly. "Now, Will, hush, these are just a couple of things for you for all the extra work you do around here. I hope you like them." Will opens the smaller package first. It's a pair of deerskin gloves, just like Mike's.

"Wow!" Will says excitedly. "These are great. They will be nice to wear while I'm doing the chores!"

June smiles. "I thought you might like them. I saw you looking at Mike's." Then Will opens the larger package; it's a pair of knee-high rubber boots. He holds them up and admires them. June explains, "I notice that down in the pigpen, the muck comes up over your over-shoes. So you see, these gifts are just to get more work out of you!" Will is delighted with the gifts. He beams as he hugs them both and thanks them repeatedly.

The holidays are over, and the winter soon turns to spring. It's March 1951, and Will celebrates his seventeenth birthday. Jake keeps his promise to Irene. One block behind the dealership, there's a big, cement block building. It has water and plumbing. It is sectioned off into rooms to live in while the owner builds the house above it. For some reason, the owner never finishes it. Jake buys the building and claims he buys it for a song. One of Jake's farmer customers tells him that he has a big old barn that he wants gone. The farmer says it isn't in the best of shape, but Jake can have all the lumber as long as he tears it down and hauls it away. This is a good deal. Jake needs the lumber to build his house. And he has four boys at home, ages four-teen, thirteen, eleven, and nine, to help. The nine-year-old is Donny. The chicken he rescued about ten months earlier is now laying an egg every morning and follows the boy around the rest of the day like a puppy. The best part of this house project is that Jake is very serious about it, and he only drinks a couple of cold ones after a hard day's work. Will agrees to help out whenever he can.

One night on the farm, a violent storm blows up. The rain comes down in hard sheets. The thunder booms and the lightning lights up the sky. Will lies in bed and listens to the storm. A few hours pass, and in the middle of the night, the phone rings. He hears Mike on the phone in the kitchen. Will gets up and asks Mike what is going on. Mike fills him in, "Well, the neighbor just called. He passed here on his way home and can see some of the cows out and one of the horses up near the road." Mike reaches for his rain gear and heads out the door. Will tells him to wait; he is going with him. Will grabs his raincoat and also a couple of apples on his way out. The two jump into the truck drive up the lane. Near the end of the lane, they spot one of the cows standing by a hole in the fence. Mike hops out of the truck and starts to chase the cow back into the fence. Will stands still for a moment. Then he sees and hears Dolly. She is up the road a little, and he can tell that she is scared. Will grabs a rope halter from the back of the truck and heads toward the horse. Mike realizes what is going on and yells, "Will, you be careful, she's pretty upset!" Will edges closer to the frightened horse and he calls her name. She turns her head in his direction and her ears perk up. She listens to his voice, her tail swishes, but she stands still. He reaches her and rubs her head. He talks softly to her and she calms down. He reaches into his pocket for an apple. He offers it to her, and as she takes it, he quickly slips the halter over her head. Will slowly walks her back to the truck. Mike finishes rounding up the cows. He tells Will that he has patched the fence well enough for the night. It should hold until they can get back out there and fix it right in the morning. He glances around. "I see Betsy already went back to the barn. Tie Dolly to the back of the truck and we'll take her back." Will shakes his head no; he tells Mike he would rather sit back on the tailgate and hold the rope. Mike agrees, and they lead the horse back to the barn. Will gets Dolly settled in. He scratches her ears and rubs her head. He breathes a sigh of relief that Dolly is all right, then he heads back to the house for a cup of hot cocoa with Mike and June.

CHAPTER 29

Time to Leave

After spring planting is done, Will explores places around town on his days off. There's a gas station and a small café that he especially likes. He buys his gas there and knows the station attendant pretty well. He really likes to go to the café too because there are a couple of really pretty girls that work there often. The girls are older than Will, and they like to tease him about drinking coffee when all the other young guys drink soda. Will enjoys the attention from the girls.

One day at the gas station, the attendant asks Will if he is looking for a job. Will tells him no, he works on a farm and likes his job. But Will also confides in him that he knows he can't stay on the farm forever. He isn't a farmer; besides, he likes it in the city. The guy tells Will that he likes his job there at the station too, but he has to leave soon. In a couple of months, he has to leave and go back east, on account of some family trouble. Will thinks about what the attendant has told him, and it weighs heavy on his mind. He really does like his job, but he wants to be around people his own age. He knows he isn't a farmer, and he really does like city life. One night after supper, he tells Mike and June what he is thinking. Mike sighs and takes a sip of coffee. He tells Will that he isn't surprised, that he always knew this day would come. He smiles and says, "I hate to see you leave, Will, but I understand. You want to be with people your own age, maybe even get a girlfriend, huh?"

June pours another cup of coffee and nods. "I am surprised you don't already have a sweetheart."

Will blushes and grins. "No, I guess I've been too busy. But if they are all as nice as you, June, maybe I'll give it a try someday." She smiles and ruffles his hair as she starts clearing the dishes. Mike scratches his head and asks him when he thinks he will leave. Will says he isn't sure.

Mike thinks for a moment, "Can you stay till we get the thrashing done? Between now and then, we got corn and beans to cultivate, then mid to late summer, the oats will be ready, and we'll do a thrashing run." Will assures Mike that he will not leave until the oats are in and put away in the bin.

During thrashing season, four to six farmers get together; that's why they call it a run. They all help each other and go from farm to farm. Each farmer gets his own field ready by cutting the oats with a machine that cuts the straw stuff with the oats on them. It ties them into bundles then drops the bundles on the ground. Then the men walk the field, taking ten to twelve bundles together and stacking them into shocks. This makes them easier to pick up later, and also keeps them from rotting if the rains come.

The thrashing run begins, and Mike's farm is first. The man who owns the thrashing machine, with his big steam tractor, gets set up. All the other farmers are there, with their wagons and teams of horses. They are out in the field, loading the shocks into the wagons. Will is out there with them, with Dolly and Betsy. Mike stays by the big machine to help keep it running and keep the straw pushed back, and the stream of oats flowing. Will is the last one to have his wagon loaded, and although it is not loaded as high as the others, he is still very proud. He begins driving his team, pulling his load. He starts to drive through the last gate; he has to make a big turn to the left. But his load isn't balanced, and when he makes the turn a little too sharp, over it goes! He looks back and sees most of the load is on the ground! Will is embarrassed and turns bright red. Even though the guys are all laughing, they help get the wagon straightened and put the bundles back on. Will smiles sheepishly and thanks them. With Dolly on the outside, he drives his team up alongside the conveyor belt. He unloads the bundles and is relieved that he gets it right. Now it's time for the food. The famers' wives come to each place to help with the meals. Midmorning, between breakfast and the noon meal, the ladies bring sandwiches and cold tea or soda to the men. At noontime, Will feeds and waters Dolly and Betsy. He stands them in the shade and gives them each an apple or two. He has his choice of ham, chicken, or pork steak, plus mashed potatoes and gravy, and of course, pie. After dinner, the men all go and lie in the grass in the shade. They rest for about thirty minutes, then it's back to the field. The afternoon goes much like the morning, except no tip-overs for Will. He learned his lesson! The ladies bring out a fine midafternoon snack, and then the day's work is done. The men gather around the well. They wash up for supper and talk and laugh about Will's tip-over. Mike pulls up some very cold bottles of beer from the well. He hands them out to each one of the guys then one to Will. Will looks at the bottle in his hand and wonders what his mother would say. One of the men tosses him the church key and tells him, "Drink up, young fella. You did just as much work as the rest of us. And one damn beer before supper ain't gonna hurt ya!" Will grins and opens the bottle. He takes a long drink and thinks how good it tastes. It really hits the spot. Will has just had his first beer! That night he has steak for supper, and when he turns out the light, he is exhausted but pleased. What a day it's been!

CHAPTER 30

A Newer Car

The thrashing run is over, and Will says good-bye to Mike and June. They tell him how much they will miss him. They know Dolly and Roger will miss him too. Will promises to stop in and see them once in a while. Meanwhile, Jake and the boys have a house. It isn't finished yet; some rooms need paint, some flooring, doors and trim, but it is livable. There's even a room for Will.

One day, Will is at the gas station, talking with his friend, Ed. The boss lady walks in and Ed says, "This is my friend, the young man I was telling you about." She glances at Will and extends a hand. She asks him his name and if he is looking for a job. Will tells her his name and that yes, he is looking for a job. He is a little surprised by her looks; she is a very stately and attractive woman in her midforties. She asks, "Can you pump gas, check oil, check tires, keep the drive clean from dirt and snow, and make change?"

He nods, "Yes, ma'am, I can do all that. Someone will have to show me how to run the cash register. I am really good with numbers though, always got an A plus in arithmetic." She gives him a little smile and turns to Ed. "When are you leaving, Ed?" He grimaces and tells her this is his last week. "Oh dear," she sighs, "I completely forgot. All I have lined up is a high school kid who can work on Saturdays and after school some." She turns back to Will. She looks at him intently. "Can you start tomorrow, Will?" She tells him to come in the next morning at seven to train the next few days with Ed. And just like that, Will has a new city job.

Will is a fast learner and picks up what he needs to know quickly. The job is from seven in the morning until seven in the evening, with Sunday off. If he needs any other time off, it has to be on Saturday or during the after school hours, when the high schooler is there. Will learns that the boss lady lives upstairs, over the station, in a nice apartment. Her husband is overseas and is due back home in a year or so. Will is good at his job. When the drive bell dings, he hustles out to the car. He knows if the customer only wants a dollar or two of gas, he needs to stay right there with the hose to shut it off in time. But if the customer says "Filler up," then he knows to put the gas cap between the trigger and the handle frame to keep the gas flowing. He can then wash the windshield, check the oil and water, and even sweep the floorboards off. He listens for the telltale gurgling sound that lets him know the tank is full. Will does a good job, and business is even picking up some. The boss lady tells Will a couple months after he has started that the station has sold more gallons of gas than ever before. The station has a café attached to it. The girl who works there has to leave shortly after she arrives each morning because she has to make a trip to the bakery for the doughnuts and cookies. She is delighted when Will offers to pick these items up for her on his way to work. Besides the café, the station has two car stalls. One has a grease rack in it; the other, where the boss lady parks her car, is a wash rack. Will keeps the drive clean, the inside of the station spotless, and the cash register is never short. The boss lady is more than pleased with his work, and he keeps her car clean too. Will gets a free meal twice a day, lunch and supper. One guy in particular comes in to the station often. He eats in the café and spends a lot of time flirting with the girls. He pulls into the drive and tells Will to fill his car with gas. He then tells Will to park it while he goes into the café and wants Will to bring him the keys. He always drives a nice car, but it isn't always the same one. His name is Kenny, and he and Will become friends. Kenny always laughs at Will's old car. Kenny is a wild guy. He is not rich, but he has plenty of money to spend. One day he says to Will, "You need a better car before winter sets in. I'll look 'em over for you." Will asks him what he means, and he tells him that his father sells cars. He tells him they own the junkyard and the Kaiser Dealership. Will is surprised and tells him that the dealership is where Jake works. "So Jake's your dad? Well, I'll be!" Kenny chuckles. "I sure ruffled his feathers the other day! I hooked the spark plug cleaner to the vise he was using and gave him quite a little jolt. He jumped a mile, threw his hammer down, and wanted to know who the hell did it! Everyone in the place thought it was funny. Everybody but him. I told the guys that if anybody told on me, I would have my dad fire them!" Will laughs, so hard tears stream down his face.

Every day, Kenny brings another car to the station to show Will. But they are all too new and cost too much money. Finally, one day he drives into the station in a black 1947 Kaiser. Will likes this car a lot and drives it after work. He asks Kenny how much it costs. Kenny tells him how much and Will is leery. He tells Kenny that it is an awfully good deal; there must be something wrong with the car. Kenny laughs. "Hell no, there's nothing wrong with it! I told my dad it's for a friend of mine!" He snaps his fingers and adds, "I'll tell you what I'll do. I'll have your dad check it all over for you."

Will grins and says, "But don't tell him it's for me!" Kenny laughs and says it's a deal, and they shake on it.

At the end of November, Will gets the car. He cleans it up and waxes it until it is nice and shiny. He drives it home and Jake sees it. Jake eyes the car, then Will, then asks him how much he paid for it. Will tells Jake the price. Jake raises an eyebrow. "That's a real good car. I know because I checked it all out. You got a way better deal than I would have gotten." Will laughs and says, "Maybe next time you should talk with Kenny instead of his dad!"

On Saturday nights, Kenny picks up Will. It's always in one of the better cars, whichever one he can talk his dad out of or get his hands on. The two drive up and down the main drag in town. Sometimes they go to the neighboring towns. Sometimes they go to the movies. They become good friends even though they are very different. Kenny is wild and reckless; he drives really fast and even scares Will from time to time.

Will gets to know and like a lot of his regular customers. Among them are a couple of brothers in their late twenties. They come into the station and fill up different cars now and then. The boss lady tells Will to keep a tab on what they buy. They are from the Ford dealership, and she will carry them from month to month. Will gets to know them pretty well. They like the way he checks their cars over. Winter arrives and with it the snow and cold. Will does a good job of keeping the drive at the station clear of snow. He has an electric block heater on his car so it always starts, even on the really cold mornings. On more than one occasion, he gives the café girls rides to and from work.

It's a cold and snowy January. One day at work, Will hears some bad news. He learns that his friend Kenny has been in a very bad auto accident. Will goes to see him and finds him in a full body cast, and for how long, no one knows. Will asks him what happened. Kenny groans, "Well, you know me. I was driving too fast. You always holler at me to slow down. I'll bet you're glad you weren't with me, huh? Anyway, I came around this curve, hit a patch of ice, and that was it. They say the car rolled four or five times, threw me out, and then rolled over me. I sure as hell hope I'm not wrapped up in this thing too long." He tries to laugh. "I got a date with that cute girl Carol this Saturday night. I guess I'll have to stand her up, huh?"

CHAPTER 31

Where's the Birth Certificate?

It's March and Will turns eighteen years old. He receives a notice from the Selective Service System that he must report for registration and a physical for classification into the draft program. He must do this by the end of the month and bring his birth certificate with him. He tells his mother and she says she will get the certificate for him. About this time, the lady who owns the station tells him her husband will be home sooner than she had thought, and she will be putting the station and café up for sale. She thinks it will be sold by about the fifteenth of June. Will can't believe all the changes that are going on. One afternoon, one of the brothers at the Ford dealership stops in to the station. He has heard that it is up for sale. He asks Will what he plans to do for a job. Will says he isn't sure. He doesn't know if the new owners, whoever they might be, will keep him on or if they will have their own staff. He tells the brother that he has decided that if a good job comes up, he will take it and not wait around to see. The man tells Will to come and see him, that around the first of June, they are going to need a permanent man on the wash rack. He tells Will the wash rack is where everyone starts out unless they are a qualified mechanic.

Will tells the boss lady the date by which he must report to the draft board, and that if he doesn't, he could go to jail. He finds out that there is a bus leaving on the scheduled day at seven in the morning from the courthouse. The bus will take the young men to Des Moines for their registration. The night before, Will asks his mom for his birth certificate. She tells him there isn't one. She remembers that a couple years after Will's birth, before she could get a copy of it, there was a fire at the courthouse. Many records were destroyed in the fire. She says, "Just tell the officials that this is all you have." With that, she hands him a piece of paper with his name, date of birth, the hospital, and city and state. He looks at it and then folds it away for the next day.

Will boards the bus and rides with the other young men to Des Moines. All the boys are taken to a room where they sit at long tables and are given papers to fill out. They fill in names, addresses, health problems, and other information. Birth certificates are collected and copies made and handed back to each young man as they leave. Will hands the official the paper from his mother and repeats what she has told him. The official tells him that the matter will be looked into.

Next is the physical examination. The hearing test doesn't consist of much. Each boy is asked a question; if he can answer it, he passes. If he doesn't hear it well, the question is repeated a little louder, and he still passes. The eye test requires reading a couple of letters at the top of a board, and they are asked if they ever wore glasses. Next, the boys take off all their clothes, except socks and underwear. Blood is drawn, the lungs are checked, and the heart is listened to. Will tells the doctor about his heart murmur. The doctor listens intently then tells Will that he doesn't hear anything wrong. And that is the end of the testing. The boys are told that in a few weeks, they will find out their draft standings.

A few weeks later, Will gets a letter from the Selective Service. He is told that they are still looking into the matter of his birth certificate. He is classified an IA. This means that when they start drafting young men from the area, in eighteen to twenty-four months, he will be one of the first to go.

CHAPTER 32

Will Meets Some Girls

The station and café sell, and Will is now the number one man on the wash rack. This entails several jobs. First job, every morning, if it's not raining, he dusts off all the used cars in the front. If there is a recent trade-in, after it has been checked over and serviced, his job is to detail it in full. He cleans the engine, washes and vacuums out the trunk, vacuums the upholstery, and washes and waxes the car. The sparkling-clean car is then put out on the lot. He washes and polishes customer's cars and keeps the boss's car clean. He washes all the new cars before delivery. Things are going well for Will; he likes his job and is making more money than ever. He even makes a few new friends. Now and then a young man named Matt comes in to the dealership. He brings his father's car in for service and a wash job. He and Will strike up a friendship. They go out once in a while and drive the loop around town. Will meets a few other kids about the same age through Matt. Matt has a sister that wants to date Will. Will and the sister and Matt and his girlfriend go on a double date, but it doesn't turn out well. But through this girl, Will meets her friend, Anne. Will likes Anne right away. Soon, they are seeing each other often. Anne lives on a farm just outside of town. She has been staying in town with her grandmother and is just starting her senior year of high school. She stays home on school nights, but on the weekends, the two go out. Will doesn't know a lot about girls, and this worries him. He feels he has a lot of catching up to do.

Will and Anne continue to keep steady company. Then in early October, Will gets a promotion to the grease rack. The parts manager retires, and the fellow from the grease rack is going to take his place. So Will gets to be the new "grease monkey." Will learns a lot in a very short amount of time in this new position. He takes care of the customers, treating their cars as if they were his own. He does lube and oil jobs and replaces filters and does other repairs as needed. The customers trust Will and like him. He will tell them if they don't need something so they don't waste money. For instance, if he can clean their air filter, he'll do it free of charge so they don't have to buy a new one. He soon knows what the car will need by the mileage on it, like wiper blades, new brakes, or wheel bearings repacked. He takes the wheel and hub off, no charge, to show them what they need. If they need it, then this extra work keeps the mechanic busy, and the boss likes this.

He learns from the old grease monkey about undercoating new cars. He is given a choice, to get paid three dollars extra for each car he undercoats or, like the older man had done, get a new Ford after undercoating one thousand cars! Will takes the new car option. The best part is, this is the only one, out of four dealerships in town, that can do the job. And it's an easy sale. Will tells customers that everyone who buys a new car in this part of the country should have it done. It protects the undercarriage from snow and the salt put on the roads; it helps keep it from rusting. And besides, it will help soundproof the car when driving on the gravel roads. The older man also tells Will to keep an old pair of coveralls around to slip into, a hat, and goggles. He tells him to smear Noxzema all over his face before he sprays. Undercoating is a dirty job. The undercoat is a thick, black, tarlike substance. It is power sprayed on, and it sticks tight to everything. It stays somewhat soft and doesn't dry hard and crack and come off.

He thinks from time to time about how lucky he is. He has a nice girlfriend and a good-paying job. After taxes, he is taking home $52.23 a week! He is rolling in the dough and thinks there is nothing more he could need.

CHAPTER 33

Pregnant?

The first of November, the boss comes to Will and tells him that he's been there five months, and he's getting a promotion. He also tells him it's time he gets a Ford to drive. The boss tells him that he has just traded for a very nice used 1949 two-door. He says he thinks it will be perfect for Will, and he will hold it for him for Will to look it over. Will checks the car out, and it is a dandy. It was owned by an older couple. It's has no dents or scratches on the outside. And on the inside, seat covers were put on it when it was new. It has good tires and has been kept in a garage. The only thing wrong with it, as far as Will is concerned, is that it is green. But he figures he can live with that! He meets with the boss to find out the terms. The boss has three options for Will. One, he can take the car just as it is, and that's the lowest price. Two, the car will be run through the shop, like all used cars; that will be the highest price. Or three, a mechanic will look it over on Saturday night when the showroom and office are open late. Will can be on his own time and service and detail the car himself for a mid price. Will thinks this is more than fair and takes the third option.

The next week, Will is very proud as he is drives his new, to him, shiny green Ford. His mother is also very proud of Will, and he gives her a ride in it. He lets Anne drive it but only once. She has a lead foot, like his friend Kenny; she drives way too fast! The next few weeks, Will stays busy working on his car. He puts mud flaps on it and blue mood lights under the dash. He adds fancy hubcaps with lights shining on them and an outside sun visor over the windshield. He even installs a through muffler that gives it a nice mellow and not-too-loud sound. And for an extra touch, he adds a wrist-breaking steering wheel spinner.

The fall goes by quickly for Will. It's soon December, with cold temperatures and lots of snow. The grease rack isn't very busy, so Will becomes the wrecker man. The wrecker is a one and half ton Ford six-speed truck with a flatbed on the back. It has a hand crank lift mounted on it to pick up either the front or the rear of a car for towing. It has solid rubber across the front for pushing cars. It's a 1948 model, but well equipped with emergency flares and a series of batteries for giving jump-starts. It has big tires with chains on them, and there aren't too many places that it can't go. The boss asks Will if he can come in one hour early on the cold snowy days. The boss will take the calls, and he wants Will to go out and take care of the customers. Will finds he likes this job; he likes being out by himself. The cars with a manual transmission he can push to start. But he has to jump the batteries on the cars with automatic transmissions. Others he just has to tow back to the garage. Sometimes, when he is on the road to a customer, he is flagged down by a motorist. He tells them he will be right back after he takes care of the first caller. The boss is surprised because Will comes back to the shop with three, four, or even five service calls, not just the one he left for.

Things are going pretty good for Will. In February, he notices that Anne hasn't been herself lately. Will thinks maybe it is because her older brother has told her parents about her going out with him instead of the nice neighbor boy on the farm next to them. For Valentine's Day, he gets her flowers, a stuffed animal, candy, and a nice card. She looks at him and bursts out crying. "I'm pregnant!" she cries. Will's mouth drops open. She sobs, "That's what the doctor says. I'm about a month along." Will's mind is racing. He thinks of the similarities, a young girl, in school, and pregnant. Isn't this so much like what happened to his mother? Will thinks about how little he knew about girls and how he has caught up on that! He doesn't say anything for a while; he doesn't know what he is going to do. He knows one thing for sure. He sure the hell isn't going to abandon

Anne and his child like his father had done to him. He tries to calm Anne down. He pats her hand and says with a sigh, "Well, I think we better tell our folks. Maybe we'll get married. What do you think?"

Will and Anne talk to Irene first. She puts on a pot of coffee and the threesome talk seriously. Irene pats her son on the shoulder. "Well, you don't need to pay me any more money. You better save all you can. Find out what will be a good night for us to visit Anne's parents so we can start making plans." The night arrives, and they drive to Anne's parents farm. Jake goes along for some reason, and he is already half-drunk. From the start, Anne's mother does not want her daughter to marry Will. And she is even more sure of this after meeting Jake. Anne's dad sits quietly and doesn't say much. The families discuss the options, and it is agreed. No matter what Anne and Will do right now, there will have to be a marriage at a later date in the Catholic church. In Anne's parents' eyes, this will be the only marriage that counts. Anne agrees with Will and Irene that she wants to get married right away. Irene places a call to her mother, Bess, who lives in Illinois. She tells her the news that she will soon be a great-grandmother. Then Bess comes up with an idea. She wants the kids, Anne and Will, to come to her place for a weekend. They can get married there then have the cottage out back for a honeymoon suite. It will also be a chance for them to all be together again. Rick has retired, and they are leaving the first of May for California. He has gotten the little ranch with horses that he has always wanted. So the date is set for the last weekend in March, right after Will turns nineteen. Anne's folks don't want to go at first; Jake doesn't either. But Jake soon changes his mind. He decides he will leave Irene with Will and Anne at Bess and Rick's, and he will go out and look up some of his old friends. The families travel to Illinois, and Will and Anne get married in secret. It is to be kept a secret until Anne graduates. After the wedding, they both go back to living at home.

The young couple is very happy, and they start to plan for the future. Anne can hardly wait for graduation. Will decides to stop shaving and grows a beard. They start to work out the details of their new life. They will need a place to live and furniture. Will says that when they get a place, he wants a television set and a telephone. But if they can't have both, he would like the television. Irene and Anne become very close. Irene tells Anne that after school is out, she will hold a baby shower for her. Will and Anne start to get excited about the future.

CHAPTER 34

Butch Passes Away

Will talks with a priest at the Catholic church in town. He meets a very nice young man who doesn't look much older than Will! They strike up a friendship, and Will likes him very much. Will begins to take instructions from the priest to become a member of the Catholic church. Classes are held two or three times a week, and Will should be done in about three months' time. This makes Anne very happy. When Will meets all the requirements and becomes a Catholic, their wedding will be blessed by the church.

Early in May, Anne's grandmother has a stroke. She isn't able to live alone anymore. At first, Anne's family plans to have her live on the farm with her daughter, Anne's mother. But the grandmother has another daughter in Minnesota who wants her to live with her. So Anne's grandmother moves out, and the young couple make plans to rent her house. The house seems perfect to Will. It has an attached garage, which he loves, and is only two blocks from where he works. The aunt in Minnesota wonders if the couple would be interested in buying the furniture too. This will help them out, plus it won't have to be moved or sold by her. Will says sure, if the price is right, because it is old furniture. He asks if she will take monthly payments. A deal is struck, and just a few weeks before graduation, Will and Anne have a place to live, with furniture. All that's missing, as far as Will can tell, is the television set.

Will and Anne move in together. Will finds that living with someone is a whole new experience. He thinks to himself, if he isn't

146

grown up enough by now, he better hurry and get that way. In the beginning, things are great for the young couple. Will and Anne make a pact. They agree to listen to and take advice from others. But at the end of the day, no matter what, it will be their choice to make, and they will make it together. As for Will, he is tired of always being told what to do. His theory is, if he is asked to do it, he will. If he is told to do it, he will do the opposite.

They settle into the new house quickly. Will loves being able to walk to work each day. And while he is at work, Anne's parents stop by most every day. The couple's friends come over some nights and they play cards. One day, a friend of Will's stops by and asks Will if he can store his motorcycle in his garage. Will says sure he can but wonders why he needs to store it. The friend tells him that he has enlisted in the navy to get away from some problems at home. He explains that he doesn't want to leave it at his house because he has a little brother he fears will wreck it or sell it while he is gone. He tells Will that he can ride it during the summer if he wants. In the winter, he asks if he will please drain the gas and turn the engine over now and then. Will is happy to help his friend out.

One day in June, when the young priest is over giving lessons to Will, he notices the motorcycle. He tells Will that seeing it brings back good memories for him, of a warm breeze on his face and the wind in his hair. He tells Will that he used to ride motorcycles. Will smiles and tells him that if he would like to, he can take it for a spin. So the young priest slips off his collar, hops on the bike, and takes off down the street. This happens several times after the lesson is done. The young priest enjoys riding the motorcycle all around town. Some nights, the priest will even enjoy a cold beer with Will.

Then the day comes when Will receives his last lesson from the young priest. Arrangements are made for a ceremony to be held on the second Saturday of July. Will will be accepted into the Catholic faith, and directly after, Anne and Will's marriage will be blessed. Everything is set, and the priest snaps his notebook shut and stands to leave. Will tosses the key to him and tells him to take a quick ride. The priest lowers his head and says, "No, my riding days are done." Will is surprised by this and asks him why. "Well, a couple of deacons from the church have seen me riding it, and word has gotten out that it has to stop." Will can't believe what he is hearing. He apologizes and says he can't help but feel responsible for getting him in trouble. They are silent for a few minutes; then Will tells the priest he is beginning to doubt if he is making the right decision about this new faith. The young priest quickly assures him that it is not the faith talking, just a couple of old men who don't want anybody to ever do anything they think is wrong. He laughs and pats Will on the shoulder. "Now bring Anne over Friday night for the rehearsal." Will says he will then asks the priest what he thinks of his new beard. The priest smiles and replies, "It looks fine to me. You keep it trimmed and neat. The bishop himself had one not so long ago, so don't worry about it."

The families on both sides are invited to the ceremonies. Anne tells Will that her mother has been complaining about his beard. She wants to make sure that Will cuts it all off before the big day. Will makes up his mind right then and there about his beard. Anne's family attends, her mother and father, brother, and an aunt and uncle who live just outside of town. Will's mother attends, and to his surprise, his boss is even there. Will is given his first Holy Communion by the bishop. Then the clergyman leans in and gives Will's beard a little tug and says, "Nice beard, young man." Will wishes that his mother-in-law could hear this. He decides not to tell her what the bishop has said; he knows she won't believe him anyway.

About a week later, Will finds out from Anne that the young priest has been transferred to Nebraska. Will is saddened by this news; he didn't get to say good-bye or even thank him. He supposes that maybe the younger priests get moved around a lot. Anne tells him no, that her brother told her differently. She tells Will, "The deacons think that since he likes you a lot, that if he stays here, you will contaminate him." Will's mouth drops open. She continues, "Yes, and that's what Mother says too." Will stands there in silence. He doesn't say a word. But he can't help thinking how unfair it is. The priest is sent out of state all because of him? And to make matters worse, Anne's mother thinks it's his fault too? It's more apparent every day that his mother-in-law dislikes him. He shakes his head. He just gets away from a man who hates him, only to get a mother-in-law that hates him too.

Summer passes quickly and June rolls into July. One hot afternoon, Will is busy at work. He looks up from the car he is working on and sees his mother standing there. She has come to tell him some bad news. His Uncle Butch has passed away. She tells him the funeral will be held in Minnesota, and he will be buried in the family plot. Irene sighs and adds that she would have liked for them to all go together, but since they weren't sure if he would be able to get time off work, she and Jake were on their way out of town right then. She gives him a quick hug, and as she leaves, she hands him a piece of paper with the address on it. Tears slip from his eyes. "I'll be there, Mom, you can count on it. No matter what, I will be there." There is no way in hell that Will wouldn't be there. He loved that man. He was the closest thing to a father that he had ever had. The boss tells Will to go and take all the time he needs.

Will hurries home and tells Anne that it's about a 175-mile drive and to pack enough for three days. They leave immediately and hope to be there by nine o'clock that night. When they arrive, Johnny comes running out to greet Will. Will can't help but notice how much Johnny has changed. He is big, like his father, not fat but well built. He takes after his father in every way. He is wearing nice clothes and expensive shoes and driving a big black Packard. Will introduces him to Anne, who is now about six months pregnant. Inside, Irene introduces Anne to the rest of the family. The mood is somber. The men stand around drinking, talking quietly. The women congregate in the kitchen. They talk, telling things they remember about Butch. Butch's mother is taking his death very hard. She listens, and the tears fall as she hears them tell fond memories of her son. But she also keeps an eye on her other son, Jake. She tells him sternly to drink just beer, no whisky. They say their good nights, but no one sleeps well that night.

The following day is the visitation and viewing of Butch. Will walks into the room hesitantly. He sees his Uncle Butch lying in the open casket and he is overcome with emotion. Johnny and Anna come to his aid, one on each side. Tears flow and he grieves for the man he loved so much. Later that night, back at Grandma's place, Jake tells Johnny that now that his dad is gone, he will be the man for him to come to. He tells him to come to him for anything, day or night, no matter what. He says, "Your dad, my brother, and I were very close, and I was just as proud as he was the day you were born. We have the same blood, and it's my job to look after you now."

Johnny nods and responds, "My father was a great man and the best damn dad, too." Will, standing alongside Johnny, hears this.

He clenches his teeth, and looking right at Jake, says defiantly, "Johnny, your dad was the very best man that I ever met." Irene, sensing the tension, walks over to Will.

She gives him a hug and says quietly, "Please don't start anything, son." Will looks at his mom and pauses. He squeezes her hand and tells her not to worry, he won't. He glances over at Johnny, and with that, the two young men walk outside.

The next day, during the funeral, Will stares hard at Jake. *You old son of a bitch*, he thinks, *is it wrong for me to think the wrong man has died here?* He mourns the loss of the man he thought of as a father while looking at the man who has always hated him. After the burial, there is a luncheon put on by the church ladies. Johnny and Will sit down at a table alone. They take this opportunity to have a serious talk. Johnny says candidly to Will, "I know you and your dad, I mean Jake, don't get along well, but he has always been a really good uncle to me and I like him very much, and I don't always know where I stand with you about that."

Will gives him a soft smile and says, "I have no problem with that, Johnny. You can do anything that you want to with Jake. I know he loves you and your brother very much." Then Will chuckles. "Hell, at one time, when we were little, Jake wanted to trade me for you with your dad! And I was at your place so much that a couple of times, your dad claimed me on his income taxes." Then he turns serious. "You know, your dad was like a father to me. They had a hard time breaking me from calling him 'Daddy' when I was small." A sad look crosses over his face, then he leans over and hugs the man he considers his blood brother. "We have no problem here, Johnny, no problem at all."

CHAPTER 35

Will's Drafted

After Butch's funeral, Will and Anne go back home, and Will stays busy at work. He undercoats as many cars as he can. Anne is getting bigger every day. Irene stops by once in a while to check on her. Of course, Anne's mother is there nearly every day. There is still some friction between Will and his mother-in-law. For one, she is not happy about the doctor that Will and Anne have chosen to care for Anne and the baby.

Summer slips by, and soon it is fall. In October, Anne and Will become the proud parents of a beautiful baby girl. They decide to name her Donna. Will can't help but be a little nervous. He doesn't know how to be a father, but he is sure he will learn as he goes along. The first week that Anne is home from the hospital with Donna, they have a lot of company. All the family stops by, and Anne's girlfriends from high school stop by too. They come to see the newborn baby and bring gifts.

The winter comes early, and soon it's the new year, 1954. Things get worse for Will with his mother-in-law. She thinks Anne should change her doctor, and she doesn't believe that Donna should get any shots whatsoever. She claims that the shots are all just sugar and water anyway. Will comes home from work many times to find Anne crying. Her mother has been there and upset her, wanting her to do things differently than Will and Anne have already agreed on. Poor Anne, she is between a rock and a hard place. She doesn't want to make her mother mad at her, and she certainly wants to keep Will happy.

For Anne's sake, Will makes a decision. The following Sunday at dinner on the farm with Anne's parents, Will has a serious talk with his in-laws. He tells them firmly that there will be boundaries set. Boundaries that they must follow. Now his mother-in-law isn't happy about this, but she halfheartedly agrees. Things seem to improve a little. They get into a routine, and the summer passes quickly for the young couple and their baby girl.

The first of September, Will gets an official looking letter in the mail. It's from the Selective Service draft board. The letter states that in forty-five days, Will is to report for induction into the US Army. All he needs to bring are the clothes on his back and his toothbrush. The letter goes on to say that the birth certificate that he did not provide at his registration has been researched extensively. They find that there is no record of a Wilton Michael Furman ever being born in that state, county, town, hospital, on that day and year. However, they do go on to say that they found a record of a Wilton Michael Johnson, born that time and place, but that person is not recorded as deceased. The letter urges him to contact his parents, check with family and friends, look in the family bible, and bring whatever information he can find with him to the induction in October. Will is speechless. He grabs the letter and heads to his mother's house. Irene reads the letter and says hotly, "I know nothing about any of this. Your records were destroyed, like I said."

"But, Mother," Will insists, "that's some kind of a coincidence, isn't it? That birth would have to have been at the exact same time as mine! You must have heard or seen something, right?" Irene snaps back, "No, Will, those damn government people are all screwed up. They have the wrong city, or state, or something wrong! There is nothing new to tell them, your records burned up, and that's all there is to it!" She sinks into the sofa and is quiet for a moment. She calms down a little and says, "But I am sorry that you are going into the service." Will's head is spinning. All he can think of are the similarities, same first name, same middle name, and same time and date! But then he thinks to himself, his mother should know, and why would she lie about something so important?

He shrugs and says with a little laugh, "Well, Mom, if the army doesn't want me because I don't have a birth record, I guess I'll just stay home then."

One day at work, Will decides to check to see how many cars he has undercoated. The count is at 886. He sighs as he closes the logbook and puts it back under the counter. It won't make any difference anyway. The man that he had made the deal with has passed away, and the deal went with him. And that means Will doesn't get the extra three dollars per car either. "Just my luck," he mumbles to himself as he heads back to the grease rack.

The weeks fly by, and it's time for Will to leave for his induction. Will says all his good-byes the night before. Early the next morning, he is on the bus with his toothbrush. He knows it is going to be a very long day. They are headed for Fort Chaffee, Arkansas, six hundred miles south. Each man is given two meal tickets and one lunch ticket and told they will be able to eat at the places they will stop for fuel. They arrive at the fort late that night, and they are each assigned a bunk to sleep in. Early the next morning, the men are escorted to the mess hall for breakfast. They are teased and called names by the guys who have already been there. Then it's off to another place where they are issued their fatigues. They are told to shower and dress, then they are given a tour around the fort. They are told to remember the name of each building and what it is used for.

The next day, they are issued their fighting gear, and the training, or "fun and games" as they put it, starts. Will stands with the others, his combat boots on and helmet in hand. The drill sergeant barks a list of names, and Will's name is one of them. To this group, the sergeant narrows his eyes and yells, "You aren't man enough to be in this man's army!" He tells these men to gather everything that has been assigned to them and hand it back in. He looks around the room as he continues. "The 'no father' rule has just come through, and you are going home. But you other men, the married men who have no children, you are here to stay and make your country proud!" So Will and the rest of the fathers ride back to Des Moines, Iowa.

They spend the night there, are looked at by doctors the next morning, then are sent back home. Will has only been gone for five days, and he hasn't told anyone that he is coming back. When he arrives back home, everyone is glad to see him. Well, almost everyone. Will thinks it's a good thing he gets back when he does, because Anne and her mother are already making plans to subrent the house, and Anne and Donna were going to live on the farm with her parents.

CHAPTER 36

Will's Smoking

Will returns from his five-day absence to work at the Ford dealership but not as the grease monkey. He is now the body shop helper. His jobs are to sand and mask off cars for painting and do glass installations. He will also install new parts when the old part can't be hammered out, like fenders, hoods, and grills. In a few months, he learns to prime spray cars. The rest of the year goes along pretty smoothly. Then in 1955, because the body man misses so much work due to an illness, Will gets to spray paint cars. One day, the boss sees some prime work Will has done, and he says he thinks Will is ready to paint. He finds a used car that is in great condition, except the paint is really bad and peeling off. He tells Will to sand, prime, and mask it all off for a total paint job and try to have it ready by Saturday night. On Saturday night he can be alone, with no one to bother him, and he can paint it. Will gets the car ready and does the job, and while it's not a perfect job, it's good enough to get Will more painting work.

One day in late October, Donna seems to be coming down with something. The little girl is just over two years old now and isn't feeling well. Anne plans to take her to the doctor that afternoon. Will returns to work after lunch. He is busy wiping a car down with a tack rag to get all the dust off for painting. Anne comes into the shop, crying. She tells Will that the doctor thinks that Donna might have polio. Donna is on her way in an ambulance to a bigger city about forty miles away, where they will put her in isolation for treatment. Will and Anne jump in their car and are not too far behind the ambulance. At the hospital, Anne calls her mother and fills her in. Donna is in an isolation room, the only ones allowed in are medical personnel. The young parents are told they won't know much until the blood work is done. Soon, Anne's mother and dad arrive at the hospital. Anne's mother is angry and upset. She chides Anne, insisting that the little girl is in the wrong place. She is adamant that they should have taken her to Dr. Grant. Will listens to his mother-in-law, a little perplexed, but he agrees. If this Dr. Grant is a better doctor for his daughter, then absolutely, she should see him. A few minutes later, the doctor comes out. He tells Will that things are under control. Donna is stable and they will know more in the morning. Will asks the doctor if the best doctor should be called in, perhaps this Dr. Grant? The doctor gives Will a baffled look; he knows of no Dr. Grant. Will finds Anne and pulls her aside. He asks who this Dr. Grant is that his in-laws are so adamant about. She tells him that Dr. Grant is the family chiropractor. Will looks at her in complete disbelief. A chiropractor? He can't believe his ears. He feels the anger rising; he clenches his teeth and tries to stay calm. He heads downstairs for a cup of coffee, fuming. He sees the cigarette machine out of the corner of his eye and then he does something really dumb. He buys a pack of cigarettes. He smokes a cigarette and it calms his nerves, and it begins his smoking habit.

Will and Anne decide to spend the night at the hospital with their little girl. Before Anne's parents leave, her mother again tells them that after Donna is out of the hospital, they should take her to see Dr. Grant. Will looks at his mother-in-law and says angrily, "No, no, and no! She is under the care of a good doctor, one that Anne and I both like and trust, and she is going to stay there." Anne's father glances over at Will and nods. He is a nice man, a very good man. He never says much, and he doesn't give them any grief like his wife does.

The next day, Donna is taken out of isolation and put in a room where Anne and Will can be with her. The doctor comes in with news. He tells them they aren't sure what Donna has; it's a virus of some sort, but the good news is it is definitely not polio. Furthermore, he doesn't see any reason why they can't take her home that evening. In a day or two, he tells them to take her for a checkup with her regular doctor. Will shakes the doctor's hand and thanks him. The young couple smile at each other. They are very relieved that Donna will be fine. And of course, Anne's mother reminds them that when Donna has her checkup, don't let them give her any shots.

Will has a good job with the dealership and is making pretty good money. He and Anne live in a nice home and things are going great. So he decides it's time he makes a big purchase. He buys a television set. And this television set comes with a remote control too. The delivery men arrive and set the television in the living room. Then the men go on the roof and put up a long pole, with a motor, to turn the antenna. In the living room, they pull up some of the carpet to run a wire from the television set to the chair. Will can sit in his chair and change the channels up and down and even control the sound. Will stands back and admires his new purchase. He smiles at Anne, and Donna claps her hands with delight. Will finally has his television!

CHAPTER 37

Another Pretty Girl

The winter arrives and with it cold temperatures and lots of snowfall. Will is driving the wrecker again. He is having some health trouble; he coughs up blood now and then. He sees a doctor who tells him it is from the paint. He advises him to wear a better mask and drink heavy milk to coat his throat. Will follows his advice, and the new mask really seems to help. The year goes by very quickly. Soon it's spring 1956, and in April, Anne tells Will she is about a month pregnant.

One morning, Irene stops in for a quick visit. She tells Anne she would like to take Donna on a little outing with her, and she will bring her back later that afternoon. Anne says "Of course" and kisses Donna good-bye as the two head out the door. At noon, Will walks home for lunch. Anne's brother has just stopped in too, and Anne begins to make them both a sandwich. As the brother pulls up a chair, he looks around and asks Anne where Donna is. Anne replies that she is with Grandma Irene. The brother is shocked! He pushes his chair back, knocking it over. He yells, "What? You let her go to their place? What's mother going to say?" Anne stares at him. Will stands up, he looks at his brother-in-law, his face reddens, and his jaw clenches.

He says hotly, "Why, you son of a bitch! You're in my house, at my table, and you tell my wife that our child can't go with my mother? Get out of here right now before I smack you in the mouth!" Will gives him a shove and he falls back toward the door. He gets up, and without a word, he lets himself out. Will is outraged! He is angry and his feelings are hurt. Strong words are said between Will and Anne. Will calms down and he and Anne talk it out. Anne agrees with him. Even though Will's family is poor, they should not be treated like that by her family.

The following Sunday at dinner on the farm, Will has another talk with Anne's family. Will says pointedly to his mother-in-law, "I don't care if you don't like me, but don't you bad-mouth my mother or tell us who and who cannot see our daughter. And stop telling Anne what to do! We will run our own lives." He continues. "You can stop by anytime you like to see your daughter and grandchild, but stop trying to be the boss." Later, the women clear the table, and Will steps outside to have a cigarette. He leans against the fence and blows out a puff of smoke, deep in thought. His father-in-law walks up to him, and he puts his hand on his shoulder.

He says quietly, "I apologize, Will. She's been like this ever since the kids were born." Then he chuckles and adds, "You're lucky. Hell, I have to live with her."

Summer arrives, and Will begins coughing up blood again, only worse now. He sees the doctor again, and the doctor tells him he is going to have to stop painting. Will decides to keep his eyes and ears open for another job. He learns that the Phillips 66 gas station is up for lease. The man who owns it is going to retire. He has let the inventory dwindle so it won't cost too much to take it over. Will is told that the money from the gasoline sales alone pays for the rent and utilities. The money from the grease rack, wash rack, and tires is all profit. The Phillips Company thinks Will is a good candidate, but he needs a little money for a down payment. Will intends to go to the bank, but his father-in-law wants to lend him the money instead. Will accepts his offer, and with this down payment, Bill's 66 is open to the public in the fall of 1956. Will thinks it's a great location. It sits on the corner of two highways. The highway going north goes to the lake, and there's a lot of traffic in the summertime. Things start out pretty well. Some of Will's old customers from the Ford dealership bring their cars in to be serviced. The boss from Ford even brings some used cars out for Will from time to time. Will tries to handle it all by himself, to give good service like he has always done, but finds that he needs help. He decides to hire the young schoolboy who lives right across the street for after school and Saturday help. Will teaches him how to work on the cars. He tells him to be fast getting out to the drive for the gas customers. He instructs him on the service he should give, wash the windows, check the tires, sweep the car out, and all with a big smile. Will really likes the kid; he reminds him of himself. He's a hard worker and isn't afraid to earn money.

One day, a flier from the Phillips Company gets delivered to the station. It says that a "mystery customer" is going around to different stations to see what kind of service they are providing. If this customer finds a station that is really exceptional, the station will receive a gift of twenty-five dollars and a write up in the local newspaper. Will shows the flyer to the kid. He says, "We do all that here and more!" The boy nods then says he doubts the man will stop there. Will smiles and says he doesn't see why not. After all, they are a pretty new place, just the type that should be checked out. The boy asks him if the "mystery shopper" does come in, how much money will he get? Will laughs and tells him ten dollars.

The station stays pretty busy. After school, some of the younger drivers like to come in. Will shows them how to tune their engines and different things about their cars. The boys like to use the hoist and get up under their cars. They install through mufflers and mud flaps. Will lets them, as long as the hoist isn't busy. If they buy gas and oil there, then it's free; if not, he charges them fifty cents.

There is a policeman in town who does not like the loud and noisy mufflers. He knows that the kids are installing them at Will's station. He doesn't like this; as matter of fact, he doesn't like Will. There isn't much he can do about it except stop them when they are out driving. He stops Will every so often too and stops in to the station.

One afternoon in November, the kid comes in to work after school. A car pulls up on the drive and Will can't get to it; he is busy finishing up a car from the Ford dealership. The kid hustles outside and takes care of the customer. The man pays for his gas and leaves. Will walks to the front and notices that the car that the kid has just finished with hasn't left but has pulled off the drive and is parked by the restrooms. The man walks back to the station and informs them that he is the "mystery customer"! He tells Will there will be a write-up in the newspaper about the excellent service he received and how nice and clean the restrooms are. The man leaves, and Will claps the boy on the back. They laugh and smile at their good fortune. Then the boy grins at Will and asks, "Where's my ten spot?"

Will hands the boy the twenty-five dollars. "Here you go, kid, you deserve it." The boy's face lights up, and he grins from ear to ear. Will laughs. "But now don't slack off, okay?" The boy works even harder, and the cash register is never short. Will lets him have a soda and a pack of peanuts on the house every so often. The two make a good team.

Soon, the cold weather arrives, and Will comes up with a few more tricks to drum up business. On his way to the station in the mornings, he drives by two motels. He stops and cleans the ice and snow off the cars windows and leaves one of the stations business cards under the wiper. Winter is in full force, and it is getting closer and closer to Anne's due date. Anne makes Irene very happy when she tells her that she can take care of Donna when the time comes to have the baby. Then it happens; Will gets an early Christmas present. A week before Christmas, he and Anne have another beautiful daughter. She is named after Will's mother; she is named Jonie Irene. Of course, this doesn't sit well with Anne's mother. The birth is fairly easy, and Jonie and Anne are back home in a few days. Anne's parents are practically waiting on the doorstep for Anne and the newborn. After seeing and holding the baby, Anne's mother starts making plans for Christmas. She decides that Will and Anne and the girls can go to Will's parents for Christmas Eve. But they are to be home early enough to give the girls a nap and be ready by eleven that evening for midnight mass. She further decides that they will pick them up then take them all back to the farm after mass for Christmas Day on the farm. Will listens for a few minutes then puts his hand up. "Whoa, stop for a damn minute. You don't decide where we will go or for how long." He continues irately, "Now, we will go to my mother's on Christmas Eve, and *if* we go to mass, we will do it on our own. And *if* we come to the farm on Christmas day, we will be there when we get there!" Exasperated, he asks, "Did you forget about that talk we had?" He continues angrily, "I got a damn good mind to just stay home on Christmas day. Now how would you like that?"

Anne's dad, a man who never says much, calmly points out, "Anne should have a say so in this."

Will agrees but shakes his head. "Well, not according to her mother, she doesn't seem to!" The in-laws get their coats and hats to leave. Will tells them he and Anne will talk it over and get back to them later on what they decide. The next day Anne's father stops by without Anne's mother. He tells Will that his wife is pretty shook up over the thought of not being with her daughter and grandchildren on Christmas. Will pats him on the back and tells him he could never be that mean. He says with a soft smile, "I promise you, we will be there on Christmas day. But it won't be early, and I can't promise you how long we will stay." His father-in-law nods and turns to leave; he thanks Will and the two shake hands.

CHAPTER 38

Gas War

Time flies by for Will. He is busy with his family and running his gas station. By mid July, Anne tells him their family will increase; she is pregnant again. Will's mother-in-law continues to be a thorn in his side. If he gives in an inch, she takes a mile. One thing does make her happy though; in July, right after Anne finds out she is pregnant, Will's family moves. Jake and Irene and Will's siblings move about forty miles to the east.

Business is good this summer, and his station sells a lot of gas. Then fall arrives, and soon the snow and cold. One particularly cold and snowy evening, Will locks up the station for the night. Before he goes home, he stops in to the little café next door to his business. He orders a cup of coffee and a hot ham and cheese sandwich as he has done many times before. He finishes his meal and steps out into the cold night air. On the way back to his car, he hears noises between his office and the workshop. He pulls his hat down to shield himself from the cold and ducks back around the building to investigate. There, in a pile of snow, he spots a young boy, facedown and thrashing around. Will notices he looks nearly frozen. He grabs the boy, puts him in his car, and turns the heater on high. Will can see he is only about twelve to fourteen years old. He reeks of a bad combination of vomit and beer. When he warms up a little, enough so he can talk, Will asks him where he lives. The boy looks at Will, his eyes wild. "Please no, mister, I can't go home! My mom will kill me!" Will scratches his head and thinks, what the hell am I going to do with him? The boy begs him, "Please, please, mister, can you just drive around a little till I feel better, maybe get some sleep?"

Will shakes his head. "No, it's well after midnight. I have to get home and get some sleep myself. I have to open my station in a few hours."

The shivering boy pleads, "Take me home with you where I can clean up, maybe sleep on your couch a few hours? I promise I'll leave early and walk home." Will sighs and agrees; he puts the car in gear and drives the boy to his house. Anne meets Will at the door. She tells him she knows the boy because his family goes to her church. His father works at the lumberyard. His mother does a lot of charity work and is known to be very, very strict. Anne gets the boy some blankets and a pillow and shows him to the couch. When Will gets up in the morning, the kid is gone.

A few days later, Will is busy at the gas station. He looks up to see the police officer who doesn't like him standing at the counter. The officer has a smug look on his face and tells Will that he is there to arrest him for contributing to the delinquency of a minor! Will is dumbfounded. At the police station, the police chief looks over at Will. He knows Will pretty well because Will services his car for him. He asks Will what happened. Will tells him the whole story, how he found the frozen boy in the snow, warmed him up, and took him home. The chief listens then says, "Well, his mother says that you bought the beer for him."

Will's mouth gapes open. "Hell no, I didn't! Is that what the kid says?"

The chief shakes his head. "The kid won't say where he got the beer. He did say you didn't get him anything. His story is the same as yours. But his mother wants to press charges, so there will be a hearing to see if there is a case or not. You will make yourself available, won't you, Will?" Will nods yes. The chief tells Will that he can go. The police officer stands and asks the chief angrily, "What? You're going to let him go?" The police chief just smiles.

The next day, Will contacts a lawyer he knows. The man assures him it will be fine and tells him not to lose any sleep over it. The date of the hearing arrives. There is no investigative committee, just a judge. The judge hears the boy's mother's charges first. Then he asks her if she saw Will buy beer for her son or if she knew of someone else who saw Will buy the beer. She says no. The judge looks at her sternly. "Then what makes you so sure that Will had anything to do with this?"

She speaks up. "Because the officer who brought my boy home picked him up coming from Will's house. And the officer told me that Will helps them boys put illegal mufflers on their cars, so I wouldn't doubt that he buys them beer too." The judge peers at her over his glasses at her.

He turns in his chair and looks at the boy. "Now, what do you have to say for yourself, young man? Did this man buy you any beer or liquor or alcohol of any kind?"

The boy hangs his head. "No, sir, he did not."

The judge continues. "Then what is his involvement in this?"

The boy answers softly, "Well, sir, he picked me up out of the snow. He got me into his warm car then wanted to take me home. But I begged him not to. I told him my mother would kill me if she saw me like that." The judge looks at him intently and asks him where he got the beer. Again, the boy looks down and doesn't answer.

The judge eyes the boy. "Is it because there are other young people like you, maybe friends of yours, that you don't want to squeal on?" The boy nods yes. The judge turns toward Will; now it's his turn. He tells the judge his side of the story. The judge nods, and everyone sits in silence for a few minutes. Finally, the judge speaks. "We have the mother, who wants to press charges, but she knows absolutely nothing about how her son got the beer. We have the boy, who doesn't want to tell on his friends and says no, the man his mother wants to press charges against did not get him the beer. Then we have Will, who says he did not buy the boy beer, and furthermore, the boy's story and Will's are just the same." There is a pause, then he slams his gavel down. "There is no misconduct here. There will be no charges filed. This meeting is concluded." Will is glad it's over. He stands from his chair and turns to leave the courtroom. He notices the mother and father have brought their younger son with them to the hearing. He walks past them then stops short.

He looks indignantly at the mother and says, "I hope that the day your younger son here tries what his older brother did, that it's a really nice warm day. If it's not, you better hope and pray that somebody other than me finds him, because I'll walk right on by and let him lie there and freeze!" With that, he shoves the door open and walks out. He knows he would never really do that. He would help someone again; he just doesn't want her to know that.

Spring rolls around, and in March, Anne goes into labor. Will is blessed with yet another very pretty, tiny daughter. Anne says that her name will be Michelle. About a month after her birth, there is trouble at the gas station. A gas war starts! There are five gas stations in town, and one of the station owners lowers his gas price by two or three cents. Then another owner drops his price two or three cents below that. Will and the other owners just try to stay the same as the lowest price and not go any lower. But prices continually drop. By the first of May, the price of regular gas is down to nineteen cents a gallon. No one is making any money at that price. Will knows if this lasts very long, he will soon be out of business. The only stations that can make it are the ones with plenty of money to back them up. Will hangs on as long as he can. He prays the gas war will end, but it doesn't. Will lets his inventory go way down, and it isn't long before the place is up for sale. Will starts to look around for a new job. The next weekend while visiting his mother, he finds out about a new co-op coming to the town she lives in. A quality egg program is in the process of starting, and they are looking for help. They need people in the field to sign up egg producers, truck drivers to haul the eggs, workers in the plant to run the machines, bookkeepers, cleanup people, and many others. Will talks with the hiring department. They like the fact that he is mechanically inclined. He is hopeful they will hire him.

On the first of June, the gas station sells. There isn't much money in it for Will because there isn't much left to sell. Will's father-in-law wants him to claim bankruptcy. Will tells him no; he doesn't feel right doing that. He owes people money, besides his father-in-law. He owes the jobber for some fuel and cases of oil, and the tanker man, they both put their trust in him. Will promises them that if they will give him some time, he will pay them back.

Luckily for Will, a few days later, he gets a call from the new egg plant. As it turns out, when an egg producer is signed up, he has to house his chickens, no free range, and they are to be fed co-op feed. This way, all the eggs coming into the plant from all the various producers will have a uniform yolk color. The eggs are to be kept in a cooler with a controlled humidity level. This also insures uniform color. There will be an egg-cleaning machine available, if producers care to buy it, or they can clean the eggs by hand. This means no washing, a dry cleaning only. This is where Will comes in. He will be given a service truck, and after a producer comes into the program, he will set them up with the proper-sized cooler and egg-cleaning machine. Will is also the service man if they run into any trouble with any of their machines. The plant is to open on the fourteenth of July. Will is sent to Minnesota, to the factory where the coolers and egg-cleaning machines are made. He learns all he can about them. Then he is back in the egg plant when it opens. He sets up his shop inside the plant to hold the first shipment of coolers, cleaners, and parts, and he is ready to start delivery of them. The coolers arrive in four pieces, a back, a front with a door, a plain centerpiece, different sizes for different units, and a drop-in compressor. Will learns quickly how to take the machines apart and put them back together and also make all the necessary adjustments. He is ready to begin his new career at the egg plant.

CHAPTER 39

A Big Boy

Will returns from Minnesota and starts his new job. He learns that his brother Kenny will also be working at the plant. Kenny's job, after the eggs have been candled and graded, is to box them, fill the cases, seal them, and wheel them into the cooler. Early one morning, Will is working in the shop area. Harold, the man who hired him, calls him into the office. Will raps on the door, and Harold motions for him to take a seat. He begins by telling Will that he will be considered a "field man." He explains that there will be himself and two others, and they will sell the program and set up the equipment. He tells Will that he will not be paid hourly but will get a monthly salary, with an expense account. He adds, "So if you are out on a job and it's going to get a little late, you can finish it. You won't have to go back to the same place in the morning. Everything is new to everybody here, and one of my guys might try to tell you something different. Well, don't pay any attention to them." He opens a file drawer and pulls out a paper. "I will assign your installation schedules." He slams the drawer shut and adds, "Oh, and if you see anything or get any ideas of how to make things run a little better, don't hesitate, let me know right away."

Will stands there a moment then says, "Well, now that you mention it, I do have an idea." Harold looks up and motions for him to continue. Will pitches his idea. "I know that the first shipment of coolers comes Monday and they are all sold and ready to be installed. The delivery truck will have two, with six more on a trailer behind it, for a total of eight. Now then, I can only take two at a time on our service truck." Harold nods and Will continues. "This is all new business for the people we are buying the coolers from. They know they will be getting a lot more business. They are willing to bend over backwards for us. So if the driver with the coolers will get here early, I will meet him here. I will have the two cleaning machines loaded on my truck, and he can follow me. Together we can deliver each cooler where it is supposed to go, and he can still be on his way back home by early afternoon." Harold leans back in his chair and begins to smile. Will adds, "The last place gets a cooler and a cleaning machine. I can install them then go back and install the other cleaning machine before I come back in."

Harold stands and shakes Will's hand. "That's good, Will, really good, you can have eight out on the very first day! I will make all the arrangements." Will steps out of the office with a smile on his face. Right off the bat, he is in good with the main man.

Will talks with Anne about looking for a new place and moving to where his new job is, but she isn't sold on the idea. He tells her that he might only be home one night a week during the week and then on weekends. She says she wants to wait and see how things go. The next few months, Will is busy setting up new customers. He likes his job. He likes being out by himself, and he does good work. Jake is on the road truck driving a lot. When he is gone, Will stays at his mom's house. On weekends he is home with Anne and the kids. He still tries to talk Anne into moving. Her mother is really getting her foot in the door with Will gone so much.

The plant is in operation about four months when one morning, Harold calls Will back into the office. He tells Will that the board of directors wants him to punch a time clock and get an hourly wage. Harold frowns and shakes his head and says he is dead set against it. He explains that the plant isn't making any money yet, but the way it was set up, it wouldn't turn a profit for at least eighteen months, but the board members are nervous.

Will looks down at his hands. "Well, I can punch in in the mornings, but what do you want me to do? Make sure that I am back by five to punch out, no matter what? You know we will have some pretty mad customers if I leave and don't finish then have to come back in the morning." Harold sighs and nods. He stands up and looks out the window.

He comments, "I see sometimes in the morning when I get here that you've already left and that sometimes you aren't back until after seven." He thinks for a moment then brightens. "I'll tell you what. Let's give them a taste of their own medicine! Don't do it on purpose, but when you have to, you finish the job. Then come in and punch out, and everything after five o'clock, we'll show it as overtime! Let's see how they like that!"

For the next month or so, that's exactly what Will does. And when he goes home on the weekends, he still tries to convince Anne to move. He is making good money. With all the overtime, he pays off all his gas station debt except for what he owes his father-in-law, and that will be next. A few weeks later, Harold again calls Will into his office. This time, he has a big smile on his face. He pats Will on the back and tells him he is back on a monthly salary. Will laughs. "I guess that means I will have to take a cut in pay then." Will thanks him and turns to leave then says, "Harold, I have another idea. You know how big our territory is getting. It's from the Minnesota border to the north and south about twenty miles past Des Moines. And east and west between this side of Sioux City and Waterloo. It's a big area. The girls in the office take the calls from customers who need service. They tell one customer I will be there in the morning then another at the other end of the territory in the afternoon. That's a lot of driving and a waste of time and money, and I can take care of maybe only two customers in a day." Harold nods and Will continues. "So instruct the girls to tell the customers that I will get to them as soon as I can. When I finish a job, I will call in and see if anyone needs me in that area. The next day, I can go the other direction and do the same. We won't let anyone wait over a day, and we'll keep everything caught up." Harold nods approvingly and says it sounds good to him. "And another thing, Harold," Will continues, "I think you should send out a letter. Tell the customers if they have a problem to first look themselves. Hell, a couple of times, I drove all the way out and the cooler wasn't working because the electric cord was unplugged! I drove all the way out there just for that. Also, customers are letting their kids run the egg-cleaning machines, and they aren't paying attention. When a cracked egg gets by them, it breaks on the soft rubber belt. When it dries, the rubber gets stiff, and it tosses the eggs out one right after another. Maybe you can say that if this doesn't stop, we will have to charge them for a service call and deduct the money from their egg checks. But I'll still go around and periodically check and replace the sanding belts and reset the tension." Harold agrees and tells Will he will have the office girls draft a letter right away. He thanks Will for all his hard work and chuckles, saying that he is still sorry about his pay cut.

The next five months go by fast. Anne is pregnant again, and she lets on to Will that she is pretty irritated at her mother. Will decides to add fuel to the fire. He tells Anne that he is damn tired of their living arrangement, that he married her and not her family. He says he is going to move there, with or without her. Now what is she going to do about it? Anne relents and agrees that it is time to move. She says that she would rather not live in the same town Will's family lives in, where the plant is. She would rather live in the next town over. It's about the same size and only nine miles from his job. Will says this is fine with him. On the first of May they decide to take a weekend and look for a place to live. Summer arrives, and Will and Anne and the family move to this nice little town. It has several churches, three big grocery stores, a movie theater, a courthouse, and even a hospital. Will is home with his family every night, and things are good.

Soon, winter arrives. Will and Anne take the girls and spend Christmas day on the farm with Anne's parents. Things are better now between Will and his mother-in-law. Anne is very big with this pregnancy and is having a lot of pain. This pregnancy is very different from the others. Early in January, 1960, Anne goes into labor. She is in labor for about forty-eight hours. The doctor talks to Will. He says, "This baby just does not want to come out, must be comfortable in there. We are going to try something to induce her, something to make the little rascal want to come out and join us." It's still another three hours, but finally Will hears the doctor say, "Wow, that's a big one!" And a big one he is, all ten pounds and eight and a half ounces of him. Will is the father of a big boy! Will calls his mom and tells her the good news. Later that evening she walks in, and to Will's surprise, Jake is with her. He is half-drunk already. He has a pair of little cowboy boots in one hand and a pint of whisky in the other. The first thing he does is congratulate Will, and then he offers him a drink from his bottle. This surprises Will. Will doesn't say anything about Jake being a grandpa, although he does call Irene "Grandma." Then Jake embarrasses everyone; he loudly tells the nurse, "Take off his diaper. I want to see his balls to make sure Will's got a boy." Irene turns bright red. She tells Will she will take Jake out of there, but first she wants to know the newborn's name. Will says proudly, "His name is Johnny Michael. Of course, the Michael is after me." He grins and chuckles. "By the size of him, I think we will call him Big John." He gives his mother a kiss and tells her good night and thanks her for coming. By this time, Anne is exhausted and sound asleep. It's still visiting hours, so Will walks down the hall. He stands at the glass window of the nursery, looking down on Big John. Two elderly ladies come to the window; they gaze in on the babies.

One lady remarks to the other, "Oh dear, I wonder what is wrong with that little tyke? That baby must be about six months old." Will looks over and sees that she is pointing to his newborn son. His baby is twice the size of all the other babies! His head is at one end of the bassinet, and his feet touch at the other end. He smiles to himself, and just then a nurse walks out. She says, "Guess what? Your baby boy there just set a record! He is the biggest baby ever to be born at this hospital!"

Will grins at the nurse. He says, "Wow, do I get a prize?"

She grins back. "Yeah, you do. You get him!"

CHAPTER 40

The Head Brakeman

The "big boy" is a big hit and the talk of the town for quite a while. Will and Anne are very proud. Anne makes friends with a couple of really nice women. One woman's husband is the chief lineman for the telephone company, and they have a houseboat. The other woman's husband is the head man for a gang of men on the railroad. They fix railroad cars and take big wreckers out and do all the cleanup work when there is a train wreck or cars are derailed. This guy, like Jake, likes his beer. He claims that's what weekends are for, drinking beer. But unlike Jake, he is very happy when he drinks and makes everyone laugh. In the summertime, every Sunday there is a party in his backyard, and he is quite a clown for the kids. Anne and Will get to know both couples very well. Both couples have young girls; they fit right in with Anne and Will's girls.

At the first of the year, there are rumors about the new egg plant being in financial trouble. Will is concerned about this and asks Harold. Harold tells him that yes, they showed a big loss when they started to export eggs, but that was expected, and of course, it will take awhile for the money to come back. He shakes his head and says, "I don't know what's the matter with those board members." Around the first of May, the board wants Will to go back to punching the time clock, but this time, they want him to arrange his work so there will be no overtime. Will can see the handwriting on the wall; he decides he better keep his eyes open for another job. As luck will have it, he finds out from his new beer-drinking friend that the railroad will be hiring men to be firemen and brakemen, and he sends Will to see the trainmaster. These jobs are really good-paying jobs, and as a rule, they only hire men from their own families. But Will's friend is also a friend of the trainmaster, so Will has his foot in the door. Will meets with the trainmaster, and the man asks Will when he can start his student trips. The man explains to him that he is required to take two weeks of student trips with various conductors, without pay, and these conductors will fill out forms about his performance. These forms will be given to the trainmaster, and he will determine whether or not Will is to be hired. Will tells him that he can start the first week of June; he will have two weeks of vacation then. The trainmaster shows Will the train yard. There are about fifteen sets of tracks, each a half to three-fourths of a mile long, all with railroad cars on them. He also shows him the roundhouse where the engines are kept and the yard office where the crew callers work from. One of the men on duty at the yard office asks Will for his phone number so he can call him for his first trip.

The first trip comes soon, and that first student trip is not a good one for Will. He meets the crew, the engineer, the fireman, the rear brakeman, and the conductor, who is the boss. The conductor points to a fellow and says, "This is my head brakeman. You stick to him like glue. I don't want you more than ten feet from him at any time. You keep your eyes wide open, your ears hearing, and stay out from the middle of the track. I don't want to be filling out any paperwork on account of you getting hurt, you got that?" Will nods yes. Their job is to take the engine to different tracks that are numbered. They will pull the cars on that track out to the switching lead, where they can switch the cars out that are to be put in a train that is making its way up north, to a little town in Minnesota. They will spend the night there then the next day bring another train back to their home terminal. Some of the cars will go with them all the way. Others will be set out in different towns they go through, and sometimes cars will be picked up in these other towns. The head brakeman's job is to stay in sight of the engineer at all times. He also must be where he can see the brakeman and conductor. Most of the time they will be back along the railroad cars, making the cut on cars.

When they give a hand signal, the head brakeman relays that same hand signal to the engineer. This is how the engineer knows whether to go, stop, or back up. At night, they use lanterns for the signals.

Early afternoon goes well for Will; he only gets hollered at six or seven times. The train is made up of about fifty cars, with the caboose on the end. This is where the conductor and rear brakeman ride. The head brakeman rides up in the engine with the fireman and engineer. At the very first town, they have cars to set out and also cars to pick up. It is raining cats and dogs. Everyone has on a rain suit, everyone except Will. He knows this doesn't excuse him one damn bit. He still works hard, but it is miserable out, and he is soaked to the skin. It's a good thing they are a pretty good distance from home, or Will's railroading career may have ended right then and there. He makes it through the day and is one happy guy when he gets to his hotel room. He doesn't eat at the café with the rest of the crew. Instead, he takes a couple hamburgers back to his room and gets out of his wet clothes.

The next morning, the sun is out and it is a whole new day. Will's clothes are dry, the sun is shining, and he heads to the café for breakfast and a cup of coffee. The rest of the student trips go much better than that first one. Will meets a lot of guys. Most are very nice; there are only a couple who aren't. The guys tell him a lot about railroading. Will listens and learns quite a bit from them. He learns so well that at the end of the two weeks, the trainmaster tells him that he has received very good reports on him. He tells Will that he is hired and that he will be put on the extra board. Will tells him that is great and that he can start the first of July. He wants to give the egg plant a two-week notice. Harold tells Will he doesn't blame him for leaving, but he sure hates to see him go. Will finishes his last two weeks at the egg plant. His replacement goes with him on the route, and he teaches him about the coolers and egg cleaners.

On Will's very first pay trip with the railroad, he brings along extra clothes, a big lunch, and yes, a rain suit. He also has all the rule books and timetables of the trains with him. He is well equipped and ready for anything. The only thing he doesn't have is a railroad pocket watch, which is required for everyone. The trainmaster says that he can wait until his first paycheck to purchase the watch. When Will shows up for his third pay trip, he is met by an old conductor who is very hard to get along with and not well liked by the other brakemen. The old man says gruffly to Will, "Show me your watch."

Will looks down and hesitates. "I don't have one yet. The train-master said I can get one after my first paycheck."

The old man snaps, "No watch? You're not going out with me." He turns to the crew caller and yells, "Get me another brakeman!" He turns back to Will. "You can go home. I'll put you back on the bottom of the extra board." Will walks out to his car; he throws his grip in the backseat and drives directly to the jewelry store that sells the railroad watches. All railroad men, either in passenger service or in freight service, all must have a particular watch that is approved by all working railroads. Will finds out he must carry a card with him that proves that the watch is inspected once every thirty days. If he doesn't have his card on him or it isn't up-to-date when an official asks to see it, he will be automatically considered out of service until the matter is taken care of. The jeweler makes a deal with Will on a good used watch. The card is signed and updated, and Will is set to make monthly payments. Will walks out of the store with a smile on his face. He fingers the watch in his pocket and feels very proud. He is now, officially, a qualified brakeman for the Chicago Greatwestern Railway. Irene is also very proud of her son. She enjoys telling people that her son, after being with the railroad for less than a month, is now the head brakeman. Will doesn't have the heart to tell her that actually, he is the low man on the totem pole. He is called the head brakeman only because he works at the front end of the train.

Some of the guys who work for the railroad are called "sharp-shooters." They hang out at the yard office all day, and they watch and see how the extra board is moving. If they get first out and if the next call is going to be for a local or work train, then they lay off. They wait, hoping to catch a through train, one that doesn't have to stop and set out or pick up along the way. But Will doesn't do this; he works each and every train that comes his way. It is a very good summer for Will. He is proud to do his job right. He learns all the hand signals and studies the rule books and timetables every chance he gets. He gets along with everyone. The engineers like him; they work with him and quiz him on the rules to help him remember them. Soon, it's late fall, and all the summer trains are gone. The work slows down when the cold weather comes in. In order for the older brakemen on the extra board to make a living, the board has to be cut. Will and some of the other younger men are cut off until further notice. They are told that they can sign up for unemployment benefits.

CHAPTER 41

A Humbling Experience

Will likes railroading. He likes to travel and see what is over the next hill or around the next curve. He knows that someday he is going to be a traveling man. *Yes, sir, someday*, he thinks to himself, *someday*. But now, since the colder weather has arrived, he is temporarily out of work. He goes to the courthouse to sign up for his unemployment benefits. While there, he runs into the city manager. He is a nice fellow that Will met through a mutual friend, the telephone repairman. He shakes Will's hand and comments, "Well, since I see you here, I'll bet it's that time of year when the railroad cuts the extra board, right?" He tells him yes, that is indeed the case. The kindly man smiles and says, "This time of year and through the snow season, I can always use one extra man. What did you do before working for the railroad?"

Will clears his throat. "Well, my last job, I had a service truck and did repairs on machinery. Before that I ran a gas station, and before that, I worked as the grease monkey for the Ford garage." The city manager smiles and tells him to come in and see him Monday morning. Will thanks the man, and walks out of the courthouse with a new job. He now works for the city. He starts working at the city shops, servicing the trucks, putting on the snow tires and the plows. He learns how to flush out the fire hydrants. He learns the route to change out water softeners for the regular man when he is out of town. Then the snow arrives, and Will likes this job the best of all, driving the snowplow. He discovers he really likes plowing snow.

Some mornings, after the early risers have already been out and are shoveling their driveways, Will drives by in his snowplow. The giant blade throws the snow right back where they just shoveled. They get mad and shake their fists. Will just smiles and waves as he plows by. Anne rides with him some evenings when he plows late, and she gets a big kick out of it.

One day, the boss calls Will and tells him to stay home and rest up because there is a very big snowstorm coming late that afternoon. He wants Will to be out plowing all night. He tells him that he must keep a lane open between the main road, the police station, and the hospital. He works all through the night and into the next morning. Finally, the storm eases up some. He sees that his favorite little café is open, and he decides to stop in for a cup of coffee and a doughnut. The bell clangs as he pushes the door open. The little café is crowded. He stomps the snow off his boots and finds an empty stool. The waitress has a great sense of humor, and everyone just loves her. She can brighten anyone's day. Will sits on the stool and sips his coffee. He asks her if she has heard any news about the storm. She looks at him with a deadpan expression and says, "It's still and clear." Will looks over his cup at her, puzzled. He asks her what the hell she is talking about. She points, "Look out the window. It's still blowing, and it's clear up to my ass." Everyone in the café howls with laughter. Will grins and shakes his head as he bites into his doughnut.

The snowstorm finally passes. The city streets are all cleared. The snow from Main Street is plowed and hauled to a field by the city dump. An older fellow, who also works for the city, works at the cemetery. He keeps the grass cut in the summer and keeps the cemetery weeded and looking nice. When there is a funeral, he is the one to open the grave site. But now, in the wintertime, when the ground is hard and frozen, opening a grave is a very difficult job. The city manager tells Will that a local man has just died and the grave needs to be opened. He asks Will if he will help the older man out. Will arrives at the cemetery and sees that the old groundskeeper has the plot all marked out. He has the LP gas flamer lit and shovels and pickaxes nearby. Will runs the flamer over the frozen ground, trying to soften the earth so they can start digging. He glances over at the old man and notices that his face is a very bright white. Will knows right away this means that parts of his face are getting frostbitten. He directs the man into the truck and turns the heater on full blast. Will stays with him a while and decides that he doesn't look very good. He tells the older man that he should probably go home. The man agrees. Will hops out of the truck and the man drives off. Will gets back to work. He digs for a while and then starts to warm up. He stops for a moment to take his outside jacket off. He looks around and feels a shiver go down his spine. For some reason he feels very uneasy. He notices the sky is gray and turning dark, and a little snow is starting to fall. He leans on the shovel and listens. The wind whistles around the tombstones and through the evergreen trees, making an eerie sound. He looks around the deserted cemetery and down at the grave plot. There is not another living soul in sight. He can't explain the feeling that comes over him. He wonders if this feeling isn't something that everyone should experience in their lifetime. He starts to shovel again. He sighs as he pushes the shovel hard with his foot. *What a humbling experience this is*, he thinks, *a truly humbling experience.*

CHAPTER 42

The Broken Promise

The winter passes quickly for Will. Before he knows it, it is spring and the flowers are beginning to bloom. He receives a notice in the mail from the railroad that he can mark up for the extra board at any time. But he is in no hurry, it is still cool and rainy, and he likes what he is doing. He really enjoys working for the city, but he knows it will come to an end soon. Then a second notice arrives in the mail; this one says that if he doesn't mark up in two weeks, he will lose his seniority. So Will tells the city boys that while he really enjoys working with them, he has to move on. It doesn't take long and Will is back into the swing of things working for the railroad. There is a lot of work, with plenty of extra trains this summer. Will still reads up on the rules and regulations whenever he can. He gets along really well with most of the conductors. In fact, some conductors, when he catches their run, will make the older brakeman ride ahead and then let Will be the rear brakeman. He watches them very closely because he knows he will be a conductor someday. The extra-board men don't get much rest. They are on call all the time, and most of the time they are only home eight to ten hours. The summer is a busy one for him.

Late one night in the fall of 1961, Will gets a call at two in the morning. He is told to report for work as the brakeman on passenger train number 13.

Will tells the man on the other end, "I think you have made a mistake. Not only do I not have a passenger uniform, but I have not been qualified for passenger service yet." The caller responds that it is an emergency, and there is no one in town who is qualified. The trainmaster has gone over the list of men who are rested, and even though he is not first out, he wants to use Will.

The man on the phone continues. "As for a uniform, wear a pair of dark pants, a white shirt, and a dark sport coat. Report at the depot, not at the yard office." Will hangs up the phone and rubs his forehead. He is nervous; he does not know anything about this job he has just caught. To make matters worse, when he gets to the depot, he finds out that the conductor he will be working with is none other than the one who wouldn't take Will out when he didn't have his watch yet. The conductor, Tom, is already in the depot. He sees Will walk in and strides over to him.

He says with a smile, "Hey, young fella, do you have a watch and card up-to-date?" Will shakes his hand and says nervously that he does, but he shouldn't be there. He is only there because it is an emergency. The old conductor nods. "I know all about it. You're scared as hell, right? I know I was when I caught my first passenger trip, and I was already qualified. But don't worry, kid, I'll get you through it, one way or another." Will smiles nervously. He glances up at Tom and notices what a big man he is. His big frame reminds Will of his Uncle Butch. The two stand and watch. There is a main line change out of crews right there in front of the depot. While they wait for old number 13 to pull into the station, Tom begins to tell him what his job will be. He explains, "Starting with the stepstool that the incoming brakeman will put down for people getting off to use, leave it there for anybody getting on. I will board first, see that everything in the coach is all right. You watch outside and see that the mailmen are all inside the mail car. I'll look at my timepiece. If I think it's time to leave, I will say to you, 'If you are ready, brakeman, let's depart.'" Will nods and listens intently. The man continues, "Then you look at your watch. If you agree that it's time to leave—by the way, what time are we due to leave?"

Will quickly responds, "Two a.m., unless we have an order from the dispatch to leave at a different time, which we do not have. I have the schedule and timetable in my pocket."

The conductor smiles and continues with his instructions. "At that leaving time, you will pick up the step, place it inside, give the engineer a highball signal, and we will head for Omaha. Next, you will walk through coach, look at the hat checks above the passenger seats. After the conductor has checked the tickets, this is where he puts the number, on the hat check, to correspond with the town the passenger is to get off at. Ten minutes before the stop, let the passenger know that their stop is next. Make sure they get off. I am only going to tell you this once, and it's hell to pay if we carry a passenger beyond his destination." Will makes mental notes of all the big man is telling him. The conductor concludes, "Now, there are only three big stations to stop at between here and Omaha, and they will all have mail to load and unload. So after getting all passengers on and off, and while the mail is being worked, walk around our train, looking for anything that could be wrong. Then see that the mailmen are done, check with me, and we will depart." He slaps him on the back. "So there, piece of cake, right?"

It is quite a trip for Will. He learns a lot from the old grouch, who Will decides is really just a very good railroad man. When they get back and tie up at the home terminal, Tom tells Will he should tell the trainmaster that he wants to qualify for passenger service. He points out, "You have all the information you need, right there in your timetables and rule books. Study up. I will set you up with the rules examiner for the test. Go to the Goodwill Store and get the right-color pants and jacket. I'll give you the shoulder brakeman bars, and you will have a uniform." He leans over and confides to Will, "You know, there are older brakemen here, older than you, but for some reason, they tend to stay away from this. But I'll tell ya, it's a warm job in the winter, and the coaches have air-conditioning in the summer. There may be times when you are six to ten times out, and you will end up going around all those guys and getting a better job than they will get." Will smiles and thanks him for the information. He starts to leave, but Tom calls after him. "And one more thing, Will, you can go out with me anytime." Will can't help smiling at this; it makes him feel really good. He gives a wave to Tom and heads for his car.

Will does get qualified for passenger service, and he does catch a trip every now and then. He doesn't get cut from the extra board at all this winter. He remembers how much he enjoyed plowing snow for the city. But this winter, he finds out it is quite an experience riding in a railroad snowplow being pushed by a big locomotive. One day after a particularly heavy snowfall, he is riding along in the train, looking out the window. He grins as he looks out at the snow whirling about and thinks, *Now this is a snowplow!*

Early in the new year, Will's second oldest daughter, Jonie, slips on some ice at the top of the stairs. She falls all the way to the bottom and has a nasty lump on her head. The doctor thinks that she will be all right, but a few months later, she begins to have eye problems. Her eyes don't seem to stay straight and sometimes cross, and Will is sure this has something to do with the fall. The doctor in this small town doesn't know what to do. An appointment is made for her in Iowa City, at the big hospital where there are specialists. Two of the specialists are very concerned and interested in Jonie's eyes, and the next few months is filled with trips to Iowa City. There are plenty of x-rays and exams and a whole bunch of different eyeglasses, but nothing seems to be working. Will feels a pain in his heart when he hears schoolkids tease her and call her names. He makes up his mind right then and there, no matter what it takes, he will make sure something is done for her. At the next examination in Iowa City, the two specialists tell Will and Anne that there is no way that eyeglasses are going to work. They cannot make glasses strong enough to correct the eye muscle, to keep it from pulling the eye over, without impairing her vision. They believe the solution, the only way to correct the problem, is surgery. They explain that they will lift the eyeball out of the socket, make a Z cut to the muscle, and the eye will retract to its normal position. They can do this in two operations, one eye at a time, a week or so apart. Will asks them, "So you are actually weakening the muscle on one side so the other muscle can pull it back?" The doctors tell him that yes, that is exactly how it works. They tell the young parents to go home and think it over and if they have any more questions to call them. Before they leave, the two doctors again tell them that they are sure that this is the best solution.

Back at home, Will and Anne go over everything the doctors have said many, many times. Will is convinced that this is the only option left, and the sooner, the better for Jonie. Anne isn't so sure, but she also doesn't know what else can be done. Anne's parents visit, and this only makes matters worse. They are upset and very, very against an operation on the little girl's eyes. They think that Jonie should see their doctor, Dr. Grant. Anne's mother's last words to her when they leave that evening are, "Now don't you let any butcher cut on her eyes!"

A few days go by, and Will says to Anne, "What do you think? What do you want to do?" All Anne can say is that she doesn't know. So finally, in exasperation, he says to her, "Well, let me make it easier for you. First of all, you sure as hell don't think that Dr. Grant is going to help her eyes by rubbing her back, do you?" Will rubs his chin and paces the floor. He has grown into the kind of man who thoroughly believes that the ends justify the means. He stops in front of Anne and raises his voice, "Come hell or high water, whatever happens between you and me or your folks, I am taking Jonie to Iowa City for the eye operation." He calms down a little then continues. "You can think this through a little more, and if you want, we can take her together. Or I can go alone, and you can tell everyone I kidnapped her and ran off with her and you didn't have a say so. Put it all on me. I don't care. You suit yourself." And with that, he storms out.

He makes the appointment for the eye operations, and although reluctant and very apprehensive, Anne is right there with him beside her daughter. In the hospital, before the surgery, the little girl is very scared. Her biggest fear is that, after the operation, she will not be able to see. She has heard the doctors say that the eyes will have to be covered to heal. Anne and Will hold her little hands and reassure her. Will explains to her that the doctors are only going to work on one eye this day and the other eye a different day. "So you see," he tells her, "you will only have a patch over one eye, and you will be able to see with the other. I promise you that." He hugs her and says, "I promise you, you will be able to see today when the doctors are done." And this is a sad and bad promise that Will makes to his already-scared little girl. Because when the surgery is complete on the eye, the surgeon comes out to talk to the parents. He tells Will and Anne that everything has gone very well. In fact, even better than he had thought. It is perfect; the eye is straight. It couldn't have gone any better. They would like permission, since everything is going so well and they are already there, to do the other eye as well. Anne and Will look at each other and smile. They are relieved that the operation has gone so well. But should they consent to the other eye being done now? They talk it over briefly then tell the surgeon yes, and that's when Will's promise is broken. Will's heart sinks. He tells the doctor that when his daughter comes out of the anesthetic, she will be very distraught on account of his promise to her. The doctor nods and tells him that he will make sure the nurse gives her something to keep her calm and to make her sleep through the night. He adds that he thinks the patches will come off the next day, after breakfast. Will and Anne are right there when she comes out of surgery, and she is indeed very upset and scared. She cries when she realizes she can't see. "But, Daddy," she wails, "you promised. You promised I would be able to see!" And this breaks his heart. Will and Anne spend the rest of the day keeping her hands off her eyes and the patches. The next day is a wonderful day. The patches are removed, and although the eyes are sore and red and swollen, they are perfect, and the little girl can see again.

CHAPTER 43

The Big Test

In the spring of 1963, Johnny comes for what he claims is a visit. But Will finds out from Doug, his brother, that Johnny is in a little trouble in the big city and has to get away for a while. Now Johnny is big, like his dad, and he likes the fine threads and the big fancy cars. He likes the fine-looking young ladies too. But where he is different from his father is that he has a con man, or "wiseguy" style. This shows up now and then, and this is what gets him in trouble. But Will loves him and never asks any questions. Johnny only stays with Will and Anne a night or two because Jake finds out he is in town. There is no way around it; Jake insists Johnny stay with his uncle. After all, it's his duty to look after his nephew. Jake gets Johnny a job driving truck where he works, but it doesn't last long. Johnny misses the big city too much and is bored to death with small-town life. He is back home in three weeks.

Late in the fall, Will gets a call from the crew caller. The man on the phone says, "Well, I don't know how you did it, but you have been assigned as temporary brakeman for two weeks on passenger train 13. There are a few men older than you who want this job." Will doesn't say anything; he doesn't know either. He hadn't even put a bid in for this job. Hell, he didn't even know that it was coming up for a bid! But he thanks the man and hangs up and he is glad he got it. When he reports to work, he finds out that the conductor is Tom, the old grouch. Tom walks over to him and pats him on the back. He says, "I hope you don't mind, but I told the regular man to keep his mouth shut about being off work, and I put in a bid for you."

Will grins at him. "Hell no, I don't mind a bit! It makes me feel good that you want me to work for you, thank you." He knows he has steady work for the next two weeks in a warm coach. He learns that on the nights when there are deadhead crews to Omaha, the guys like to get together in the lounge and play poker. Tom especially loves to play poker.

The next morning, he stands at the station, waiting for number 13 to pull in. A deadhead brakeman, who is older in seniority than Will, walks over to him. He says, "Hey, lucky, how did you get this job?" Will shrugs and says it was just luck. Before they leave the station, Tom asks him if he can handle things while he plays cards between the stations. Will assures him he can. He tells him he knows which stations to watch for, and if anything comes up, he will be sure to get him. Tom likes this arrangement. The two get along just fine, and Tom trusts him completely. It's a nice two weeks, but it flies by too fast for both of them. A few days later, the trainmaster calls Will into his office. He glances up at him as he walks in.

He says, "First, I want to congratulate you. All the old heads around here say that you are going to make a very good railroad man." Will smiles and thanks the man. The trainmaster continues. "I heard that old Tom, whom you worked with a couple weeks ago, spends a lot of time in the lounge car. Is that true?"

"Well, sir, I don't think so," Will answers.

The trainmaster swivels in his chair. "I am talking about the nights there are three or four deadhead crews on the train, how about those nights?"

Will looks at him squarely. "Well, as you know, they play cards, and every so often they get a little loud. He has to go back and tell them to keep it down, and that can turn into quite a few times. But I understand that's part of our job, to keep it quiet so the passengers can sleep." The trainmaster thinks for a moment. "Yes, you are right. I suppose some of the men who lose too much can get pretty loud and get mad and talk too much and say things they shouldn't, right?" Will nods in agreement. Moments tick by, then the trainmaster stands. "All right, Will, keep up the good work." Will breathes a sigh of relief as he leaves the office and the door closes behind him.

About a week later, Tom spots Will at the yard office. He comes over to him and says, "I heard you got called into the office the other day." Will tells him he did. Tom eyes him. "What the hell was it all about?"

Will laughs and tells him he is sure he already knows. Tom grins. "Yep, I heard that some people get loud and talk too much and someone else has to go and tell them to be quiet and keep the noise down." Will grins and nods. Tom pats him on the back. "Thanks, I owe you one."

He shakes his head. "No, Tom, I think you are all paid up, and thank you!"

Early in the spring of 1964, Will walks into work one morning. He sees a sign on the bulletin board that reads, "Firemen who want to be engineers and brakemen who want to be conductors sign up before June 1. Tests to be June 15." He is one of the first to sign up. There are two firemen who want to get promoted to engineer and five other brakemen besides Will who want to be promoted to conductor if they pass the test. Will finds out some information about the test. The test takes five days, and is held in the conference room of the hotel. The test is over all 1,200 rules in the rule book and the current timetable. The test starts at 8:00 a. m, with a fifteen-minute break midmorning, a lunch break, a fifteen-minute afternoon break, then ends at 5:00 p. m. The men are allowed to refer to their books on break or at lunch. The rules examiner is the person in charge. There are no true-or-false questions and no yes-or-no questions. Each question must have a minimum of one sentence in the answer. An example question: What is a train? Answer: A train is one engine or more coupled together with or without cars displaying markers. Will knows it will be grueling, and he studies every chance he gets.

The test date arrives, and Will and the others assemble at the hotel. They test each day. At the completion of the testing, on the fifth day, the rules examiner congratulates the group. He tells them they have the next two days, Saturday and Sunday, off. On Monday, there will be a bulletin posted with the promotions. Each man will receive a letter in the mail with his own score. He walks over to Will and asks, "How long have you been a brakeman?"

"A little over four years now," Will responds.

The man nods. "I was thinking you hadn't been here very long." He continues. "I don't know what's going on, if the company has changed its policy on promotions, but you are going to set a precedence here. You are the first brakeman with less than ten years of service to even be allowed to try for a promotion. Good luck to you." Will thanks him and leaves the hotel, relieved the testing is over. And now all he can do is wait. Ten long days go by. No bulletin, no letter, nothing. Then Will gets a phone call from the president of the O. R. C. & B. (Order of Railroad Conductors and Brakemen Union). He would like Will to come into his office, immediately.

Will meets with the man a few days later. He tells Will that the superintendent of the railroad has informed him that his secretary made a mistake on the bulletin. It should have noted a cutoff date for brakemen hired before January of 1960, and therefore, Will should not have been allowed to take the exam. But they add that they will pay him for the five days of his time. The union man tells Will that he asked when they found out about the mistake and was told they knew three days into the testing. He said he further asked them why Will wasn't taken out of the class at that time. He was told that they thought that since Will was such a young brakeman, that he wouldn't pass anyway, and the experience would be good for him. The union man chuckles and says, "So I say to the superintendent, well, he must have passed, or we wouldn't be having a problem. So before we agree on anything, I want to see all the test results for the firemen and brakemen." He shuffles some papers on his desk and looks up. "I must say, Will, you did damn good. No wonder the superintendent wants to buy you off! You got the second highest score! The only one to beat you was one of the fireman, and that was only by three points. You scored way ahead of the other brakemen, although everyone passed." Will can't believe what he is hearing. The man continues. "I have already been in touch with the B. of R. T. [Brotherhood of Railroad Trainmen], and together, we are not going to let them get away with not promoting you to conductor." Will is relieved to hear this. The president adds, "I agree that four years of service doesn't sound like enough time, but on the other hand, you outscored the men who did have the service time in." He stands and extends a hand to Will. "I will keep you posted, but rest assured, you will be a conductor on the CGW Railroad!"

The man is true to his word. A few weeks later, he gets a signed document stating that to this date, he is the only man with only four years' service to be promoted from brakeman to conductor. He is so excited; he can't wait to tell his mother! Irene and Jake are running a little bar and steakhouse a few miles from where they live. It's in a small town, with only a handful of houses. Besides the steakhouse, there's only a hardware store and a post office. The steakhouse has great food. Irene is one of the best cooks around. This town is surrounded by four other towns, all only a few miles away, and it's very popular. All the guys who live around here are either truck drivers or railroaders who are on call a lot. What they like about Jake's Place is that it opens at four in the afternoon, and besides the bar and good food, there is a jukebox and a big dance floor. Best of all, there is no phone service. No one can get a call from work or the wife telling them to come home. The young guys love this place. On Saturdays, they come in and drink a couple beers then go home and get their wives and return to dance a little and enjoy a really good steak.

It's Saturday afternoon and Will is off work. He and Anne decide to go to Jake's Place. Donna will babysit. If she has any trouble, she can go right next door to the nice lady who lives there. They sit in the café part, not the bar part, where Jake is with Will's brother, Kenny. Kenny is a lot like Jake. He likes his beer and he likes to fight. Anne and Will are seated at a table. A waitress that he has never seen before comes over and hands them their menus. She returns to take their orders. Anne orders first, then Will says, "I will have your fried chicken, but I want it just like my mother used to make it." The girl takes their menus and heads into the kitchen. She tells Irene that some smart aleck out there wants his chicken just like his mother used to make it. Irene smiles and pokes her head around the kitchen door. She turns back to the girl and says, "That's just what we will give him, chicken just like his mother makes it!" Then she laughs and tells the waitress that the customer is her son. The girl is surprised. She thought she knew all Irene's kids. Irene gets caught up on her work in the kitchen and comes out and sits with Anne and Will. She is really proud to hear of Will's promotion. The talk turns to the rumors around town. She tells him she has heard of some arguing between the railroad men and the truck drivers. She is happy they haven't had any trouble; everyone there just seems to have a good time.

Jake is still driving trucks on Monday, Tuesday, and Wednesday. On Thursday, he and Kenny or Mel stock and clean the place. The bar and steakhouse is open on Friday, Saturday, and Sunday. A few weeks later, Will thinks that Jake will be gone, so he stops by to see his mom. He walks into the living room and he sees Irene in the kitchen. Jake is at the table with a bottle of whisky. His truck is broken down, and he isn't in a very good mood. Jake looks up at Will and sneers, "Look, Ma, it's the railroad man." He continues sarcastically. "I hear they call him Mr. Conductor now." Jake takes a big swig from the bottle.

Will looks at his mother. "I'll stop again another time." He turns to head for the door as Irene steps toward him, but Jake reaches out and grabs her roughly by the arm.

He snarls, "Mr. Conductor can come in here if he wants to and talk with us." Irene struggles to pull her arm away from Jake's grasp. Will looks at her arm and sees black and blue marks covering it.

His mouth drops open and he looks at her. "What happened there, Mom?"

Jake hisses, "None of your damn business, Mr. Conductor." Will can't hold back anymore.

He looks Jake directly in the eye and says hotly, "Well, Mr. Truck Driver, that's my mother, and it is my business." And that's just what Jake is waiting for, for Will to mouth off to him. He lunges at him, but Will knows that Jake is already drunk and there won't be much fight in him. Will shoves him back hard, with both hands, in his midsection. This knocks the wind out of Jake. He falls back in his chair, gasping for air. Just then, Kenny comes running in. Will didn't even know he was there. He looks at his dad, struggling to catch his breath. He shoots a look at Will.

He asks angrily, "What the hell happened?" Before Will can answer, Irene tells Kenny that she and Jake had been playing around and she accidentally knocked the wind out of him. She tells him he will be fine in a minute or two. Kenny snaps at Will, "What are you doing here?"

Will's eyes narrow and he says, "No! What's this doing here?" And with that, he picks up his mother's arm and points to the bruises. Kenny shrugs and says he doesn't know. Will glares at him, "Well, I don't want to see it again."

Kenny smirks, "What's that supposed to mean?"

Will glares back. "You figure it out." He storms out of the house and slams the door shut behind him.

CHAPTER 44

The Passing of Jake

The rest of 1964 is a very strange time for Will. His younger brother Kenny is getting to be more and more like Jake. He drinks a lot and gets into a lot of fights. Kenny's best friend is a big tough guy. They spend a good deal of time together, and this guy is, without a doubt, the toughest guy in town. The town has four bars, go-go girls, and a dance hall. There is a small railroad yard there and also two big trucking companies. There are a lot of heavy drinkers in the town. And Kenny is now the tough guy's sidekick. The tough guy, Ron, has an older brother, like Kenny has Will. Ron can and does several times beat up his older brother. And that's what he wants Kenny to do to Will. He says it's something about younger brothers should rule or some theory like that. This attitude shows up in Kenny when he is drinking or with his buddy Ron. Will also has a new friend, Joe, who is an ex-paratrooper. Joe can definitely take care of himself. His uncle gets him a job on the railroad, and he likes working with Will. The two of them get along very well. Joe has a wife and kids too, and Anne and his wife become good friends. Whenever they get a chance, the four of them like to go to Jake's Place for dinner and dancing.

One night, Will and Joe are on their way home from work. Will stops in to his mom's house, but there is no one home. Joe's eyes light up. "Hey, I hear this is a real live town. Let's go have a beer and look at a go-go or two!" Will thinks about it for a moment. He knows that Joe, after a beer or two, won't back down from any trouble, especially when he is in one of those moods. Will knows these moods and usually steers clear of him when he is in one. Joe knows this and it doesn't bother him. He tells people that it's Will's job, as the sensible one, to keep him out of trouble. But Will agrees to a drink, and they head to the bar. They order a beer, and then spot Kenny and Ron, walking over to them. Will tells Kenny he stopped by the folks' house and no one was home. Does he know where they are? Kenny shrugs then asks him what he is doing there. Will answers, "I just stopped in to show my friend Joe the place and have a beer or two." Ron puts his face close to Will's.

He sneers, "We don't like strangers coming into our place."

Will laughs at him. "Well, in case you haven't noticed, that's my little brother standing beside you."

Ron snarls back, "You mean the little brother who's gonna kick your ass?" Will takes a drink of his beer. Ron smirks. "Hell, I drank a beer with your dad, Will, and he says you're a wuss." Kenny chimes in, "Dale says that when we were little you always got him in trouble." Will sets his beer on the bar. Joe has been listening to the conversation.

He turns to Ron and says, "Hey, Ron, why are you in this? Why don't you let the two brothers be?"

Ron shoots back, "It's none of your damn business, hotshot, what I think or do. What do you care?"

"Well," Joe says carefully, "Will is my friend, and I don't like to see brother against brother. It ain't right."

Ron snaps back, "Well, big mouth, it's right if us young guys say it is." Will has heard enough. He stands and puts money on the bar and tells Joe they should leave. Ron elbows his friend. "Come on, Ken, let's escort these old guys out, make sure they don't get hurt on the way." Will knows what's coming. He steps out of the door, followed by Ron and Joe. Ron throws a punch at Joe, but Joe sidesteps it and Ron's fist just barely touches him. But Joe's punch catches Ron right on the nose and down he goes. Ron hollers for Kenny to help him. Will looks over at Kenny; he warns him to tell his friend to stay down. But of course Kenny doesn't. Ron gets up swinging, and Joe pops him a couple more times, and then it's over. Will looks at Kenny, and Kenny's mouth gapes open. Will asks his brother, "Do you still want to try to kick my ass? And I say try, because you ain't gonna get the job done. I'll never hit you first, Kenny, but I promise you I will protect myself and then some." Kenny looks down at the sidewalk.

He stammers, "No, Will, no. Are we good?"

Will sighs, "Yeah, Kenny, we're good. Now you better get your friend home. The next time, just stay away, unless he changes his attitude. Hell, then we might even buy him a beer."

Joe and Will walk to the car. On the way home, Joe turns to him and thanks him. Will looks at him, puzzled. Joe grins and tells him he had a really good time. He shakes his head. "You did? Look at you! You got a red mark on your face, and your knuckles are all skinned up."

Joe laughs. "I can't wait to meet the rest of your brothers and their friends!"

After that incident, Kenny and Will have a very good relationship. Kenny is still pretty much the same, but he is better around Will. And Jake treats Will with just a little bit more respect. Will still stays away from Jake as much as possible though. Jake and Irene move into a big old two-story house that's only a few miles from Jake's Place. It's a good thing the house is so big, because Mel and his family have fallen on hard times and move in with them. Jake is having a lot of trouble with his truck, and money is pretty tight for everyone. Even though a couple of Will's brothers are in the service, Irene still wants to have a big family get-together at Thanksgiving. Will and Anne take all the fixings for the dinner to Irene. The women all pitch in and help. The meal is delicious, and everyone enjoys the holiday.

A month later, at Christmas, Will and Anne decide to help out again. They fill three or four boxes with the staples, cans and packages, and foods that won't spoil. A day or two before Christmas, they take the food over for the big dinner. On Christmas Day, they bring over the rest of the meal. Irene is very pleased. They also have two gifts, one for Irene and one for Jake. Neatly wrapped and with a bow is the license and registration for the following year for Irene's car, and the same for Jake's truck. Jake does not really thank Anne and

Will. He only mumbles a thanks. But he does chuckle and say, "Now here's a present that will last all year!"

At the first of the year, there are rumors that the railroad will be changing hands, or there will be a merger of some sort. This talk makes the old heads a little nervous. Late in the evening on January 5, 1965, Will gets orders for train number 91. It's a westbound freight train, and it looks to be a good run. There is only one stop to make on the way to set out a few cars. There is only one superior train, passenger train number 14, to take the siding for, then it's home free to Omaha. They arrive and begin to tie up the train in the terminal. Will receives notice from the dispatcher that he has had an emergency call and should call his mother right away. Will wonders what is going on. He phones Irene and finds out that Jake has passed away. It happened early in the morning, from what they think is a heart attack, and she wants Will to come home as soon as he can. The dispatcher tells Will that he is marked off the schedule and to take all the time he needs. There is a hotshot train ordered to go back east in thirty minutes. The clerk makes Will a DH pass and gives him his condolences.

Will gets home late in the afternoon. He heads straight to his mother's house. He notices that she is holding up better than he thought she would be. Mel is a great help, and most of the other kids are already there. Dale is on his way, and brother Donny, who is in the navy, will be arriving in Omaha later that evening. Will, who has the better car, is elected to go pick him up. Will looks out the window and sees it is beginning to snow. He knows he better get a quick bite to eat and get on the road because it's a 280-mile trip. He gets behind the wheel, Mel hops in the front seat with him, and Kenny grabs a couple of beers and slides in the back. The snowfall continues and gets heavier and heavier. Will has the heater on high and drives with his head out the window, trying to see the road. Mel does the same on the passenger side. Luckily, they get behind a big rig truck, and Will just follows the taillights, which is about all he can see through the swirling snow. They make it to the airport, only to find out that Donny isn't there. His flight has been diverted. Will calls Irene and she tells him Donny is now in Des Moines. Will tells her, "Tell him if he can get a ride with someone, take it and let you know. I will call you back before we head south." Donny never gets another ride, and he sure is glad to see his brothers when they arrive in Des Moines. The brothers get back to Irene's place and have breakfast, and Will tries to get a little sleep. Dale arrives late in the afternoon. The neighbor ladies bring over food, and the day is spent discussing funeral details. Late afternoon the next day is to be the viewing and visitation and saying good-bye to Jake.

Will walks into the funeral home. He walks slowly toward Jake lying in the casket and stops short. He thinks, *I have pictured this a thousand times, you old bastard, and there you finally are.* He slowly shakes his head, thinking, *I should be happy and glad, you son-of-a-bitch, but I'm not. Why? Damn you, Jake, you made me hate you.* He looks at the man he has hated for a lifetime, lying in the casket. He can't help but wonder, *Why do I have these mixed-up feelings and emotions? Why do I feel like this?* He remembers, *There are times that I wish I could've put you in that box myself, like the time you shot my dog, do you remember that? Damn you, Jake, you bastard. I remember it. You and Bubba took me and my dog hunting with you. He was on the other side of the ditch, smelling things with his nose, working back and forth, just like a real hunting dog, and I was so proud of him. That's when you raised your long gun up and said to Bubba, "Watch this, target practice."*

I said, "No, no, please don't!" Then I heard the big boom and saw him go down. But the shot didn't kill him, and he lay there, crying and yelping in pain. I grabbed your .22 pistol from your holster. That's when I should have shot you, but I didn't. I ran as fast as I could, with Bubba right behind me, hollering for me to stop.

And you, you were hollering, "Damn you, Will, bring my gun back to me right now!" I got to my dog, I put the gun to his head, I pulled the trigger. After that, all the crying and yelping was coming from me. Bubba took the gun away from me and walked me back to where you were. You said, "Boy, when I tell you to do something, I mean right now!"

Bubba said, "Leave it be, Jake, leave it be." Do you remember it now, Jake, you bastard? I do. I remember it very well. I hate you, Jake, don't I? Then he breaks down and he weeps uncontrollably. Tears flow freely and he sobs. Tears for all the hatred and resentment and fear, tears for all the years of unjust and unfair treatment, suffered at the hands of a man who never loved him and a man he could never love back.

Johnny and Irene come to his side. Irene puts her hands on Will's head. She cups his face and whispers, "I know, son, I know." But Will knows that no, she doesn't know. The only one who could possibly know is Johnny, and Will never told him all of it. Johnny throws an arm around Will's shoulder, and Irene holds his hand; they help him walk away from the casket. They walk by a row of mourners, and Will hears a lady comment to the woman beside her.

She leans in and says, "Now there's a son who really loved his father." Will wipes his tears and whispers, "Wrong, lady, wrong, you could never be more wrong."

The funeral is held the next day. A few weeks later, Mel gets a job. Jake's truck is sold, and a local fellow buys out Irene's interest in the bar and café. Irene is such a great cook, they ask her to stay and work for them; she'll be in charge of the kitchen. Things fall into place for the family, and Will decides that everything is going to be all right.

CHAPTER 45

The Merger

There is talk about town of a merger with another railroad, but nobody really seems to know much about it. Will is in Minnesota on an outlying job. When no one bids a job that is away from home, the youngest conductor gets assigned to it. He does get to come home on weekends. Several weeks later, he finally gets off this job. He is home one afternoon when he gets a call for a westbound train. He hasn't seen his friend Joe in a few months, but Joe calls him and tells him that he is ordered to go with Will. He is pleased; he likes to work with Joe. Joe tells him he will stop by and pick him up and give him a lift to work.

Will is busy packing his grip for the job. Soon, there is a knock on the door. Anne answers it then moments later storms into the room where Will is. Angrily, she says, "What the hell is going on?" He looks at her in bewilderment. She points back at the door and says hotly, "There is a cute little pregnant girl at the door, and she is looking for Will Furman!" He follows Anne back to the door. On the step stands an obviously pregnant girl. Will looks at her and says hello.

She states, "I am looking for Will Furman."

Will answers her, "Well, that would be me."

She says indignantly, "No, you are not Will Furman."

This makes him chuckle. He says to the girl, "I think I know who I am." Just then, Joe pulls up in front of the house to give Will the lift to work. He honks the horn and waves. The girl looks over her shoulder and spots Joe.

She exclaims, "There! That's him! That's Will Furman!" She runs over to the car. A moment later, she slides into the passenger seat and they drive off. Will and Anne exchange puzzled looks. They don't know what to think. Will shakes his head and shuts the door and drives himself to work. Later, he finds out that Joe has been using his name. Joe is a married man but has been seeing the girl and has gotten her pregnant. Things do not go well for Joe after this. Joe's wife finds out about the pregnant girl and divorces him. He quits the railroad, and Will never sees his friend again.

Then the merger happens, only it really isn't a merger. Will is now working for the CNW, the Chicago and Northwestern Railway. The CNW buys out the CGW completely, lock, stock, and barrel. Things start to change immediately. Jobs, terminals, and seniority are to be dovetailed in with their men at the different locations. The CNW has a lot of men who are younger than Will, so this works out well for him. The bad thing is that they change the home terminal. The agreement states that any employee who has to drive fifty miles or more to work will get compensated for it. Plus, their homes will be bought and paid for, among other benefits. But this doesn't hold true for Will. The new home terminal is fifty-five miles away by road, but it's only forty-eight miles away by railroad. He opts to drive the fifty-five miles for a while until the dust settles. He figures he can always bump in somewhere later on.

CHAPTER 46

So There Is a Birth Certificate

The rest of 1965 and the following years are very busy ones for Will. The railroad is short of manpower. Some men leave, some retire, and some go to work at different terminals, where the workload isn't as heavy. Will is working a job where he gets only Sunday off. He doesn't get much time at home during the week because he has to tie up for ten to twelve hours at a time. Will's kids are growing up fast. He can't make it to many of their school functions and doesn't get to see them much. The good thing about this job, though, is that the pay is great. He buys a used camper to go fishing with on the weekends with Anne and the kids. Will and Anne also purchase a home. They get a great buy on a house and with less interest than the bank charges, from his friend Tom, the old grouch passenger conductor. Will makes the payments right into Tom's bank account. Tom tells Will that since he is a qualified brakeman for passenger service, he needs to finish the job and qualify as a conductor too. Will thinks this is a good idea and takes a couple days off to take the short test. The other five railroads, the UP, Wabash, Illinois Central, Rock Island, and Milwaukee, each require a signed card to be qualified. Will takes the test and passes. As luck will have it, he catches one trip as the conductor on old number 13 passenger train before passenger service is ended and the railroad goes to strictly freight service.

The first part of 1968 finds Mel and his family in their own place. Irene gets a new place too. She finds a nice little apartment that she is very proud of. It's only four or five blocks from Will and

Anne's house, and she comes to visit the grandkids anytime she wants. Summer arrives, and Irene starts to feel a little under the weather. Weeks pass and she doesn't seem to get better. The local doctors aren't sure what is wrong with her. Will takes her to Iowa City for tests, and they discover that she has cancer. The doctors think it is coming from her thyroid gland. This is the start of many, many long trips to Iowa City for treatments. On these long trips back and forth, Will and his mother have some lengthy talks.

On the first of February, Irene tells Will that she has something for him. She says it is something that she should have given him a long, long time ago. On his next day off, Irene comes to see Will. She walks into the house and she hands him an envelope. She looks at her son with sad eyes and says, "I am very, very sorry, son." Will takes the envelope from her. He gives his mother a puzzled look and opens it. He can't believe his eyes. It is his birth certificate! And the name on it is Wilton Michael Johnson, not Furman. It's the same name the army had shown him fifteen years ago. He is stunned. Speechless, he stares at the document. He looks at his mother with eyes wide.

He stammers, "What the hell, Mother? Why did you lie to me? Why? Why? I don't understand this one damn bit!" He sinks into the sofa and slowly shakes his head. "That son of a bitch didn't want me to have his name and would not adopt me. So you just let me believe that for all these years I was a Furman?" He thinks back. "Now I know what my grandfather meant all those years ago, when he wished that someday I would do the right thing. He wished that I would carry the Johnson name, because I was the only male left!" He looks at his mother in disbelief, "My god, Mother, what have you gotten me into? Every damn legal document and paper that I have ever signed is wrong! The house, car, marriage license, hell, I could be committing income tax fraud. Christ, there's no end!" His mind races as he struggles to come to grips with this.

His mother sits down beside him. She says apologetically, "I know, Will, and I am so sorry."

He looks at her angrily and continues. "If you would have shown me this so many years ago, I would have accepted it. I would have lived with this name and would have been proud to do so. I would have had my own name." He stands and starts pacing the floor. With fire in his eyes he says, "That old bastard never wanted me in the first place, and you always knew it. He went to his grave thinking that I was responsible for his daughter's death." He paces a few more minutes in silence. Finally, he regains his composure. He turns to his mother and says, "I am sorry for yelling at you, Mom. It's just that I was completely unaware, caught off guard." He looks back down at the birth certificate in his hand. "So this Pasquale, who signed this? Is he my real father?"

Irene lifts her eyes and looks at him. She nods. "Yes, he is."

He looks back down at the paper. "Did you love him, Mom?"

She answers him quietly, "I did, but then, a fifteen-year-old girl can fall in and out of love very easily."

Will thinks for a moment. "Maybe I should go and see him someday."

Irene nods her head yes. "Maybe you should. You know, he has kept tabs on you through the years, through your Grandma Bess."

This surprises Will. He retorts, "If he was so damn interested, why didn't he come and see me for himself? Out of sight, out of mind, huh?"

Irene sighs, "Maybe, I don't know. I do know that he has missed a lot by not getting to know you." He shakes his head. "I don't know what to do about this name thing. I guess I'll have to talk with a lawyer." He looks out the window for a moment then back at his mother, "I know that I would like to have my own real name." Then he sighs, "But with four kids, as old as they are, to change our last name now, that would be asking a lot. I think this will be a big mess." Later that night, Will and Anne talk it over. They decide they will just have to seek legal help to figure out the best thing to do.

A few days later, Irene stops in again. She says to him, "I have the name problem all taken care of. Come with me to the attorney's office. He has documents drawn up for you to sign in front of his secretary, who is a notary. Everything will be taken care of, your name will still be the same, and everything you have signed up until now will be all nice and legal." Will looks at her, a little surprised.

He says in exasperation, "Mother, maybe I wanted to find out what my options were! Hell, maybe I don't want the same name!" But he relents and goes with his mother to the attorney's office. The lawyer tells him that this isn't the only way to handle this problem, but it is by far the cheapest and the easiest. Will takes a deep breath and sighs, "I suppose Jake will be turning over in his grave to know that I am going to carry his name. I am not too thrilled about it myself. But I guess it's the only way to do it this late in the game." Reluctantly, he takes the pen and begins to sign. He doesn't really read the papers; he just takes his mother's word, and the attorney's word. He assumes the document is written the way it should be. Will always signs his name for something legal as Wilton Michael Furman; otherwise, he signs Wilton M. Furman. The document he signs claims that although he was born with the last name Johnson, he has lived all his life as a Furman. As of this date, February 28, 1969, his legal name, and anything signed previously, will still be legal. He thinks to himself, what a hell of a birthday present. Will is about to turn thirty-five years old, and he is taking the legal name of the man who hated him his whole life. He feels a sadness creep over him, and he hopes that this matter is over and done with. Glumly, he hands over the pen and walks out of the lawyer's office.

CHAPTER 47

The Cancer Gets Worse

Will stays busy with his job and taking his mother to Iowa City for cancer treatments. She isn't getting any better. The doctors still think that the cancer is coming from her thyroid gland, but they aren't sure and can't seem to find it. After each treatment, Irene needs rest, and then she starts to feel better, then it's time for another treatment. Early in the summer, Will plans a nice outing for her. He takes his fold-down camper to the beach. He sets it up with the sides all folded down. Irene rests inside, yet she can still get fresh air and watch her grandkids play. She really enjoys this. Later in the summer, Jerry, Irene's youngest son, and another kid, pick up a camera they find on the beach. Someone sees them using it and turns them in to the police. After a month or so of trying to get Jerry's offense reduced to a minor charge, because he has never been in any trouble before, they give up. The district attorney brings him up on charges, and Jerry is sentenced to eleven months in a correctional facility. This makes for more trips for Will, because Irene wants to go and see him on visitation days.

The next few months go by very fast, and Irene seems to be getting worse. In June and July, she is in and out of the hospital. By late July, she is in very bad shape, and he knows that she won't make it out of the hospital on her own. He tells Grandma Bess that she should come and see her daughter. He talks to the warden in the facility where his brother Jerry is. He finds out that Jerry can get out, but for one day only. If he uses the one day now, then later, he won't be able to use it again. Will thinks they better wait. Will lets Irene's apartment go to someone else, but he doesn't tell her that. He lets his mom think that she still has her apartment to come home to when she gets better. With the help of his brothers and sister, they pack up her belongings and store everything in Will's garage. Will takes some time off work, and the first of August, he sets his camper up at a campground not too far from the hospital. He spends every day with his mom, and the hospital has his number at the campground to reach Will at night. Will tells his brothers and sister how serious things are for their mother, and if they want to spend any time with her, they better do it soon. The last few days of her life, Will and Mel are right there beside her. She weighs about ninety pounds and is very frail, and pneumonia is setting in. On the last day of her life, he watches his mother as she tries to tear away the oxygen mask from her face, the very thing that is letting her breathe, so she can have a cigarette. This image sticks in his mind forever. Then her back arches, a big lump comes in her throat, and her struggle is over. Will's mother, Irene, is gone. She passes away on her daughter Linda's birthday, August 12, 1971.

Will takes on the role as executor of her estate. While making funeral arrangements, he is shocked to find out that there isn't a plot for her beside her husband, Jake. Jake is buried in his father's family plot, about eighty miles away. He always assumed that there was a place for her since Dale is buried in Minnesota. So he decides, since there is no room for her near Jake, he will buy her a plot in his town. He buys three plots in the same cemetery where he himself had actually opened up a grave site. He buys three plots, one for Irene and one each for him and Anne. The rest of the family is very unhappy that Irene can't be laid to rest beside her husband. But this certainly isn't Will's fault. He makes the necessary arrangements for Jerry, the youngest, to be able to attend the funeral. There will be a guard with Jerry at all times, inconspicuously. No handcuffs or shackles needed, but Will must pay in advance for one day's guard pay and transportation costs there and back. After the funeral, there is a luncheon put on by the church and neighbor ladies. Will talks with the guard, who is a very nice fellow. He tells him to feel free to get a plate of food and join them. Johnny takes him aside and tells him that the other brothers are making plans for brother Jerry to make a getaway. Will's mouth drops open. "What?" He can't believe what he is hearing. "The hell they are, not on my watch!" He thanks Johnny and asks him to help him keep an eye on them. He rounds up the brothers, one by one, and gathers them around the back of the lot. He glares at them then says angrily, "I don't know what the hell you guys are thinking, but you sure as hell don't want to start anything here on the day that we are laying our mother to rest!" He narrows his eyes at them. "Now, have you got that? Or do I have to make things plainer?" The brothers lower their heads and mumble as they walk away. Will and Johnny keep an eye on them the rest of the day, but everything goes smoothly.

A few days later, he gets his siblings all together to divide up their mother's personal things. To make it fair, he has everyone draw a number out of a hat, with number one taking the first item and so on. They give most of her clothes away, and everything is divvied up, except for her car. One of the younger boys really wants it. Will tells him they have to sell it to help pay the bills, but if he wants to pay a little for it, then he can have it. Will keeps good records of everything, just in case any of his siblings has an issue with anything. He makes a few final notes in his ledger. He sighs as he closes the book. He sits there for a moment with a heavy heart. It makes him sad to think that his mother, the one person he has loved his whole life, is gone.

CHAPTER 48

Big Vacation

After Irene's funeral, Will gets a letter from the hospital in Iowa City. They finally found the source of Irene's cancer. They were so sure it was from her thyroid gland, but it wasn't. She had breast cancer. He crumples the letter and thinks to himself that this news doesn't make him feel one bit better. It doesn't take long before he gets back into the routine. He works steadily and bids on better jobs every chance he gets. On one of his days off, he takes Anne to a terminal about forty-five miles south. It's one of CNW's larger terminals, and he likes what he sees. They have trains that run to Omaha and back and to Chicago and back. A lot of the trains are through trains, and it's all double-track railroad. With his seniority as a brakeman, he can hold some pretty good jobs. They offer switch jobs, extra bid jobs, and regular jobs. He likes all these options and decides that someday he will be coming to work at this terminal. At the first of the year, the employees put in bids for their vacations. Will always bids for a summer vacation, but he never gets one because he doesn't have enough seniority. He knows he has a chance this year though, because he has ten years of service in. He is pleased when he finds out he gets his first summer vacation for the month of June. It's perfect since his oldest daughter Donna is graduating from high school in May. The family can take the camper and vacation for the whole month of June. While on the engine one day, he pulls a cigarette from his pocket and starts to light up. He remembers his mother, then he takes the whole pack from his pocket and throws them out the window. The engineer gives him a funny look and asks why he did that? Will tells him that he has just quit smoking. The man remarks that he could have given the pack to him, but Will smiles and says, "Nah, they're bad for you!" So besides his vacation pay, he has all his cigarette money saved.

Donna graduates with very high grades. She has plans to get a little apartment after the vacation, and she already has a good job lined up. The family is excited about the big vacation. A few days before the trip, a trainmaster clerk that Will knows and really likes gives him a call. He wants to give Will a heads up. He tells him that the trainmaster is going to set his vacation back to the fall because of a manpower shortage. Will does not like the sounds of this, so he pays a visit to the local chairman of the union. He tells Will that as long as the crew caller can't reach him, there is nothing that the railroad can do to him. They cannot reprimand him, take him out of service, or fire him. When the terminal was in the same town, the crew caller could come to your home to find you, but now that it is fifty-five miles away, Will doesn't have to worry about that. If the crew caller does reach you, one way or another, and you aren't ill, then you must go to work. Anne is nervous, but he keeps packing for the trip. The day before they are to leave, the crew caller calls. He tells Will that his vacation has been set back to a later date. Will is exasperated; he explains that he has tickets bought and everything planned. The man says he is sorry, but that it is not his fault. Will hangs up the phone unfazed. He has plans of his own.

The next morning, bright and early, the family is on the road in their seven-passenger station wagon, pulling the new Starmaster camper behind. Will loves being on the road, going over the next hill, and seeing what lies around the bend. *Someday*, he thinks, *someday, I will be a traveling man.* The family is away for an entire month. They sightsee through sixteen different states. They camp in national parks and see deer, buffalo, and bighorn sheep. The girls especially like the moose and even name them. They travel through Las Vegas and see the beaches of California. They get to spend time with Grandma Bess. They all have a wonderful time and are sad when the vacation comes to an end.

When the vacation is over, Will sits in the trainmaster's office. He listens while the man yells at him. The man tells Will that he will not get his vacation pay and he can have the month of September for his vacation. Will smiles to himself and politely thanks him. Then he can't help himself; he stands and says, "You talk about protecting my job. What about hiring some men instead of trying to work the ones you have to death? Then maybe we would quit trying to look for loopholes so we can rest and be with our families!" He storms out of the office, and on his way out, he notices some of the clerks smile and nod at him.

Anne helps Donna move into her new apartment. They buy dishes and curtains and fix the place up. Donna likes being on her own. The next week, she invites her parents over for a home-cooked meal. The meal turns out to be a hotdog and a beer!

CHAPTER 49

What Did Will Start?

It doesn't go like the trainmaster says, because Will does get his vacation pay. He puts it back into savings, and he is pleased. He has learned many tricks over the last ten years, tricks like ways to bid jobs and get bumping privileges. He uses all the tricks he can, and this makes the trainmaster mad. He is out to get Will. What really angers the trainmaster is when Will gets him in trouble with his superiors. A trainmaster is supposed to test all the crews two or three times a month to make sure they are following the rules. One night, Will and his crew have the train put away and the bookwork done. Will looks at his watch; it's 5:28 p.m. He writes down 5:30 p.m., like he has always done. A few weeks later, he is called in for stealing time. The investigation is being done by the superintendent, a man Will knew before he was promoted to that rank. The proceedings start, and the trainmaster states that conductor Furman was caught stealing time. He claims Will had signed his name to a report and was stealing two minutes of time. The superintendent looks over the report. He asks Will if this is true. Will says yes, but there was no pay involved. The superintendent just shakes his head. He sends Will home and tells him he will handle the trainmaster. The news soon gets around, and the trainmaster is a laughing stock.

Will has some time off, and he and Anne decide to go to Chicago to see Johnny. He hasn't told anyone, but he secretly thinks it's time he meets his real father. They stay at Anne's aunt's house. They get settled in then meet with Johnny at the nightclub where his younger brother Doug is the bartender. He confesses to Johnny why he is really there. They have a few drinks and reminisce, and Johnny agrees to help. He tells Will that Doug has connections and knows a lot of people. Doug says he will start asking around for anyone connected with the Pasquale family.

They meet the next day and start the search. They look in the phone book and come up with nothing. The next stop is the library. They look through old newspapers for any mention of the Pasquale name. It gets late and the library closes. They head back to the night-club to see if Doug has turned up anything. They walk in, and Doug nervously tells Johnny that two men had been in there looking for him. They wanted to know who was the guy with him and why they were so interested in the Pasquale family. Doug warns them that he thinks something is going on. They aren't sure what to make of it, but Doug and Johnny are worried. Johnny and Will decide to change clothes and pick up the women and go out for dinner. They drive to Johnny's apartment, and Johnny is edgy. He looks over his shoulder constantly and parks in a grocery store parking lot, not at his apartment building. Will is puzzled by this, and now he starts to get a little nervous too. They walk up the three flights of stairs and reach the apartment. They notice that the door is ajar. Johnny stops and listens for a few seconds, with Will right behind him. What Will sees next makes him really nervous and scared. The place is a mess! Johnny's apartment is totally trashed. Johnny throws Will his car keys and tells him to pull the car around while he grabs a few things. Will helps him load his stuff. Johnny says he thinks they need to leave town quickly. They drive a few blocks to get Angel, Johnny's wife, who lives with her grandmother still. He tells her to pack some clothes. They get Anne and fill both cars with Johnny and Angel's things. Anne demands to know what is going on. Will tells her he doesn't know, except that is has something to do with him looking for his father. He tells her he is glad they are heading home and that Angel and Johnny will be coming back with them for a little while. They stop at a truck stop outside of Chicago for gas and a bite to eat. Johnny thanks Will for not asking too many questions back at the apartment. Will tells him he figures that if there is anything he wants him to know, he will tell him when he is ready. They drive back to Will and Anne's. The next morning, over breakfast, they make plans. Johnny says he will go to the trucking company where he and Jake used to work and see if they will hire him back. Anne says she will help the couple find a furnished apartment. Johnny asks Will if his brother Doug has Will's address or phone number. He shakes his head no. They decide that maybe this is a good thing.

CHAPTER 50

A Brand-New Home

Johnny gets hired on with the trucking company, and he and Angel find a nice little apartment. When he is on the road, Angel spends a lot of time with Will and Anne and the kids. To Will's amusement, little Johnny, his twelve-year-old son, is madly in love with Angel. On weekends, they like to take the camper to the river for some fishing. Little Johnny can always be found somewhere near Angel, baiting her hook and sitting beside her.

It doesn't take long, though, and Will can tell that big Johnny is getting fed up with the simple life. He is restless and can't wait to get back to the bright lights and the big city. As soon as spring arrives, Johnny and Angel head back to Chicago. All the stuff that won't fit in their car they leave boxed up and in Will's garage. The plan is for Will to rent a truck and bring the stuff to them later and make another attempt to find his father.

Not long after Johnny and Angel leave, Will gets bumped on his job. He can bump in somewhere else, and he has three days to do it. Another railroader, older than Will and with way more seniority, has been thinking about relocating to the bigger terminal too. Now that their seniority has been dovetailed in, they know there are a lot of really good jobs they can hold. Will and this man decide to make the move to the bigger terminal. The only conductor jobs that Will can hold are on work trains, so he opts to go as a brakeman. The two take turns driving back and forth. Will catches on quick, and it isn't long before he is very comfortable with jobs out of this new terminal.

They run many trains a day, and a lot are hotshot trains, with regular jobs and days off. He likes this and knows that this is where he wants to stay.

Johnny calls and tells him that he and Angel both have jobs and are settled in a place. They set up a weekend for Will and Anne to bring their stuff back to them. Will rents a U-Haul, and they make the trip. They unload the truck; they return it to the dealer and make plans to go out for dinner and drinks. The foursome enjoys a nice meal, and soon the conversation shifts to Will and his father. Will is quiet for a few minutes, then something inside him changes. He doesn't get loud or mean, but he sets his jaw and says a little belligerently, "You know what? That man has never done a damn thing for me. No calls, no cards, no gifts, nothing. He never looked me up. So why in the hell should I try to find him?" He sets his drink down on the table. "Piss on him, I am done." Johnny can't believe his ears. Anne and Angel look at him in surprise. Johnny wants to know if this decision has something to do with what happened the last time they tried to find his father. He assures him it doesn't. He says proudly, "It has to do with what my mother told me a couple years ago. She said he missed out by not knowing *me*."

Throughout the summer, Anne drives to where Will's new home terminal is. He has talked her into moving there, and they look at houses and property. In the winter, he can't always make it home because of bad weather. He stays at a hotel close enough that he can walk to. Anne drives to see him when she can. They finally purchase a lot and decide to put a manufactured home on it. It isn't a stick-built house or a pull-together house. It comes on a truck with large sections of walls, floors, and roof. It is a split-foyer house, and it is the first house of its kind to be put up in this town.

First, the foundation, the four cement walls for the house to sit on, needs to be poured. Will is excited and can't wait for spring so the project can get started. The contractor puts up the walls, but there is a small setback. After three of the walls are up, the contractor leaves his young apprentices alone. Will stops over after work to check on the progress. He notices right away as he walks up that something is not right. He takes out his tape measure and level, and the fourth wall is six inches off! The boss comes back and shakes his head; he can't understand how they got it so messed up. Just then, the door of the house next door opens, and out comes a pretty young lady in her bikini. It is a hot summer day, and she is out lying in the sun, not thirty feet from where the young men are working. Will and the boss share a grin; they just figured out the distraction. The boss tells him that he will fix it by adding some concrete to make it level. Will shakes his head no; how can they be sure that the bottom of the wall is strong enough to support that? He argues with the man and tells him that he will talk to the bank and an attorney until the contractor agrees to knock down the whole wall and start over.

Since this house is the first of its kind to be built in the area, the company that makes the house has advertised in the local paper for people to come out and watch the beautiful home being erected. The day arrives, and there are lots of townspeople around. The big trucks pull up with floors, windows, and walls. The only thing that doesn't arrive is the first and most essential piece, the twenty-foot steel I beam to be placed between the concrete walls! Will can't believe it. He doesn't know whether to laugh or cry. The piece arrives later, though, and the house is erected. The rest of the week, the finishing team comes in and installs carpeting and appliances. Will takes a week off work to paint and stain. He fills in the backyard with sod where the big trucks dug it up. He works every day and late into the night. He is excited; he now has a new home for his family to move into.

His children come and check out the new house. They will each have their own bedroom, and they really like the place. But like all kids, they would rather stay where they are at, in their school with their friends. The oldest, Donna, will be staying behind in her own place. Will wants the rest of the family to be together, and the moving date is set for July 1. This is where he makes a mistake, a bad call. He doesn't make arrangements for his second daughter, Jonie, to stay behind with her sister. She pleads with him to let her stay behind to finish her last year of school. She is in her senior year of high school, and word is out that she will be prom queen. She is the same daughter that he lied to about her eyes. He doesn't know how he misses this. He reasons it's because he wasn't thinking about anybody else, just how much he wants the family to be together. She doesn't want to, but she moves with Anne and the other two kids. They all attend school in the new town. Jonie graduates a few months later with kids she doesn't even know. He feels bad and hopes she isn't too mad at him.

CHAPTER 51

The Divorce

The kids make a really good effort to fit in at the new school. The girls babysit and do odd jobs, and one works at the local pizza place. The boy gets a newspaper route and cuts grass. They aren't very happy in the new town; it's a whole different life for them. They don't complain to Will, but they do to Anne. She isn't happy either, and slowly but surely, things start to come apart. Will knows that his marriage is in trouble. He is irritable and hard to get along with, and that doesn't help matters. Will and Anne decide to seek some professional help. They talk to the parish priest. After a few sessions, he is convinced that the answer is to go back to live in the other town. He also says Will needs to change jobs. Will is dismayed. He tells the priest that he has fifteen years of service in and is halfway to getting a good pension for retirement. Besides, it's a good-paying job for raising a family with four children. And although he has sacrificed a social life for the first fifteen years and missed out on the kids' activities, he is at the halfway point. He can now hold good jobs with regular days off. And, he tells the priest, he likes his job. Sure he could sell shoes or something, but he won't be happy. The priest tells him that Anne feels like she has raised the children while he was working, and soon she will be suffering from the "empty nest" syndrome. She fears that with the children gone, she will be alone most of the time.

They make another appointment, this time with a licensed certified marriage counselor, and the whole family attends. The counselor talks to everyone as a group then asks individual questions. He has Will and Anne do a role reversal. The next session is pretty much the same, except he pays a lot of attention to Jonie. He asks her the most questions and asks her repeatedly about wearing eye makeup. Will starts to get irritated. He doesn't see what this has to do with anything. Then he wonders if the man is a little infatuated with her. After all, she is eighteen years old and a beautiful young lady, with a figure to match. She is outgoing and likeable. The third session, the man starts in again questioning Jonie. She starts to cry, and this is the straw that breaks the camel's back for Will. He jumps from his chair and explodes, "It's none of your damn business how my daughter fixes her eyes! But I'll give you a hint. When she was little, she had two eye operations. As you can see, they turned out beautifully. And furthermore, what the hell do her eyes have to do with my marriage?" He whirls around and points to the man, "And by the way, how long have you been married?" The man mumbles that he is divorced. Will is incensed. The man can't keep his own marriage together, yet he gives advice? He shouts, "If the money from these sessions is paying for your Cadillac parked out front, then you better get another source of income. You won't be getting another cent from us!" His daughter shoots him a grateful look, and he motions his family out the door. This is the last session the couple ever attends.

The school year comes to a close, and Jonie graduates. Will and Anne call an end to their marriage, and Anne and the kids move back to their hometown. Will has a talk with each of his kids, and they seem to be fine. Will is worried about his son though. The boy is a very good athlete. He plays baseball, basketball, and wrestling and has become very good in all three sports. Will feels bad and worries because he rarely gets to attend any of his games. Will drives back to see his kids whenever he can. Sometimes he takes the camper and stays for weekends. The divorce is final a few months later, and the youngest daughter, Michelle, is the homecoming queen that year.

CHAPTER 52

Dicks by the Sea

Will pays alimony and child support and is never late with a payment. Anne gets the payments from the first house they had sold. He sells the new house, and they break even on it. He gets a nice trailer house to live in with a basement and a yard. The next few years go by fast. He sees his kids when he can, and they drive to see him too. He meets a woman named Lynn. She is from the southern part of the state, and they strike up a relationship. She wants to move in with him, but he instead rents her his trailer house and he rents another one for himself. His children meet her and like her. She still wants to move in together, so he suggests they take a trip together to see how they get along.

He buys a motor home, and he and Lynn travel together and it works out great. They move in together and then start to plan a big trip to the coast. They plan to stop in Las Vegas and get married. Johnny, Will's son, is nineteen years old now and just graduated from high school. He wants his dad to take him along; he tells him that he will be the best man. They stop at Lynn's brother's house in Colorado for Thanksgiving. Will has it planned that they will be on the road for about six weeks. He is happy because he is a traveling man again, just like he loves. Johnny enjoys the trip too. Lynn's brother has three pretty daughters. They take Johnny snow skiing and sightseeing. They have a great time in Las Vegas, and Lynn and Will get married.

After Las Vegas, the threesome travels to northern California then over to the coast and south on Highway 1. They stay as close as they can to the ocean and camp on the beach. On New Year's Eve, and they look for a place to stop. They are near Oceanside, California, and they spot a little place right on the beach. The bar and restaurant is called Dick's by the Sea. They pull the motor home around back and park. The place is packed. They sit at the bar and have a few drinks and hors d'oeuvres.

Soon, things start to get strange. Johnny tells Will to take a look at the beautiful blond female singer, who they notice is no longer a female! The men are pairing up with other men and women with women! Johnny's mouth drops open. "Dad, where the hell are we?"

The bartender overhears him and can't help but laugh. He says, "I guess this is your first time in a gay bar?" He tells them with a twinkle in his eye that it will be fine, he is straight himself, and he will look out for them. Johnny is nervous, though, and he refuses to use the bar restroom; he goes out to the motor home instead. They ring in the new year in the gay bar. They head back to the motor home, and a drunken Johnny hollers out of the door, "Happy New Year!" Then he falls back on the bed and passes out. Will chuckles to himself and throws a blanket over him. All in all, it turns out to be a great trip, and the traveling man hates to see it come to an end.

CHAPTER 53

The Bus Ticket

Years later, Will sells his trailer and buys an acre of land about seven miles outside of town. He has a basement built, then he puts a modular home that comes in two units on top of it. He keeps this place for a few years then sells it and makes a little profit. This money he puts toward five acres of land. He builds a split-foyer home. The lot has plenty of timber and the new place keeps him busy. He puts solar panels on the roof, and he keeps wood cut for the fireplace. There's a big yard to mow in the summer and a long driveway to shovel in the winter. He puts in a rock garden around the house and plants some evergreens.

For vacations, he starts to put two vacations together. He uses the month of December from one year then the month of January from the next. This gives the traveling man eight weeks to travel, and he loves it. Slowly, he and Lynn begin to drift apart. She has always been a city girl and finds that she doesn't really like living out in the country. Things come to a head one summer day while he is packing his grip for work. Lynn thinks the shirt he is packing is much too nice for work. She asks him heatedly what is going on. He explains that Johnny is meeting him at his layover point. The two are going to dinner and then having a drink and catching up on things. He looks at the shirt in his hand. It is an old shirt, with a frayed collar even. He can't understand what her problem is. He looks at her and comments, "You know, the way things are around here, I feel as though I am living with a sister more than a wife."

When he gets back from work, he notices that the car is gone, but he doesn't think too much about it. But inside the house, in the kitchen propped up on the counter, is a note. It reads, "You don't have to live with your sister anymore. Your sister has left." He thinks this is strange, but maybe she just needs a little time to herself. He waits a few days then calls her. She is at her brother's house in Colorado. Will really likes the brother; the two get along great. But unfortunately, it's the sister-in-law who answers the phone. She tells him that Lynn is there but doesn't want to talk to him. The second call is the same. Ten days later, she again tells Will the same thing, that Lynn doesn't want to talk to him. "Damn," he says, "I really have to know what to do." There is a long pause on the other end, then the sister-in-law tells him to do whatever the hell he wants to do then hangs up.

He hires an attorney, who advises him to file for a divorce. Lynn is piling up credit card debt, so he stops that right away. There is a freeze on his checking account, so he is glad he hasn't deposited his last check yet. It takes a long time to try to finalize the divorce, with Lynn in Colorado and Will in Iowa, but it finally goes through. She will get the car, some equity from the house, and the IRA accounts that are in her name, and this is going to be bad for Will. When he first opened those accounts, you could open a big one for the wage earner and a smaller one for the spouse. He was told, for tax purposes, to put the larger one in his wife's name. Now this decision is coming back to haunt him. Also, she wants alimony until she remarries or retires. He puts his foot down and says no, no alimony. The judge hearing the case says the alimony will cease when she remarries. Will blurts out, "That's just it! Who in their right mind is going to remarry and put a stop to this income?"

The judge glares at him. "Are you saying that your wife is a crook?"

"No, I am saying that the court is going to turn her into one!" he replies. Will gets slapped with a contempt-of-court fee, and his lawyer gets the alimony payments reduced to five years. His children are out of school now, so the child support he had been paying will now go to alimony payments for wife number two. He is paying alimony to wife number one until she remarries or retires and now alimony to wife number two for five years. All the guys at work tease Will about paying alimony to two ex-wives. They ask him, what does he get, a third of his check? He smiles and says he gets a fourth. One-fourth goes to wife number one, one-fourth to wife number two, one-fourth to the IRS, and a fourth to him. This makes the guys all laugh, and he can only shrug his shoulders and laugh along.

His divorce is now final. He can't help but think that, with two failed marriages, he should stay away from women. *Hell,* he thinks to himself, *I can't afford another one.* He bids for good-paying jobs to help get his finances in shape. He sells the house and land and makes a little profit. He goes to work, stops in to the bar now and then for a drink, then goes home alone. This routine works pretty well for several years, and then he meets Diane. They get along great, and he dates her for the next few months. The only problem is his kids don't seem to really like her. She wants to move in with him, but he comes up with the same plan. He tells her that his vacation is coming up soon and they should travel together. They can be together for a whole month and see how things go. She lives with her sister and only works part-time and has no problem taking a month off work.

The first few days of the trip don't start out well. Diane is bored riding in the passenger seat. Then she complains that she can't be expected to cook in that small of a kitchen. She does not enjoy the sightseeing. Each day, she tells Will what to wear. She even tries to tell him what pocket to carry his money in. Will can't believe his ears. He is wondering what he has gotten himself into. He got away from a woman who was like a sister to a woman who is like a mother! Thinking back, Will recalls that the night before they left for the trip, Diane's daughter said to him, "Good luck, she is a very demanding woman." Now Will knows what she was talking about.

He is driving toward Daytona Beach and is just a day or two away from there. He pulls into a rest area on the interstate for the night instead of a campground. He pulls into a level spot and gets settled in. He points the antenna toward a television station and pops a beer. He tells Diane that he will heat up some chili and hot dogs for them. Just then, a motorcycle pulls in beside them. There is a knock at the door. Will answers it and sees a nice-looking young man standing there. The young man tells Will that he is going into the army in a few days. He is on his way home to see his family and store his motorcycle. He says that he has a sleeping bag, and he is going to go over to a secluded spot to try to get some sleep. He wonders if it will be all right to leave his motorcycle close to the motor home so no one will mess with it. Will tells him sure, he will keep an eye on it. He shuts the door and is confronted by Diane, who is frantic. She screams, "We can't stay here! We have to leave! It's starting already!"

Will looks at her in dismay. "What are you talking about? Get yourself together. What in the hell is wrong with you?" She continues to cry and carry on. Will tries to get her to take a drink to calm down.

She shouts at him, "You don't understand! I had this dream where this was going to happen! A motorcycle gang is going to come in here and beat the hell out of you, and poor me, they are all going to rape me!" Will shakes his head. He tries to get her to settle down. He explains to her that there is only one really nice young man out there, no gang. And nothing is going to happen and everything will be fine. But she won't listen to him. She tells him that he is wrong and that her dreams always come true. She angrily tells him that she is going to hold him personally responsible for whatever happens.

He goes to bed, but he doesn't sleep well that night. He keeps one eye on her and wonders what the hell he has gotten himself into. They are only halfway through the trip. He wonders if he should turn back or keep going. Diane sits in the driver's seat the whole night. In the morning, he brews a pot of coffee. He hears the motorcycle start up. He goes outside and wishes the young man good luck. The younger man winks at Will and wishes him good luck as well. Will glances over at Diane, pouting in the corner. He wants to ask her about her dreams always coming true but decides against it. They do not speak the rest of the day. That afternoon they arrive at the campground. He gets the motor home set up in a level spot. He hooks up the water, sewer, and electricity. He hooks up the television antenna and tells her the television set is hers for the night, and he will see her in the morning.

He sets off down the beach. He finds a little bar with only one other man in it and the bartender. They both appear to be about

Will's age. He orders a shot with a beer backup. He chats with the bartender and tells him he has a woman back up the beach who is driving him nuts. The other patron and the bartender both commiserate with Will. The three of them have a lot in common and take turns buying rounds. Later, they decide to join a party on the beach. The bartender closes up shop, and the three of them take off for the party. At the party there is free beer, food, a bonfire, and dance music. Will meets a lot of people and has a great time. He mingles with some of the single people and has a bite to eat. He gets comfortable close to the fire and falls asleep.

He wakes up to the warm sun on his face. He finds a restroom and splashes some water on his face before heading back to his motor home. He goes inside and finds out that Diane isn't there. He brews a pot of coffee, and it isn't long before she returns with some boxes. She tells him that she spent the night with some really nice people who think that she is great and too good for him. Will nods and sips his coffee. Then she states that she will pack what doesn't fit in her suitcase in the boxes, and Will is to take her to the post office to mail them and then to the airport. Will tells her she can leave the boxes. He will get them to her when he gets back home. She is surprised by this. "You won't destroy my stuff or throw it away?" He tells her of course he won't; he is not that kind of guy. She snaps, "I am going to fly home, and you are going to pay for my flight." Will sets his coffee cup down. He shakes his head no.

He says calmly, "No, I am not. If you want to fly, you buy your own damn ticket. If you want me to pay, I'll take you to the bus station." He pauses for a moment. "So what's it going to be?" She complains all the way to the bus station. Will buys her ticket and stands aside. He would like to leave, but he stays; he wants to make sure she gets on the bus. She boards the bus and he tells her good-bye, and he never sees her again. He heads back out on the road by himself. The traveling man thoroughly enjoys the rest of his trip, alone.

CHAPTER 54

Takes a Big Diamond

Will is back home in time for New Year's. Diane's daughter and her husband come and get Diane's boxes a few days later. He has been back in town for a week or so, and late one afternoon after work, he heads to his favorite watering hole for a drink. The bar is a hangout for mostly single people, and he knows most of them. As soon as he walks in the door, the teasing starts. He walks to the nearest barstool and takes a seat. A single man, a guy he knows from work, stands up at the other end of the bar and begins to clap. Will looks at him in bewilderment. The man shouts, "Now there is the man of the year!" Will can feel his face turn red and wonders what the hell is going on.

Another fellow walks up and slaps him on the back. He grins, "Ole Will here, now he knows how to get rid of a woman you can't get along with, right, Will? You just put her on the first bus out of town!" He laughs loudly, and the whole place erupts into laughter with him. The jokes continue to fly, and Will feels a little sheepish.

One woman hollers out, "Hey, Will, if you ever date me, we're staying in town!" He takes all the good-natured ribbing and smiles as he drinks his beer. Then the door opens and in walks Rod. Everyone knows him and also knows that he has had his fair share of trouble with women. Rod has a very loud voice.

He booms, "Hey, thank you, what a great idea! I don't know why I didn't think of it!" And out from his pocket he pulls a Greyhound bus ticket. The place roars with laughter again, and Will smiles and nods and hopes the topic will die down soon. He is the talk of the town for the next few weeks, so he decides it's time to change his dating habits.

He decides that he will only date a girl two or three times. He'll take her to a dinner theater or dance hall. He likes to wear his boots and dance, and a lot of women seem to like to dance with him. But the word gets out that he is a "two-time" dater, and not all women are interested. But that's fine with him; it'll keep him out of trouble. As a rule, he only goes to two different bars. But he hears of a new place in town. Rumor has it that the place is owned by a good-looking lady, and she has a staff of nice-looking girls. He decides to check the place out. It's called Quiet Times. He walks in and thinks the name suits the place perfectly. It's very quiet in there; there's just a small group of people at a corner table. Will surveys them; they look pretty young. They are talking about their exes and their jobs. He sends them a round of drinks then plays the jukebox. He asks if there are any dancers in the group, and that's when he meets Natalie. She is a cute little thing and pretty much full of wine. She asks Will how old he is. He smiles and tells her that he is probably older than her. She says she doesn't mind because age is just a number. After a few dances and more drinks and small talk, he has made his first date with Natalie. The date is to be on his next day off, which is his grandson's birthday, October 26, 1992.

He finds out that since her divorce, Natalie doesn't have much trust in men. He thinks this might be a good thing because then she won't want to get too involved. He really likes her and breaks his new dating rules. He sees her many times, and they have a lot of fun together. She is a good dancer and everyone likes her. Her relatives come to visit, and he takes everyone to Des Moines to a country dance hall. They have a great time. It doesn't take long before Will realizes he is getting more involved with her than he intended. She is a smoker, and since he quit, he doesn't want to be around smoke, plus she is younger than he is. He tells her these reasons then stays away from her.

Four or five weeks go by, and one day he is in the bar, throwing darts and drinking a beer. Natalie and her girlfriend walk in. The friend slides into the first booth, but Natalie, in her high heels, tight jeans, and low-cut blouse, walks over to Will. Sarcastically, she says, "Hey Mr. Nonsmoker Furman, I don't smoke either." With that, she walks away and joins her friend in the booth. He stands there, his mouth gapes, and he can't help but think how good she looks. She has the attention of his fellow dart players too. He sends over drinks and then finishes his dart game. He walks over to the booth and congratulates her on quitting smoking. They talk about smoking and how hard it is to quit. They talk the rest of the night, and one thing leads to another. Before he knows it, Will and Natalie are a couple. His children meet her and really like her. Even his first wife, Anne, likes her and invites her into her new place. This makes Will smile because he hasn't even been invited in yet.

The next few years are interesting for Will and Natalie. They go on several trips together because Will wants to make sure they can get along in tight quarters. Natalie's stepdad passes away, and she moves in with her mother. This arrangement doesn't work out too well. Her mother can't manage her income, and she always has to help her out financially. Natalie works three jobs to make ends meet. One of her jobs is managing the bar that Will's friend owns. She is a good manager and very trustworthy, and the customers love her. Will soon takes advantage of her position. On nights after a run, he calls her and tells her to leave the back door open. He and the crew come in late for a few drinks before going home. There are a lot of divorced and single people in the town who like to hang out there. On Christmas Eve, the boss tells her to close the bar early. But Natalie tells him that they don't have any place to go, and she would like to keep the place open. The place is soon full of people who have no place to go either.

Will can see that Natalie is having a hard time keeping up with finances. Between helping out her mother and her kids, there isn't much money left for her. He asks her if she would consider moving in with him. He also asks her to put aside a set amount each week into a jar kept on top of the refrigerator. He pays all the bills and sets aside a little from his paycheck too. On the weekends that Will is off, they like to take the camper to a lake near his oldest daughter and Anne. Will's sister and her husband join them and they cook out and fish and have a great time. Every once in a while, they take longer trips. They travel to New Orleans, and Will meets Natalie's oldest son. Will tells her that he plans to retire in 1996. He intends to sell everything but the motor home and become a full-time traveler, his lifelong dream. He has asked her about this before. But her answer is always that she is not sure what she wants to do. She tells him this is a big step and a very big commitment.

The railroad continues to make changes. The Union Pacific railroad buys out the CNW, and now he is a conductor for the UP Railroad. There are many more changes coming, with a hint of some buyouts. He is hopeful, he knows a buyout now will be good for him. He keeps up with all the changes. He watches the bulletin board to make sure he doesn't miss any notices. There are a few buyouts offered for engineers but nothing yet for conductors.

Late one afternoon, after mowing and raking his yard, Will experiences trouble with his throat and his breathing. He sees his doctor, who tells him that he is concerned that he is having heart trouble. He thinks he just overdid it on the yard work and blows it off. He is thinking more about Natalie and the issue of a commitment. Christmas is fast approaching, and he thinks now might be a good time to do something about it. He finds out that his youngest daughter is getting married in January. This will be her second marriage, and she would like him to be there. This worries him because it's a bad time to travel, especially to North Carolina.

He goes Christmas shopping and buys a diamond ring. It's over one carat and beautiful. He places it inside a hand-painted figurine, made just for a ring yet looking like a statue. He wraps it in a pretty box and can't wait to give it to Natalie on Christmas Eve. But it doesn't work out that way. Will's train derails outside of Chicago, and his crew is the only crew that doesn't make it home for Christmas. So Natalie keeps the bar open for the all the single people and people with no place to go. He gets home a day late, and they have their Christmas together. Natalie opens what she thinks is all her gifts. Then he points and says, "I think I see a little present back there, behind the tree." She excitedly reaches for the box and opens it. She sees the little figurine and isn't too excited anymore but comments that it will look nice on her dresser. Will can't stand it. He grins, "Well, aren't you going to open it?" Her smile widens as she opens the statue. She gasps as she looks at the beautiful diamond ring. She throws her arms around his neck. "Now," he says, "is that enough commitment for you?"

CHAPTER 55

Are the Travel Plans Over?

Things look very good for a buyout soon from the railroad, and Will has only eight months to go until his retirement. He knows this a buyout will be the icing on the cake for him. January roars in with a major snowstorm. He is out shoveling snow, trying to dig his driveway out from the huge amounts of snow left behind. Then it happens again. He feels the pain and weird sensation like before, when he was doing yard work, only worse this time. He sees his doctor that afternoon. The doctor tells him not to go to work, to stay home and rest until he can get an appointment with a heart specialist in Des Moines. A couple days later, the specialist gives him a series of tests and does complete blood work. Two days later, he returns for the results. The doctor delivers the bad news, that he needs a double-bypass operation. Will doesn't hear another word he says. He is shocked. He thinks this can't be true. He is ready to retire. He is going to finally be a traveling man! He didn't see this coming. He regains his composure and can't help the tears in his eyes. He hears the doctor say that he will make him an appointment with a colleague for a second opinion.

Will meets with the second doctor. He is a big man, very soft-spoken, and he reminds him of his Uncle Butch. Will sits in the room with the big doctor, two other doctors, several nurses, and a lot of equipment. He looks around the room, and now he is scared. The big doctor tells him he is going to take one hell of a test, but not to worry, he has everything ready if anything should happen.

This doesn't make Will feel any better. He sees the machine with the paddles connected to it and thinks to himself that if this is a dream, he needs to wake up right now. The nurse hooks up some wires, and he is given an injection. The doctor tells him to get on the treadmill. It will be elevated, so the test is going to be difficult. He instructs him to walk until his heart is pounding; he is gasping for air, and he feels he can't raise his foot one more time. Then he is to fall over on his left side onto the bed, and the doctor will take over. When Will hits that bed, he knows that he is a goner. He feels his heart beating wildly, and he is gasping for air. He thinks he isn't going to make it. The doctor is behind him, monitoring his pounding heart. He tells him to hang in there and breathe in all the air he can. On the wall is a big screen with a picture of Will's heart. Will watches; it looks like his heart is trying to jump off the screen. There are red and blue flashes of electricity triggered by the heart contractions. Will thinks it looks like a colorful bad storm. He doesn't know how much time passes until he is able to catch his breath and his heart rate slows down. He thinks maybe he's dead, that his heart has stopped completely. He isn't dead; he is exhausted. Several hours pass, and he is allowed to go home. The doctor tells him to get a good night's rest and return in a few days for the results.

His daughter has been trying to call him to find out why he isn't there for her wedding. He tells her that the railroad buyout is going through and he needs to be home. She isn't very happy about this, and he hopes that she will understand. He doesn't want to tell her about his heart problems. And he doesn't want to tell her that with all he has going on, he has completely forgotten about it. He knows he should have called her, and he feels badly that he hasn't. But he reasons that he had been there for her first wedding and had given her away. He is sorry he isn't going to make it to this one, and he hopes she won't be mad at him.

Will sits in the waiting room, nervous and worried. They call his name, and he goes back to an examination room. The doctor walks in, and Will stands and shakes his hand. The big man tells him he has very good news for him. He tells him he does not need a double bypass or even a single bypass. In fact, he needs no operation at all. Will feels an overwhelming relief. The doctor continues, explaining that he did have a mild heart attack not long ago. The problem is with the small ventricles in the lower tip of his heart. Some are plugged up all the way; some are plugged up half the way. He further explains to him that the ventricles will branch off into separate ones, and even create new ones. In Will's case, this has already started. He tells him he will prescribe a medication that will make this happen faster and that there was very little heart damage. Will is extremely happy and relieved with this news. He smiles broadly as he thanks the doctor. He walks out of the office feeling like a new man. He looks to the sky and says a silent prayer. "My travel plans are not over. Thank you, Lord, thank you!"

CHAPTER 56

Surprise, Surprise!

Will spends the rest of the winter working and planning toward his retirement. He tells his landlady that he will be out by mid September. He talks with the railroad retirement board and fills out all the necessary paperwork. In the spring, he and Natalie hold several garage sales. They start to sell everything they won't need and that won't fit in the motor home. All his follow-up doctor visits go well. Natalie's mother moves to Wisconsin to be near Natalie's sister. Natalie puts in her notice at her job. Everything is falling into place. The last few weeks of August, they hold more garage sales, and what they don't sell they donate to charity. Natalie only keeps what will fit in the motor home; Will does the same. They sell both their cars, and he sells his work truck. They buy a small car to tow behind the motor home. Will's last railroad trip is set for the end of August. Ironically, his last run on the railroad is with the son of the first engineer he worked with as a conductor. The landlord sells the house, and they set up camp in Des Moines until everything is finalized. They meet with friends for drinks and say their good-byes.

Will is busy doing paperwork one afternoon, and Natalie keeps insisting that they go to their favorite bar. The bar is the one she managed and is owned by his good friend Tony. He tells her he would like to, but he can't; he has things to do. But she insists; she says she promised a friend that they would come in to say good-bye, and it must be that afternoon. He sighs and closes his notebook; he figures he can finish his paperwork later.

Will walks into his favorite hangout. He is met with a huge chorus of "Surprise!" He is caught totally off guard and can't believe it. He stands there with his mouth open. The place is packed with people. All of their friends are there, including many of the railroaders he has worked with over the years. His sister and her husband, his brothers, Natalie's kids, and Will's kids and grandkids, all are there smiling at him. There's a huge "Happy Retirement" banner and even a DJ playing music. Will is greeted with cheers and handshakes and hugs. He can't help but notice that the only one missing is his daughter, the one whose wedding he missed. He is soon handed a beer, and he makes his way through the crowd. He finds out that the whole party was planned by his kids, with the help of Natalie and Tony, the bar owner. His kids have been in town, planning and decorating, and he didn't even know it. The crowd enjoys the food Tony cooks up, and there is even a keg of beer. It is a grand party with style. The night is full of fun and dancing, and everyone has a wonderful time. Some of his friends tell him that when they retire, they want his kids to plan their parties too. No one wants the night to end, but it finally does. He knows he will have these wonderful memories for a lifetime. It really sinks in. This party seems to make it official: Will is retired.

His children return home the next day, and the following week he ties up all the loose ends. Then at ten o'clock in the morning on September 15, 1996, he drives his motor home away from the campground. He is officially retired from a thirty-six-year career with the railroad, and his lifelong dream is coming true. He smiles as he looks out at the open road. He looks over at Natalie in the passenger seat. He says gleefully, "I am officially a certified, bona fide, guaranteed, full-time traveling man. I am on the road, and I can't wait to see what is over that next hill and around the next bend!" He is indeed, finally, a traveling man, and he can't be happier.

CHAPTER 57

Houston, Do You Copy?

Now armed with maps and campground books, Will and Natalie are ready. They know that they are not "snowbirds." No, they are full-time travelers. Anything that looks interesting in the direction they are going, they will stop in and see. And they will take all the time they want. As a matter of fact, Will decides that to travel a distance of two hundred miles a day will be a big day for them. The plan is that they will find a camp spot and set up. Then they will have a couple of drinks, eat supper, and do whatever they want.

First, they head to South Dakota, and there is plenty to see. They travel through the badlands and watch big herds of buffalo. They travel from there on to Wyoming and through Yellowstone National Park. The weather starts to turn colder, so they head for northern California and the redwoods in Yosemite. In California, away from the big cities, Will discovers that he can't get good television reception, and this means no news of any kind. After talking it over, they decide to purchase a little dish antenna. It's on a tripod with a long cable. This way, if there are a lot of trees around, they can still get reception. The man at the shop sells him everything he needs and shows him how to hook the receiver to the television set. He tells him that wherever he is, all he has to do is turn on the television and the receiver then type in the local zip code. On the screen will be the correct settings to set his dish to with a compass. Will thinks this will be a piece of cake. He is told that the first time he uses it, set it up and get locked in on a signal, then call the programmer. They will send the package that he ordered right to his television set. Will can't wait to get it all hooked up.

They get to a campground that evening, and Will gets everything hooked up inside. He double-checks it; everything looks good. In the morning, in the daylight, he will put the dish outside. The next day, the dish is level and right out in the open under a clear blue sky. He turns it on inside, gets the correct numbers, and has the compass. Natalie has the window open so she can see the television and still hear him. He points the dish in the right direction and waits to hear the beep. Natalie watches to see if the chart comes up with the numbers from eighty to one hundred. For a good quality picture, it needs to be in the eighty to one hundred range. According to the compass and elevation marks, Will is pointed in the right direction; he just needs to do some fine turning. He moves it back and forth and up and down, ever so slightly. He hollers to Natalie, "Do you see anything?" She doesn't see anything on the screen. He continually asks her, "How about now? Anything yet?" This goes on for a few hours. He stops to eat lunch and decides to recheck everything. He is back at it in the afternoon, turning the dish this way and that way. Still nothing. He decides there must be something wrong. He puts the dish away for the night and plans to try again the next day. The next day is the same thing all over again. By the third time, Will is convinced that the satellite must have fallen from the sky. He calls the company, and they assure him that the satellite is fine and that it sounds like he is setting it up correctly. He hangs up the phone and scratches his head. He rereads all the instructions.

The next night they are in a campground near Candlestick Park, outside of San Francisco, California. Will likes it here; it's neat and clean and a beautiful place. He gets the motor home leveled and hooks up the electricity, water, and sewer. He sets the dish in a clear spot. He goes inside and enters the zip code and gets the correct numbers. He heads back outside and tells Natalie that they will have television tonight. She doesn't know it, but they are close enough to the big city to get regular stations on the TV antenna anyway. She is at the window, and Will is busy fine-tuning the dish. And then he hears it, the *beep beep*. Natalie starts hollering. They have a signal! It's not very strong, only at thirty-five, but he turns the dish a little more and gets it to ninety-two. Will stands back and laughs. He jokes, "Control to Houston, we have a full signal. Do you copy?" He calls the programmer, and they send the channel package along with free movies for the rest of the month. Will leans back in his chair and hangs up the phone. A smile crosses his face and he says, "Thank you, Houston, over and out."

CHAPTER 58

Worst Day in Will's Life

Will and Natalie travel to San Diego and spend Christmas with Natalie's cousin. The two grew up together and are very fond of each other but haven't been together in a long time. They continue on to Mexico and then to Las Vegas, a city they both love. They spend time along the gulf coast and make their way to Georgia, where Will's daughter and grandchildren live. From there, they travel to North Carolina to see Will's son and youngest daughter. Then it's on to Wisconsin to visit Natalie's mother and sister. In June 1997, they pull into their favorite campground and get settled in. It's their favorite campground because it is in the center of where most of the family and friends live. To his surprise, his brother Mel is there to greet them. Will asks him how in the world he knew they were arriving there on that day? Mel just grins and tells him that all he did was call the campground and ask! On weekdays, Will and Natalie see friends and go to the bar where she used to work. On weekends, the kids and grandkids come to visit. There is a lake to swim and fish in, and Will cooks out for everyone. At times, there are as many as twenty people. Everyone sits around the campfire. They drink beer and tell stories, and everybody, young and old, has a great time.

The couple then travels north about fifty miles to a bigger lake. It has a nice beach and is just outside the town Will's oldest daughter, his sister, and brother all live. The sister and her husband bring their RV to the lake and camp beside them. Will always lets Rod, his brother-in-law, do all the cooking. He is the expert, and he cooks a great steak. Besides that, he is a really nice guy. Jokingly, he always wonders how in the hell his sister ever got him trapped! Mel and his wife spend time with them too. Mel always brings something, like games for the kids and sodas. He likes to bake and brings Natalie her favorite, pineapple upside down cake.

Soon it's time for the traveling man to hit the road again. This time, he has a whole new route planned, with new things to see and experience. It's earlier in the season, so he can go farther north before the snow and cold weather set in. And this time, they are traveling with a new and tiny companion. His name is Roadway, and he is a one-pound, four-ounce apricot poodle. He has an orange tint to his fur, and he is the cutest little guy ever. They get the name Roadway from Will and Natalie's friends. They host a dog-naming party, and everyone submits names having to do with travel, like Interstate, Parkway, Parking Lot, and Highway. The name Roadway wins the contest, and it fits him.

The first stop is central Minnesota to see Natalie's brother and his family. Then on to Sault Ste. Marie and into Canada. It's quite a sight seeing the locks and dam and the grant ore ships. They see Niagara Falls on the Canadian side then travel back into the United States. The weather starts to turn cold, so they turn south and follow along the coastline, through Delaware and across the Chesapeake Bay Bridge. They spend time in Cape Hatteras and continue on to the Florida Keys and Key West.

In early June 1998, they return to their favorite campground in Iowa. As before, brother Mel greets them and with a pineapple upside down cake for Natalie. Will is busy setting up because people will be coming over soon. He is putting out the awning and setting up lawn chairs when he hears an announcement over the PA system. There is a call for him at the office. He walks in the office, and the manager hands him the phone. It's his oldest daughter on the line. She tells him that there has been a terrible accident. She tells him the horrible news that his youngest daughter has been killed. Will's knees go weak and he can barely stand. He doesn't know what he says to her. The tears start to flow and he can't speak. Natalie knows right away that something is terribly wrong. He manages to tell her that his little girl has been killed in a car accident. Natalie is in as much shock as Will, but she manages to get him to sit down and pull himself together. He finds out that his daughter Michelle and her husband had been out for a motorcycle ride. A truck ran a red light and hit them, and she was dead at the scene. Her husband is alive but in very bad shape. Anne, his ex-wife, is frantic with grief; she wants him to come there right away.

Will throws some things into the car, and he and Natalie arrive there shortly. Anne is really glad to see him, and all she can say is "Will, I want her back." His sister and three of his brothers are there plus Anne's friends. The next day, Will's son arrives. The poor boy has just had to identify the body of his sister and escort her body on the plane back to Iowa. They make funeral plans and decide that she will be buried in the Catholic cemetery about a mile from where Will's mother is buried. The first night is a long one; no one sleeps. Family continues to arrive, each grieving in their own. way. The next few days are tough on Will and his family. The next afternoon is the viewing and visitation for family and friends. It's a good thing that Natalie has a tight hold on him, because when he walks into the room and sees the casket, his knees buckle. He sees the sweet and adorable face of his little daughter, and the room reels. He is helped into a chair, and that is where he stays for quite some time. The tears flow, and he vaguely hears people talking to him and patting his shoulders. He is helped by Natalie back to the casket. He looks down at his daughter, and now he knows what hurt is. This, he thinks, now this is pain. He remembers what he felt at his mother's death. That pain, and now this pain, and it's nothing like he felt at Jake's death.

The service begins. Will's children get up, one by one, and talk about Michelle. They talk about their sister and their wonderful memories. The attendance is huge. The place is overflowing with people. One after the other, Michelle's friends and townspeople get up and share a story or favorite memory. When the service is over, Will's sister finds him. She is worried; she knows he has been having blood sugar problems lately and that he probably hasn't eaten anything. She brings him a sandwich and warns him if he doesn't eat it, she will stuff it down him.

The burial is the next afternoon. It is a beautiful summer day. The sky is blue and there is not a cloud in it. A luncheon is held in the church basement afterward, and again, it is standing room only. Will overhears some people talking, saying what a beautiful funeral it was. He wonders if there is such a thing as a beautiful funeral. He reasons that maybe there is, but it depends on who you are burying.

CHAPTER 59

9/11/2001

The next few months in his travels, he sees that little daughter just about everywhere. He sees her get into a car in North Dakota. He spots her again in Montana, walking across the street. Then he sees her again in Idaho, just leaving a gas station. Natalie tells him that he is looking for her and he needs to stop, because sadly, he will never be able to find her. They follow along the Colombia River, between Washington and Oregon, and through Portland to Highway 101. At the coast, they turn south and head to Coos Bay. They spot some whales traveling south right alongside them, and they watch them for several days. He had always heard about Coos Bay, and he wants to check it out. It turns out to be a quaint little fishing village full of nice people and good seafood.

Roadway is a very good traveling dog. He is smart and he, like Will, loves to travel. They continue on south until they reach South Padre, Texas. They enjoy a café there that has an early bird special if you eat before five o'clock. The café across the street has a special that starts after five o'clock, so Will figures he can't go wrong. The seafood restaurants have "fresh catch of the day" specials. Will loves sampling all the different foods. From there, they head to Corpus Christi and the Gulf Coast. About thirty miles north, they find an Indian casino and campground called Coushatta Red Shoes. Will likes it here. They offer a free shuttle to the casino, the food is good, and the campground is really nice.

Soon, it's time to start heading back to Iowa. They stop and see family and friends along the way. They stop in Chicago to see Johnny. Johnny has cancer, and Will knows that he isn't doing well. Will sets up in a campground close-by and stays a week or so. He and Johnny enjoy reminiscing and talking about the good old days. Early in June, they arrive in their favorite campground in Iowa, and as before, brother Mel is there to greet them.

The next few years, the traveling man crisscrosses the United States. He and Natalie travel from ocean to ocean, border to border. Will loves every moment of it. In September, he gets word that Johnny has passed away. Sadly, six weeks later, his brother Donny passes away, too. He is saddened by the news but glad that he is retired and has been able to spend some time with both of them.

The next year, when Will leaves Iowa, he has some special plans. He plans to visit New York and a few other states he and Natalie have not been to yet. He can't wait to see the Statue of Liberty and Ellis Island. He plans to travel to New Brunswick, then Nova Scotia, and put the motor home on a ferry to Boston. He has it all mapped out. The day before, they pull into a campground to spend the night. In the morning they will head to see the Statue of Liberty. It's the morning of September 11. Will is shaving and Natalie is making the bed. The television is on, and he can't believe what he hears. He steps out closer to the television to hear better, and Natalie stops and listens too. The reporter is saying that a plane has flown into the tower! And another plane has flown into the Pentagon! Will sits down in shock. He and Natalie, like the rest of America, watch the television the rest of the day. Natalie wonders, what are they going to do now? He walks into the office of the campground and extends his stay for another day. That evening they decide to alter their plans. Instead of driving north and east, they turn around and head back south. Instead of going to New York, they drive to Savannah. From there they travel to Cape Canaveral, where they watch an unmanned rocket launch. The rest of the year they travel to national parks and monuments and any place they find of interest. They meet and make friends along the way, and the traveling man is having the time of his life.

CHAPTER 60

Vegas, Baby!

While spending time in Las Vegas, Will checks into getting married without Natalie knowing about it. One morning, he grins at her and mentions getting married, right now, today. Her answer is that it's short notice and she will have to think about it. This stops him in his tracks and catches him totally off guard. He is surprised by her answer. He waits a few minutes then brings up the subject of marriage again. This time, she says that after eleven years together, she doesn't see why not. Will smiles; now this is more the answer he was hoping for. The two exchange vows in a beautiful, quiet little ceremony.

A few months later while in Georgia visiting his daughter, Will notices that Roadway loses his balance and has trouble standing up. They make a doctor appointment. At the groomers, before they can get him to the veterinarian, he becomes completely paralyzed. Fortunately, they are in a large city, and there is a pet hospital that is open all night. The first doctor says that the dog has one or two ruptured vertebrae in his neck, and there is nothing he can do. But the second doctor tells them that a specialist can help him. The specialist looks at Roadway and says that he can help him, but the operation is a very serious one. It is also very costly and needs to be done right away. Natalie and Will pay half the cost up front, and the operation is scheduled for the next day. Roadway is hospitalized for the next ten days, with no visitations. It's a long ten days for Will and Natalie. When they finally bring Roadway home, they are sad and disappointed. He is still paralyzed from the neck down. They are told he will need four to six more weeks to recuperate. They help him go to the bathroom and eat. They keep him clean and work his legs back and forth every few hours. They follow all the doctor's instructions carefully. Then one day, the dog moves his front leg, then a few days later, the other. Soon, his back legs start to work and he can stand again. It isn't long, and their precious dog, "little boy," as they call him, is back to his old self. Will is relieved and grateful. He ruffles the fur on the little dog's head and can't help but think how much he loves him.

While drinking coffee one morning and watching television, Will notices the forecast is particularly bad. A storm named Katrina is heading for the New Orleans area. Will and Natalie are not too far from there. They are at their favorite casino, Coushatta Red Shoes. They watch the news closely to see if the storm will stay on the predicted path or veer off. It is still three days away and headed straight for them. Even though they have paid to stay for two more weeks, he decides that they should leave in the morning. He reasons that this will give them two full days to travel somewhere else. He figures maybe they can get a jump on the traffic.

They leave early the next morning and travel north. The traffic on the interstate is bumper to bumper. It is slow going all the way to Shreveport. From there, he notices that most of the traffic is heading east. He tells Natalie that since most of the heavy rain and tornadoes spawn off the east side of a hurricane, he thinks that they should go west and stay on the backside of the storm. They travel to Fort Worth, Texas, and set up camp. Will watches the news and knows he made the right decision. The gulf area and New Orleans are pounded by Katrina. The whole area is hit hard, and the storm destroys everything in its path, including the oil platforms in the gulf.

It doesn't take long before there is a shortage of oil and prices soar. Fuel prices are extremely high, and this really affects Will's wallet. Not only are gas prices outrageous, but campground prices soar too. They cope the best they can after Katrina. They stay longer at places to get the extended-stay discounts, and they cut down on their driving time. Will tries to wait it out and hopes the prices will go back down. But in the months that follow, things don't improve, and he knows he is going to have to make a decision. He doesn't want to give up traveling. He loves being a traveling man! He still wants to see what is over the next hill and what is around the next bend. But he knows that with the current prices, the traveling expenses are much too high. They talk it over and weigh all their options. They finally agree that the time has come to quit traveling. With a heavy heart, Will asks Natalie where she wants to settle down. To his surprise, she says without hesitation, "Vegas, baby, Vegas!"

Chapter 61

Not Again, That Birth Certificate!

They arrive in Las Vegas and set up in their favorite campground on Fremont Street. They collect papers and brochures from various condos and apartment buildings throughout the city. They search for several weeks until they find an apartment to rent that they both like. They decide to trade the truck and fifth wheel in. Will knows the best place to do this is with a dealer in Mesa, Arizona, that they have dealt with before. Over the last twelve years, he has traded RVs five times. In the past, he always liked to drive the big diesel motor home and tow a small car behind. But with a truck and fifth wheel, he found he got a whole lot more living space. Over the years, Will always manages to trade up, and he has become very knowledgeable about motor homes and fifth wheels.

They travel to Arizona and make the trade. They get a class C motor home. Will knows it's really just a large van with everything the big RV has everything except space. They know it will be nice to have to make trips back east to see their families though. In the next few days, they pick out new furniture for the apartment and have it delivered. They hold a parking lot sale, and Will sells hoses and cords and all the things he knows he won't need any more. Before they move into the apartment, they spend a few nights in the new class C motor home. They notice the difference right away; with so much less space, they are very cramped.

They move into the new apartment, and Will can't help feeling sad. He isn't very happy about this new big change in his life. He sighs and thinks how much he enjoyed being a bona fide, certified, guaranteed traveling man. But he knows all good things come to an end. It takes a few weeks, but he and Natalie finally settle into the new routine.

A few weeks later they go to the Department of Motor Vehicles to register the new motor home in the state of Nevada and get their Nevada driver's licenses. They notice that things are much different in this state than in the state of Iowa. They stand in a very long line and find out that's only to make it to the first counter. At this counter, all the information is checked over, and from there, you wait in line for a second counter. They find out at the first counter that they don't have all the necessary information. Natalie has to go to the social security office and update her card since her marriage to Will. This office isn't much better than the DMV. They check and recheck and make sure they have all the right paperwork. Again, they stand in line and make it past the first counter. They are handed a number; it's 189. Will glances up at the monitor and cringes; it is on 90. They take a seat and wait. Will shakes his head as he watches all the little kids running around screaming. Finally, it is their turn. The lady at the counter takes the paperwork and looks everything over. She hands them the registration and plates for the new motor home. She then looks at Natalie's papers. She instructs Natalie to read the eye chart then hands her a document to sign with her full legal name and date.

Now it's Will's turn. The woman looks over the papers. She hands him a paper and tells him to sign his full legal name. He signs Wilton Michael Furman and hands it back to her. She looks down at the paper then hands it back. She says she can't accept it since it is not the correct legal name. Will's mouth gapes open, and he stares at her in disbelief. He can't believe what he is hearing. After all he has been through over the years with his birth certificate, she is telling him that his name is still not right? The woman behind the counter points to his signature. She says, "You have no middle name, just the initial M." She pulls another paper from the stack and continues. "You see here in this document you signed on February 28, 1969, you changed your name from Wilton Michael Johnson to Wilton M.

Furman." Will looks hard at the paper and is speechless. She continues, "If it isn't supposed to be that way, all I can tell you is that somebody goofed, and if you want your driver's license, you will have to sign it the way this document shows it." He feels sick to his stomach. How ironic, he thinks. His mother wanted him to have the Furman last name so badly that in her haste, she inadvertently changed his middle name to just the initial M. He no longer has the middle name of Michael, the one name that his mother wanted him to have, after the brother she so dearly loved. He stands there, looking down at the paper. He thinks of his mother. The one name that she so wanted her firstborn son to have and carry all his life he no longer has. He also thinks of Jake. He is still carrying the name Jake never wanted him to have. He sighs as he picks up the pen. He can't help but notice another irony. He is seventy-one years old, and for the very first time in his life, the bastard son is signing his correct full legal name.

Well, dear reader, do you remember at the beginning of this book when I told you that I would reveal to you how I know so much about this story? If you haven't guessed it by now, I was, and still am, the bastard son.

Any regrets, you ask? Yes, I have one huge regret. I wish that I had kept on looking for my real father until I found him. I would have stood right in front of him, looked him right in the eye, and said in a very loud voice, "Junior! What in the hell happened?"

A LITTLE SOMETHING
ABOUT THE AUTHOR

He has been married three times. Wife number 1 gave him four wonderful children, three girls, and a boy. God bless her, she raised them to be very good, responsible, caring adults. And she did raise them, because he was always out chasing trains.

He did work as a conductor on the railroad for thirty-six years, and that's a whole other story. He was married to wife number 2 for less than ten years. They did make a few RV trips together, and that's when he found out that he wanted to be a traveling man.

Wife number 3 is the last one, and she is something else. She stood by him and helped him very much through some difficult times, especially the death of his daughter. She stayed right by his side, even while knowing that someday he was going to be a traveling man. When he did retire and hit the road, she was right there with him. They had a great and wonderful life together traveling through the United States for better than ten years. They saw a lot of beautiful places and made a lot of nice friends.

A tip from the traveling man: it is his personal opinion that Utah is the prettiest state in the United States. Zion National Park, Bryce Canyon, Capitol Reef, Archer National Park, and the city of Moab are all high on his list. He says you haven't seen anything until you've seen Dead Horse Point State Park. Mere words can't begin to describe the beauty of it.

He is now in his eighties. He and his wife still live in Las Vegas. They spend a lot of time on Fremont Street. If you are ever in Las Vegas on Fremont Street, stop by the El Cortez Hotel Casino and say hi. He will be on his favorite video poker machine!

About the Author

The author knew very early in life that he would be a traveling man. He wanted to see what was over that hill and around that next bend. He loved his job as a conductor on the railroad and traveled the rails for thirty-six years. When he retired, he and his wife-to-be sold everything, bought a big RV, and traveled the continental United States for twelve years. They met many people and saw some beautiful places. They now reside in Las Vegas and pull a handle now and then.

CPSIA information can be obtained
at www.ICGtesting.com
Printed in the USA
FSOW01n0800180417
33261FS